Everything She Never Knew

ALSO BY ANNETTE CHAVEZ MACIAS

Big Chicas Don't Cry

Too Soon for Adiós

When We Were Widows

Everything She Never Knew

a novel

ANNETTE CHAVEZ MACIAS

This is a work of fiction. Names, characters, organizations, places, events, and incidents are either products of the author's imagination or are used fictitiously. Otherwise, any resemblance to actual persons, living or dead, is purely coincidental.

Published by Montlake, Seattle

www.apub.com

EU product safety contact:
Amazon Media EU S. à r.l.
38, avenue John F. Kennedy, L-1855 Luxembourg
amazonpublishing-gpsr@amazon.com

ISBN-13: 9781662530425 (paperback)
ISBN-13: 9781662530418 (digital)

Cover design by Caroline Johnson
Cover image: © Thomas Barwick, © ManuelVelasco, © trekandshoot / Getty

Printed in the United States of America

For my sister, Yolanda. I couldn't have asked for a better best friend.

CHAPTER ONE

THINGS I NEVER KNEW #14: I ACTUALLY LIKE SCHOOL AND WOULD BE SAD IF I MISSED MY FIRST DAY OF FIFTH GRADE

Dear Diary,

Gloria has been gone for four days now. I asked Abuela if she was ever coming back, and she called me a tonta and said that of course she's coming back. That she just went away with Arnold for a quick vacation.

I didn't remind Abuela that my mom's note actually said she and Arnold would be back after one night. Or that they were just taking a quick trip to San Diego to pick up something from their friend's house. I didn't remind her because I don't have the note anymore to prove it to her. Abuela snatched it out of my hand as soon as I walked into her living room after Gloria dropped me off four days ago.

I thought Abuela would be mad that my mom didn't even call to ask if I could stay with her this time. But all she did was tear up the note and ask me in Spanish what I wanted to eat for lunch. That was Saturday. Now it's Wednesday and I'm starting to get worried.

School starts next week, and I don't have any notebooks or pens or even new tennis shoes. How am I supposed to start fifth grade at a school that's not even in the same city as Abuela's house?

That's why I had asked Abuela if Gloria was coming back. I need to know for real so I can start making plans. I need to figure out the best bus route to get me from East LA to Baldwin Park. I need to start calling some friends and ask if they can let me borrow some supplies just until Abuela gets her Social Security check in a few weeks and we go to the market.

It's not the first time my mom has run off with a guy. Last Christmas she left me with Abuela so she could go skiing with one of her coworkers. I was supposed to stay with Abuela until New Year's Day, but she ended up coming back two days early because she found out the guy had a girlfriend.

Since Gloria isn't back yet, Arnold must not have a girlfriend or wife. I guess that's good for her. Not so good for me, though. Because what if she decides to stay in San Diego with him? What if Arnold becomes my new stepdad?

I've only met him a few times, and he seems decent enough. But the bar isn't that high when it comes to the long list of losers Gloria has brought home over the years.

It would be just my luck that Arnold ends up being The One but doesn't want an eleven-year-old girl as his kid.

Part of me wants to tell Abuela that I'm old enough now and she can tell me the truth. I can handle it. This is the longest Gloria has ever gone without calling me. But maybe she's already called Abuela to let her know she's starting a new life somewhere with Arnold and I'm not going to be a part of it. I don't want to believe I'll never see her again. As much as I hate that sometimes my mom acts like she wishes she never had me, at the end of the day she's still my mom. Don't get me wrong. I wouldn't mind living with Abuela permanently. I mean, I already spend a lot of time here. But when the worst thing in the world is going to happen to you anyway, you kind of want it to go ahead and just happen so you can figure out what to do next.

I just hate waiting. I'd rather rip off the Band-Aid and scream it all out.

The pain will go away. Eventually.

CHAPTER TWO

I screamed as my knee hit something hard and pointy.

As I lowered the two heavy paper grocery bags I was already struggling to hold, I looked down to see what I'd collided with. It was the handle of the dryer door. Someone had left the door open against a plastic hamper, blocking the path from our attached garage through the laundry room, which then led into our kitchen.

The burning pain almost matched my annoyance. How many times had I asked David to close the dryer door after emptying it? He'd left that morning for a business trip, so I knew it had to be him. He was probably running late as usual and grabbed stuff directly from the dryer to throw into his carry-on suitcase. I'd stopped taking him to and picking him up from LAX years ago due to the traffic. But because I'd been feeling guilty about an argument we'd had the night before about him leaving again for a work trip after only being home for a few days, I'd offered to take him to the airport to give him some extra time to get ready. But he'd insisted on calling an Uber like he always did. Truthfully, I was relieved he didn't take me up on the offer. I had a day full of appointments and errands to run and wanted to leave the house as early as possible so I could drop Maya off at her friend's house. She'd been invited to tag along on a weekend trip to the San Diego Zoo and wouldn't be back until Sunday. And since David didn't need to get to the airport until closer to noon, I didn't try to change his mind about me taking him.

That meant I'd left him to empty the dryer on his own and, apparently, leave the door open. Again.

I pushed it softly with my uninjured knee to get it out of my way and headed to the counter island just a few feet away. I set the bags down and began to put things in the refrigerator and cupboards. The groceries were the last things on my to-do list and were standing in the way of me, a glass of wine, and a relaxing Friday summer night all on my own.

A rare treat indeed.

Once the bags were empty, I folded them and entered our walk-in pantry to place them next to the dozen or so reusable grocery bags I kept forgetting to put back in the trunk of my car. I considered doing just that when a painful twinge made my right knee buckle a little.

"Dammit," I said as I looked down and saw a fresh red scratch covered in red dots of blood just below the hem of my denim shorts.

The reusable grocery bags would have to wait it out in the pantry just a little longer.

As I made my way to our bedroom at the back of the house, I thought about what I wanted to order for dinner. Even though I'd just restocked the fridge, I was not going to cook. It was the first night of a child-free and husband-free weekend, and I wasn't about to waste it by making something I could eat any day of the week.

That meant I could order a nice salmon dinner or even a seafood boil. David always refused to eat shellfish and didn't even allow it in the house since he hated the smell of anything that came from the sea. Or I could get a couple of dishes from China Gate down the street, since I didn't have to worry about having to pick a restaurant that also served chicken nuggets or mac and cheese for Maya—the pickiest eater I knew.

I decided on Chinese food so I could have leftovers for lunch tomorrow after my hair appointment. Then maybe Rachel and I could go out to dinner and have some grown-up refreshments. It had been a while since the two of us had done that. Even though she lived next door, it seemed like forever since I'd had the chance to hang out with my best friend like we used to. That was partly my fault, and I knew it. I'd way overcommitted myself to Maya's summer activities. Swimming lessons at the recreation center, arts and crafts at the YWCA, horseback riding at the stables, and various story time hours at the library had me spending most weekdays in my car driving my daughter all around South Pasadena. Weekends were then filled with the errands and shopping I didn't get to Monday through Friday.

I missed her.

After cleaning up the scratch with some soap and water on a washcloth, I dabbed it with a little bit of Neosporin on a Q-tip. I decided to let it air-dry before applying a Band-Aid and began to put my first aid supplies away in the tall storage cabinet in the bathroom connected to my bedroom. That's when I first noticed something was different.

Something seemed wrong. Off.

It took me a few seconds as I scanned the counter next to the cabinet. Why did it look . . . empty? Then it hit me. All David's hair and skin products were missing. I opened the double medicine cabinet in search of his deodorant, body spray, beard wash, hair gel, prescription-strength eczema cream, and other various bottles and tubes. When I didn't find them, I headed toward our walk-in closet to look on his dresser. But I stopped at the doorway. Only a handful of his jackets and shirts were hanging on the racks, and most of his drawers were pulled open. I could see from where I stood that they were no longer stuffed with clothes.

None of it made sense. As a senior account manager for a big Los Angeles advertising agency, David had left that morning to head to San Francisco to prepare for a major presentation to a client on Monday. Although he didn't usually travel on the weekends for business, he'd said the client had requested that he also attend a dinner with some company executives on Saturday evening. I had thought he was going to be home Monday night, so I'd promised Maya we'd take her to the movies on Tuesday. She'd become extra whiny whenever David was home, and I figured she needed some quality time with him. But when he told me last night that he'd be home by late Tuesday evening instead of Monday—I lost it. He swore up and down that that had always been the plan. I was so mad that I went to sleep in the guest bedroom without speaking to him for the rest of the night.

Maybe if I had slept in my own room, I would've noticed that he'd packed more clothes than normal. That still wouldn't explain why half his side of the closet was nearly empty.

I turned around and scanned our bedroom for answers. That's when I saw it. Or rather, I didn't. The photo of Maya and David taken last Christmas that he kept on his nightstand was gone.

With my heart pounding in my ears, I ran back to the kitchen and yanked my phone off the counter to text David. He would've landed in San Francisco at least two hours earlier. I realized at that moment that he hadn't messaged to let me know. My pulse, and probably my blood pressure, skyrocketed even more.

I sent him a flurry of texts.

Call me.

Please call me.

David!

What is happening right now????!!!!!!

After a few minutes of no response, I texted Rachel. She was the one who could always talk me off the ledge and tame the dark conclusions I tended to jump to thanks to my wild imagination. There had to be a reasonable explanation as to why David wasn't texting me back and why most of his personal belongings were missing.

I *needed* there to be a reasonable explanation.

Call me! I texted.

911!

Something is going on with David!

I tried calling her. Then tried his phone again. Both went straight to voicemail.

My brain couldn't compute why both of them had gone radio silent. Their lack of responses only fueled the growing sense of terror in my gut.

I was about to run next door to Rachel's house and bang on her door when my phone vibrated. The screen showed it was an incoming text from David, and I nearly cried with relief.

Until I read his message:

Check your email.

My email?

In my panicked haze, I reasoned that something must be wrong with his phone, which was why he couldn't call me or answer my calls. Or maybe it was my subconscious trying to protect me from the truth for just a few seconds more. Deep down I knew something was horribly wrong. But I had no idea how bad it was until I opened the Gmail folder on my phone and spotted the email from him with the very ominous subject line "I'm sorry."

> Claudia, there's no easy way to write this so I'm just going to do it. I want a divorce.

It was as if someone had punched me in the stomach. I flinched in pain and nearly dropped the phone. I squeezed my eyes shut a few times and shook my head because I couldn't possibly have read what I thought I'd read.

Slowly, I opened my eyes and scanned the beginning of the email again.

> Claudia, there's no easy way to write this so I'm just going to do it. I want a divorce.
>
> I resigned from Goodman a few weeks ago and accepted the position with Brighton—the one you didn't want me to take. And as of today, I've officially moved to San Francisco. I took whatever I could fit into the two big suitcases and I'll figure out how to get the rest of my stuff later. I plan to make a trip back in a few weeks so I can see Maya. In the meantime, I'll make sure to call her as soon as I get settled.

Tears blurred my eyes, and I raised a shaky hand to cover my mouth. My whole body felt cold and numb. I didn't want to read the rest. Yet I also couldn't *not* read it. I wiped my eyes dry with the back of the hand not holding my phone and forced myself to continue.

> I know this is a crappy way to do this but every time I tried to have this conversation with you in person, something else came up and there was never a good time to do it. My moving up north might seem like it came out of nowhere, but you and I both know that this divorce has been in the works for a while.

"I didn't know a damn thing!" I screamed like a banshee. My head was now throbbing in agony. Just like my heart. But the torture wasn't over. I had to read the rest.

> There's one other thing. I didn't come here by myself. Rachel left Nick. We've been seeing each other for several months now. She's going to send you her

> own email a little later. You have every right to hate the both of us. Just know we never meant to hurt you. Please don't try to call me or text me right now. Nothing you say is going to change my mind about the divorce. I'll call you in a few days so we can figure out next steps. David

I had to reread those last few sentences again. And again. And then three more times.

He was with Rachel?

My Rachel?

That's when the nausea hit. My stomach violently lurched as bile filled my throat. I clamped my mouth and ran to the kitchen sink and heaved up my lunch. Wails of despair pierced my ears, and I covered them before realizing the cries were coming from me.

I slid to the floor in front of the sink, crying uncontrollably, until the sobs began to choke me and I was gasping for air.

This was not happening. It could not be happening.

My husband and my best friend? No. I refused to believe it. This had to be a nightmare.

It wasn't that I thought we had the perfect marriage. We'd had our ups and downs like all married couples. There was even a time when I suspected David was cheating with a coworker. But he'd denied it, and eventually I'd convinced myself that I was just being insecure as always.

But to have an affair with Rachel? The woman I'd been friends with since I was fourteen?

Nothing about this made any sense.

It was one thing to cheat on me, but to cheat on me with her?

Had any part of our marriage been real? How many of their lies had I foolishly believed over the years?

Scenes of all the big happy moments in my life played in my head like a movie, followed by some of the hardest. Rachel was there for all of them—either celebrating right alongside me or giving me her shoulder to cry on. I loved her like a sister. How could she do this to me?

It was unfathomable.

Unbelievable.

Unsurvivable.

To be betrayed by the one person in the world I never thought would hurt me like this was a wound I didn't think I could ever heal from. In that moment, I honestly believed it would be the death of me. At the very least, my life would never be the same again.

I balled my hands into fists and pounded viciously on my thighs. *Wake up, wake up,* I told myself. My body, racked by anguish, grew weak until I couldn't even hold myself up any longer. So I slowly fell onto my side, curled into a fetal position, and quietly sobbed into the cold kitchen tile.

Pound. Pound. Pound.

My eyes flew open. For a few seconds I wasn't sure where I was. I blinked a few times before I got my bearings and realized I was lying on my back on the couch in the family room. I had no memory of getting up off the floor. But I must have at some point.

Everything hurt. My head. My eyes. My back. My stomach. Even my toes, for some reason.

I stared at the ceiling, dazed and numb. The solar lights from our back patio cast shadows into the otherwise darkened room. The sun had gone down, which meant I must have been lying here for hours. The day had abandoned me too.

What time was it, anyway?

Pound. Pound. Pound.

"Open the door, Claudia!" I heard a man's voice call out. It was muffled, but loud still. It startled me. My heart lifted at the thought that maybe David had come back.

But he wouldn't be yelling at me to open our front door.

Pound. Pound. Pound.

Groggily, I pulled myself off the couch and shuffled to the front of the house. Even without looking into a mirror, I knew I must've looked as bad as I felt.

All I wanted to do was go back to sleep so I could try waking up from this non-nightmare nightmare. I just had to get rid of the very rude man pounding on my door.

Had I been thinking more clearly, I would've tried harder to ignore him.

But I didn't. Add it to the list of things I wished that hadn't happened today.

"Nick," I gasped.

Rachel's husband gave me an ice-cold stare that chilled me to the bone, despite the warm mid-August evening breeze that wafted over me as soon as I'd opened the door.

If "disheveled" were a person, it would be Nick. His company polo shirt was tucked into the waistband of his trousers on one side and hanging out on the other. His usually slicked-back dark hair was tousled in all directions as if someone had been pulling at it.

And although I knew for a fact that he stood more than six feet tall, the man in front of me seemed smaller. Less than.

"Did you know?" he asked harshly. The bite behind his words made me flinch.

His absurd question left me speechless for a few seconds. I didn't understand it at first. When the realization hit me, I immediately stiffened at his accusatory tone. As if I'd given his wife permission to fuck my husband.

Of course I hadn't known.

God, the four of us had just had dinner at their house last week. There was no special occasion. Just another Friday night hanging out with friends, enjoying each other's company and some pizza and wings. Something we'd done together at least a hundred times before.

How could this man really think I would've just sat there quietly sipping my wine while knowing about this level of betrayal by both of our spouses?

I was about to ask him just that when I noticed how his face was etched with visible anguish, and his watery eyes reflected the same pain I was still in the throes of. For a moment, his agony seemed bigger and more important than mine. But I ignored the fleeting sense of empathy because his question let me know that he obviously didn't feel the same for me.

The fury that had been spilling over ever since I'd read the first sentence of the email erupted from my belly like lava once more. It burned my soul as it traveled up to my chest and then my throat, instantly making me sick and nauseous again.

Before I could vomit a tirade of curses, I slammed the door in his face.

CHAPTER THREE

THINGS I NEVER KNEW #68: I HATE CARNATIONS

Dear Diary,

I don't even know where to begin. Today started out like any other day. I got up. Got ready for school and then headed into the kitchen to pour myself a bowl of cereal. To my shock, Gloria was already there and seated at the table drinking a cup of coffee. A friend had gotten her a job a few months ago at the warehouse where he works, but on the night shift. She usually isn't even home by the time I leave in the morning. So I asked her if she got fired again, and she just laughed and told me she took the day off and that I wasn't going to go to school either. When I asked her why, she said, "Because it's a special day and we're going to spend it together."

Now, normally I would've asked more questions. Maybe it was because I was still half asleep. Maybe it was because I didn't feel like going to school anyway. Or maybe it was because there was a part of me that wanted to believe her. Whatever the reason, I pushed aside my usual suspicions and decided I'd go along with whatever she had in store.

Our first stop was the mall. She told me she was going to buy me a new dress and something for herself. Even though I explained to her I didn't need a new dress and would rather get a pair of jeans and tennis shoes, Gloria insisted I needed a dress for where she was taking me later. Of course, I had lots of questions AGAIN about where we were going and, of course, she wouldn't answer any of them.

"It's a special surprise, and you're going to ruin it for me if you keep asking me for info."

So I shut up and let her buy me a short-sleeved maxi dress with a floral print. Then I watched as she tried on a million outfits at JC Penney's before finally settling on a light-gray pantsuit. Next we went to some salon to get manis and pedis. I actually liked that, especially since she didn't care which nail color I chose.

I had begun to think that maybe Gloria had actually remembered what today was.

We stopped at our favorite diner for a quick lunch. I got my usual cheeseburger and French fries. Gloria nibbled on a salad and downed two Diet Cokes. She seemed nervous, even more than usual, and I wanted to ask why but didn't because it had been a nice day up to that point and I didn't want to ruin it by trying to have a real conversation with her.

But today seemed different. She seemed different. And somewhere between not making me go to school and letting me get my nails painted neon green, I had become excited thinking about what could be her last surprise for me.

After lunch, we stopped at a florist in downtown LA. I stayed in the car while she went inside. Less than ten minutes later, she was back with two small matching bouquets made up of white carnations and light-pink baby roses. When she handed them to me, I couldn't stop the questioning this time. "For me?" She told me one was for me and the other was for her.

For a few wonderful seconds, I actually thought that Gloria had bought me flowers for my birthday. She hadn't, though. Because after those few seconds were over, she told me what the big surprise was all along: she was getting married today at the courthouse.

To Simon.

Her boyfriend of four months.

So, Diary, that's how my day went. Now my mom's wedding anniversary will also always be my birthday.

I already hate being 13.

CHAPTER FOUR

"Mommy, where's my pink skirt—the one with the circles?"

Slowly I cracked open the eye that wasn't pressed into the sofa cushion and then shook with shock when I saw my daughter's face just a few inches away from mine. Not that her sweet face was scary. I just hadn't expected to see it so close and so early in the morning.

I pulled myself off the couch and raised my arms in a long stretch. My neck and right shoulder throbbed in response, and I shrugged a few times to get the kinks out.

"Mommy, where's my skirt?" Maya asked again.

"Why are you awake so early on a Sunday?" I replied, not answering her question.

"It's Monday. I'm going to school today."

I froze mid-yawn. "It's Monday?"

Maya reached out and handed me my phone. "It says seven three five. Leila's mommy will be here to pick me up at seven four five. Where's my skirt?"

I looked at the screen and confirmed that my daughter was right. It was 7:35 on Monday. Then my brain seemed to finally turn on, and I was fully awake.

But that meant the blissful oblivion that had let me forget everything for a few hours every night was gone. The stark reminder of our new reality slapped me in the face like a splash of freezing-cold water. And I remembered all over again that my husband had left me to start a new life with my best friend.

Immediately, my usual morning routine of tears stung the back of my eyes. I squeezed them tight in an effort to make them dissolve before my daughter noticed. Then I tried to quell my queasy stomach and dry mouth with a swig from a nearby water bottle.

Another day, another heartache hangover.

A few minutes later, I was in Maya's bedroom looking for her favorite skirt. But we couldn't find it anywhere in her closet or dresser. I even searched under her bed and inside her toy box.

"It's probably in the laundry room hamper," I finally admitted after pulling off all the blankets from her bed to make sure it wasn't somehow hiding in between them. "Sorry, I don't think it's clean. Wear some jeans today instead, okay?"

She hung her head. "There's no jeans in my drawer either."

She was right again.

"Okay, let's look in the closet and find a dress."

"I'm running out of clothes, Mommy," she told me in a soft, small voice.

It was a simple statement, but it slammed into my heart and broke what was left of it. I took her hand and brought her closer to me for a hug. Tears welled in my eyes, blurring everything around me. I held on to my daughter as tight as I could.

"I'm sorry, baby. I'll wash your clothes today, I promise."

"You can teach me, Mommy," she said against my middle. "That way I can do it myself until you feel better."

Emotion nearly choked the life out of me. My eight-year-old thought I was sick. And even though she was close to being right, she shouldn't be worrying about taking care of me or her own laundry. Guilt and shame made me want to scream. I had failed at being a wife, and now I was failing at being a mother. The one thing I swore I would never do.

I kissed the top of her head and then wiped my eyes. "We'll see. Let's get you ready first, okay?"

I continued to fight my overwhelming sadness as I helped Maya get dressed and combed her hair into two ponytails. It had been almost two weeks since I'd opened the email from David that had turned my life—our life—inside out and upside down.

Those first couple of days, I had tried to shield her from it all. She was used to her daddy being away for days at a time because of work, so I just told her that he'd be away for a little longer this trip. Whenever I'd feel like I was about to burst into tears, I'd run to the bathroom and bury my sobs into a towel. It was probably one of the reasons why I'd been sleeping on the couch in our family room instead of our king-size bed down the hall. I'd rationalized that my late-night sobbing sessions would be harder to hear if Maya was sleeping several feet away from them. At least, I'd hoped they were.

But after a week, my very inquisitive and bright eight-year-old kept asking when her daddy was coming home and why he hadn't called her like he usually did when he was away. His replies to my texts, when I did get them, were vague and noncommittal.

I'll call her after work.

I'll call her this weekend.

I'll call her soon.

I knew he was just being a coward. He could barely tell me the truth these days—I was sure he had no idea how to tell it to a child who still adored him.

After waving goodbye to Maya from the porch as she got into the Silvas' gray Toyota Sienna minivan, I headed back to my spot on the family room couch. Despite the overwhelming urge to go back to sleep, I forced myself to grab my phone from the nearby coffee table.

With trembling fingers, I pulled up David's number and pressed the call button.

He didn't answer, of course.

So I continued calling until he did. Nine more times in total.

"What?" he said when he finally answered.

The fact that he couldn't even say hello made me physically hurt. I ignored the urge to hang up. I had to do this. I had to be strong for my daughter. I couldn't give her her favorite skirt this morning, so I was going to make damn sure I gave her this.

"You need to talk to Maya tonight. She keeps asking for you. Last night she cried for almost an hour before bed because she misses you."

There was silence on the other end. I kept going. "You don't need to call me. We can still communicate by email or texts like we've been doing. But you NEED to call her."

"Fine," he said softly. His gentler tone snatched my breath. It was a flashback to who David had been before . . . this. He sounded as if he actually cared about us. My body ached from the memory, my knees buckled, and I fell down onto the couch.

"Call her at six," I said after clearing my throat of all the emotion I was feeling. "If you don't . . ."

"I will." I noticed he didn't promise, but I'd have to take it.

"Okay."

The silence was back. I waited a few seconds and was about to hang up when he said my name.

"Yes?" I said, trying not to sound too hopeful . . . or pathetic.

"I was going to email you, but since I've got you on the phone, I might as well tell you now."

"Tell me what?"

Sorry? I miss you? I'm coming home?

It was as if my heart suddenly came back to life and sent shock waves of wishful thinking up to my brain.

The damn fool. She still hadn't learned her lesson. Which meant I couldn't prepare myself for what he said next.

"I think we should use a mediator instead of hiring attorneys."

His words seemed to hover in the air for several seconds, and then, once my brain had processed them, it was as if they'd fallen down on top of me, knocking the air out of my lungs.

"Oh." I didn't say anything else because I couldn't say anything else. Literally.

My mouth went dry, closing up my throat and seizing my vocal cords.

David continued. "I know I didn't go about this in the best way, and I just don't want to make it any uglier. I've been talking to people, and lawyers just seem to make things messy."

He'd been talking to people about the divorce? About me? What people?

He didn't have any family he was close to, well, other than me and Maya. His parents passed away in a car accident when he was a teenager, and he barely spoke to his older brother. They'd had a falling-out years before he'd even met me—something to do with their inheritance and property their parents used to own. I also couldn't imagine David staying in touch with anyone from his former agency. He'd left them for their biggest competitor. The advertising business, as I'd come to know it through David, was cutthroat. I'm sure he'd burned bridges when he'd left for San Francisco. Maybe I should call up his old boss so we could commiserate on our shared betrayal.

Minus a few college friends who hit him up whenever they were in town, David didn't have "people."

Who he did have was Rachel. That must have been who he'd been talking to. And it made sense that she didn't want him to spend any more money to deal with me and the divorce.

Now that my rose-colored friendship glasses were off for good, I could see clearly about the type of person Rachel had always been—especially when it came to money. Maybe because I'd grown up with a single mom and was used to making do with what I was given, I couldn't care less about designer labels or expensive vacations. Rachel, however, seemed obsessed with both. Even though she didn't come from a wealthy family like David, she'd usually gotten whatever she wanted as a teenager. That included a brand-new car when she turned sixteen and then a second one at seventeen after she'd crashed the first. But that wasn't the case when she moved out on her own. She hated the fact that she couldn't buy anything she wanted, despite having a good job. When I'd first met David, I thought she was joking when she'd asked if I would introduce her to his estranged brother because it had always been her dream to marry rich so she wouldn't have to work anymore.

I guess since she didn't marry rich, she had to have an affair with it instead.

My new jaded view of my former best friend allowed me to believe that she was indeed the reason why David was talking about mediators.

Part of me wanted to tell him I was still going to hire an attorney, just to be petty. But I also didn't want to spend any money I didn't have to, especially since my money was basically still David's money.

I'd stopped working as a business manager when I'd gotten pregnant so I could be a stay-at-home mom. Although I refused to call it an allowance, any money I needed came from David. I'd transfer money from our main checking account into a credit union account every month to use for anything I needed just for me. Then I'd pay the mortgage, utilities, groceries, and anything else for Maya and David using the main account. In one of his emails last week, David had announced that his last paycheck from Goodman would be that account's last direct deposit. Until things like spousal and child support were finalized, he'd transfer money from his new account to cover the larger bills. But he'd made it clear that this wasn't going to be forever, and he was expecting me to figure out my finances—including finding a job and deciding whether I wanted to keep the house and buy out his half or sell it and get a percentage of the money.

My head began to throb, as it always did when I thought about the house, money, and what I was supposed to do next.

"Are you still there?"

David's question brought me out of my migraine-inducing thoughts.

I coughed to make sure my throat worked. "Yes. I'm here."

"Well? What do you think about using a mediator?" He sounded annoyed now, which made me not want to continue the conversation any longer.

"I'll think about it."

"Claudia . . ."

"I said I'll think about it. Don't forget to call Maya tonight. Goodbye."

He didn't deserve the courtesy of a goodbye. But I didn't want him to use me hanging up on him as yet another excuse not to call his daughter.

Although I still didn't quite understand why or how his feelings for me had changed, I was more confused by his seeming lack of concern for Maya. Sure, some of it had to be guilt or not wanting to explain why he wasn't coming back. But didn't he miss talking to her? The same question I'd been asking myself for weeks reared its ugly head once again: How could he have left her too?

As far as dads went, David had always seemed like a good one. Since I had no real-life example to base that judgment on, the bar was admittedly low. Still, he changed her diapers and got up with me in the middle of the night when it was time to nurse her. He took her to the park so I could nap and would contort his body into her playhouse in the backyard in order to make her laugh. Things did change, though, when he started in his new role at Goodman two years ago. It was a position that gave him more money but also meant he'd be traveling more than he ever had. In the beginning, he told me he hated being away so much. He made it a point to spend quality time with us when he was in town, especially with Maya. But eventually, he seemed to always be at the office, even when he was home.

One of our regular arguments was about how I felt like a single mom because I was always the one doing things with Maya or taking her to all her activities.

"That's what a stay-at-home mom is supposed to do," he'd yelled at me once.

Despite all of that, I'd still believed that David loved our daughter and loved being her dad.

So why was he acting like neither of those things were true anymore?

What had changed?

Rachel.

It was the only explanation I could think of. And I hated it so much.

My stomach churned from both hunger and fury. It wasn't like I'd expected the call to be fun or even easy. What I didn't expect was for it to trigger yet more unsettling thoughts about Rachel. It was bad enough she'd played me for a fool all these months. Apparently, she wasn't done with finding new ways to destroy me.

I'd had to do some pretty amazing mental gymnastics to not think of her during my every waking hour. In fact, I hadn't left my house during these entire two weeks for fear of seeing Nick, which I knew would send me spiraling into another episode of "I must be the most ridiculous woman alive."

In his email, David had written that they'd been seeing each other for several months. But what did that mean? Since April? Since January? I'd spent every day of the last two weeks replaying every interaction between the three of us that I could remember since last Christmas.

There had to have been signs that I'd missed. Or ignored.

I had to admit one of them was our sex life. Before Maya was born, we couldn't keep our hands off each other. We'd christened every room in this house—even the backyard, thanks to a very sturdy hammock. But that all changed once we were parents. If we weren't too exhausted, then we were interrupted. It got better for a while once she was a little older and started sleeping in her own room and through the night.

Then it slowed down again. First, I was the one who was always too tired or even too resentful about him being away all the time to be in the mood. Then, the last few months, David had been the one to turn me down.

Now I knew why.

For a moment, my mind drifted to Nick. Was he doing the same as me and going down some kind of twisted memory lane known only to sadists and gluttons for punishment? Judging by his totally offensive question at my door two weeks ago, he, too, had been blindsided, but Rachel had made comments previously that had led me to believe their marriage was on shaky ground. So maybe Rachel's cheating hadn't come out of the blue, but rather he was more shocked about whom she'd been cheating with?

If I was a fool for not seeing what was happening between them, then Nick and I had been fools together.

Last night, after I couldn't sleep even after three glasses of wine, I'd gone into David's home office in search of incriminating clues that could lead me to an explanation—something neither David nor Rachel had offered me yet. The fact that they didn't feel the need to answer any questions or help me understand why they did what they did to me was almost as disrespectful as the affair.

The only thing I'd managed to find in David's desk was printed copies of credit card statements I'd already gone over at least three times online. And the only thing that stood out to me then and last night was the double purchase of a $500 espresso machine from Williams Sonoma. The mystery wasn't that David had bought that same machine a few months earlier—it was still on my kitchen counter. I just didn't understand why there were two charges just days apart.

Then, as I sat there, in the bright unforgiving light of my third Monday morning without a husband, the reason finally came to me.

I jumped off the couch and ran to the kitchen and stared down the espresso machine as if it were my new mortal enemy.

"You," I whispered.

Of course I didn't expect the inanimate object to admit its identity. But that didn't stop me from flipping it off anyway.

When I'd seen the box in the trunk of David's Lexus, it didn't raise any suspicions. I figured he just hadn't had a chance to bring it inside the house. So I did just that.

If anything, I was happily surprised that he'd remembered this was the exact one I'd mentioned wanting to buy the week before. I'd even shown it to him on the store's website. I had been stupidly impressed at his thoughtfulness.

The next day, he'd returned from one of his business trips and seemed surprised when I gave him a second kiss and thanked him for getting the new espresso machine.

"What are you talking about?" he'd asked. "The one we have works just fine."

I was confused. "Um, it doesn't. I told you the water sometimes doesn't heat up or doesn't come out the way it used to."

David still didn't seem to understand. He pointed to the shiny new appliance on the counter. "Wait. Where's the one we had before?"

"It's in the garage. I'll throw it out on trash day."

"That's the espresso machine I had in my trunk?" he'd said after walking over to it.

My wifely Spidey senses should've buzzed as soon as David's eyes widened. I thought it had been realization. I knew now it was panic.

"You took it out of my trunk, set it up on the counter, and threw the old one in the garage?"

I remembered how confused I'd felt at his response. He'd seemed angry.

"It was old, David. We've had that thing since before Maya was born. I told you that was the machine I wanted to buy, and you bought it instead. What's the big deal?"

His olive-colored neck flushed with pink streaks. "The big deal is that I don't know why you'd go through my trunk without telling me."

It was my turn to get annoyed. "I'm telling you now. And why are you making it seem like I did something wrong? I drove the Lexus the day I had to take in the RAV4 for servicing. I had thrown Maya's gym bag in the trunk when I picked her up from practice, and I saw the box when I went to take the bag out. Why are you acting like this?"

The moment I'd said that, his entire demeanor changed. His glare softened, his shoulders relaxed, and he gave me a sheepish smile.

"It was supposed to be a surprise," he'd said, reaching for me.

"A surprise?" I asked after he'd pulled me against him.

"I was planning to surprise you on Sunday with breakfast in bed and a piping-hot espresso made with the new machine. I'm sorry for getting annoyed. You get annoyed, too, when Maya goes snooping under the Christmas tree for her gifts."

I bristled at his explanation. "I wasn't snooping."

"I know. Sorry, that was the wrong word. I've been up since the crack of dawn, and the flight was delayed. I'm tired and cranky, and I'm sorry for taking it out on you." David then lifted my chin with his index finger so I could look at him. "Do you forgive me?"

Although my gut still wasn't sitting right with his reaction, I told myself I didn't want to fight. He'd be leaving again in a few days, and I didn't want to spend what time I had with him in a bad mood. So I'd told him that I did.

I'd forgiven that pinche pendejo.

Because what I now remembered as I looked at the espresso machine was the fact that the only other person I'd told that I'd wanted it was Rachel. We'd been shopping at Williams Sonoma for a wedding gift for one of David's coworkers when I spotted it. She made a comment about how lucky I was that I had a husband who enjoyed espressos, since Nick was strictly a no-sugar, no-cream coffee kind of man.

"He'd never let me buy it. He'd say it wouldn't be worth the money, since I would be the only one using it."

"You work, though," I said. "If it's your money, then he can't say anything."

"That doesn't matter. Even if I bought it with my own money, that wouldn't stop him from saying it every time I used it. And then I'd stop using it just so I wouldn't hear him complain. Which would make him right anyway—it wouldn't be worth the money I'd spent."

"Sorry," I replied. My usual response whenever she'd say something negative about Nick.

"You were smart, Claudia. You married rich. I married practical."

Rachel always classified our husbands that way. I'd gotten used to her self-deprecating comments, especially when it came to her marriage. Rachel and Nick had only been married nine years, and I'd bet she was only happy—truly happy—for about two of them.

Honestly, I'd expected for her to leave him sooner rather than later.

But I never expected that she'd take my husband with her.

I stared down the espresso machine again. I knew I could never use it again after realizing that David had bought it for Rachel in the first place. But because I'd taken it out of his trunk and put it on the counter in our house, he'd had to go buy her another one.

I wondered how she'd explained that to Nick.

Or maybe he never knew because that espresso machine had gone to San Francisco too.

Anger swelled up inside me, and I let out a guttural yell. I yanked the machine's plug out of the wall socket, grabbed it with both hands, and stomped out to the side of the backyard. But right before I was going to toss it inside the trash can, a thought came to me, and I set it on the ground.

A few minutes later I returned with the mallet I used to pound chicken breasts flat. Then I began hitting the espresso machine hard, over and over again. If it had been a chicken breast, it would've disintegrated into the concrete. Instead, the machine shattered into a million tiny pieces.

Just like my heart.

By the time the murdering of the machine was done and I'd swept up the evidence and disposed of its remains into my trash can, I was an exhausted, sweaty, and panting mess.

It was the most exercise—most activity, period—I'd had in two weeks.

Satisfied with what I'd done, I blew away the loose hairs that had escaped my already-messy bun and wiped the sweat beads off my forehead with the hem of my faded purple Lakers T-shirt.

But my pride was short lived as soon as I walked back inside and my reality set in. I looked around my kitchen with its sink full of dirty dishes, cluttered kitchen island, and dingy floors and immediately became overwhelmed. Destroying that stupid espresso machine had given me a false sense of accomplishment.

My life and my house were still a complete and utter mess.

Tears filled my eyes. Suddenly, I was too tired to even take a very needed shower. All I wanted to do was sleep.

As I headed back to the couch in the family room, I heard my doorbell ring.

It had been a mistake to answer my door the last time, so I hesitated to do it again. Given my emotional state, I couldn't trust that I wouldn't break down if it was Nick coming back to ask me more ridiculous questions. I also couldn't trust that I wouldn't grab that chicken mallet out of the trash if he dared point an accusatory finger at me.

I waited a few seconds for the pounding and yelling to continue. When I didn't hear anything, I decided it must be a package delivery. I vaguely remembered ordering some things off Amazon a few days ago.

The silence seemed to confirm my assumption, and I walked slowly to my front door.

When I opened it, though, there wasn't a box or padded envelope waiting for me on the other side.

My eyes took in the woman's appearance, starting from her fashionable black leather high-heeled sandals up to her flowy fuchsia skirt and matching short-sleeved blouse. Her makeup was impeccable and fresh, judging from the shine of her glossy pink lips and shimmery pink cheeks. Her previously long black hair was now short and all silver. She removed her black Prada sunglasses to reveal the same hazel eyes I'd always known, now framed by age spots and lines.

"Hello, Claudia," she said with a smile.

I squinted my eyes, again trying to reconcile what I was seeing. Correction. *Who* I was seeing. Finally, I opened my mouth. "Mom?"

Gloria's smile immediately turned into a frown as she scanned—and definitely judged—me up and down.

"Good Lord," she said with a hint of disgust. "You look way worse than I thought you would."

CHAPTER FIVE

THINGS I NEVER KNEW #86: FUNERALS ARE FOR THE LIVING

Dear Diary,

My heart is broken. My beloved abuela is gone.

I'm still not sure what happened. All Gloria said was that she got an infection, and by the time she went to the emergency room, there wasn't much the doctors could do. She died after only two days of being in the hospital.

I didn't even know she'd been sick. She and Gloria had had a fight the week before, and we hadn't gone to see her since. I'd called her a few days before, and she'd told me she was fine. But I should've known that she wasn't.

After she died, the women from her church asked my mom if they could pray the rosary for the next nine nights at Abuela's house. Gloria said it was called a novena. I didn't understand why it had to be nine nights or why they had to do it at her house. But my mother just told me to stop asking so many questions and that her friends could do whatever they wanted to do if it helped them with their grief.

So I asked her what I was supposed to do. She told me that I could help her clean Abuela's house from top to bottom to prepare for the novena. But that wasn't what I had meant. I was asking what I was supposed to do without her.

Gloria and I are staying right now at Abuela's tiny two-bedroom rental house instead of our own apartment. The owner gave us two more weeks to clean everything out, so that's what I'm going to be doing after school most days. My abuela has always been a very private person. She would yell at me if she caught me looking in her closet or in her dresser. I know she's probably having a heart attack thinking about me and Mom going through her things and deciding what to keep and what to throw away.

During the nine nights of the novena, people I barely knew came and brought us food like enchiladas and pozole so Gloria wouldn't have to cook. Others brought pan dulce and coffee for everyone to snack on. Then we all prayed the rosary so Abuela's soul would find heaven. I've been to church enough times to know the basics. The one thing I loved the most about it all was that my mom let me pick one of Abuela's rosary beads to use. Then she said I could keep it after. I chose the one I knew Abuela prayed with every night. It had sparkly blue beads on a silver strand with a silver cross in the middle. She'd told me a friend had brought it for her after visiting Italy. But after the novena was over, I told my mom she should be buried with it instead so she could still pray every night for us in heaven. Then I picked from her jewelry box a small bracelet rosary with clear beads and a white plastic cross to keep instead.

Today was her funeral. There was a Mass at the church, and then we all met at the cemetery. I found out a few days ago that Abuela had prepaid for everything for the services, from her plot to the flowers they put on her burgundy-colored casket. But instead of being relieved, I overheard Gloria tell one of her friends that "even in death, the woman didn't trust me." I don't understand what she meant by that. But ever since Abuela died, I've learned life is easier with Gloria if I stop trying to figure her out.

I probably cried all day. I still can't believe she's gone. I don't know if I really believe in heaven or God, but it's nice to think that Abuela is somewhere up there living her best afterlife. The arthritis in her hands is gone and so is the pain, and she's going to spend eternity snacking on pumpkin seeds while watching her favorite telenovelas. I also want to believe that every now and then, she'll come back to check on us. Because I really don't know what me and Gloria are going to do without her.

I love you, Abuela. I will miss you always.

CHAPTER SIX

Gloria had been in my house for several hours, and I still had no idea what she was doing here.

Sure, she'd explained that she'd come to help me during my *awful* situation, but I knew it was bullshit. And I'm pretty sure Gloria knew that I knew it was bullshit. But she was doing what she did best—evading the truth.

If I counted on one hand the number of times my mother had shown up to help me get through so-called awful situations, I'd still have three fingers down.

The first time was when I broke my arm trying to roller-skate in the parking lot of our apartment complex. I'd come home crying, and she immediately grabbed the car keys and raced us over to the nearest emergency room. Then she turned into Shirley MacLaine from *Terms of Endearment* after five hours of being in the waiting room. She threatened to sue the hospital if my arm didn't end up healing right because it had taken so long for a doctor to examine me. I was actually impressed and even started calling her "Shirley" for a few weeks after that. I thought it was hysterical that she had no idea why. I guess Abuela had never made her watch the movie over and over again like she had made me.

The second time was when Rachel and I got wasted at a party our senior year, and our dates abandoned us once the police showed up. We'd somehow managed to walk ourselves to a nearby liquor store and called her to come pick us up. Even though it was nearly midnight, she arrived in less than ten minutes. She bought us some Gatorades, drove us back to our apartment, and switched off holding our hair back as we each puked our guts out. I found out later that she'd even called Rachel's mom at some point to let her know that the boys had ditched us at the party and Rachel would be staying the night—but thankfully had left out the whole underage drinking part.

Still, Gloria had never seemed interested in being the type of parent who'd drop everything after finding out her daughter's husband had left her for her best friend. I blamed the wine and the self-pity party on night number three after David's email for not letting her call go to voicemail like I usually did. Instead, I'd answered and told her the whole sordid story.

Had I asked her to come in my inebriated state? God, I hoped I hadn't. I never thought there would be enough alcohol in this world for me to get to the point where I'd ask my mother for anything ever again.

Gloria did not like stress or confrontations or being uncomfortable in general. So my suspicions had been on high alert ever since she'd walked through the door with two rolling suitcases and announced she could stay with me for as long as I needed her.

She either didn't hear or ignored my "I don't" that I'd muttered right after, because she'd proceeded to recount her harrowing travel experience that began at five that morning in Florida and included not one but two Uber drivers and one broken nail. Then she said she was exhausted and had a migraine and asked where she could lie down for a nap.

That was four hours ago.

"I'm starving. Let's go out to dinner," Gloria said after finally emerging from the guest bedroom.

"It's not even three in the afternoon," I said.

"I'm on East Coast time. My body thinks it's almost six and dinnertime. Well, technically we usually eat dinner around four. Carlos likes to eat earlier because he's in bed by eight."

Carlos was my mother's current partner. He owned a fleet of car dealerships across central Florida, and they'd been together for about three years now. They'd met on some singles' cruise, and she'd moved in with him just a few weeks after they'd docked. I'd never met him in person, even though Gloria had asked me numerous times to go visit them. I'd nearly run out of excuses not to go. Truth was, I saw no need to meet Carlos when I knew he most likely wouldn't be around much longer.

And that's when I had a paranoid revelation.

I walked over to where she was sitting at my kitchen table. "Did you leave Carlos? Did he kick you out? Oh my God. Are you here because you think I'll let you move in with me?"

Her eyes grew wider with every question. Then she rolled them. "I did not leave Carlos, and he would never kick me out. That man adores me. I'll have you know we are still happily together."

"Then why are you here?" I asked, not even trying to hide the suspicion in my voice.

"I already told you. I came to help you. And by the looks of it around here, you definitely need it."

Although I'd had a chance to shower and change during Gloria's nap, I hadn't done very much to clean around the house. I had at least emptied the dryer and put one load of Maya's clothes into the wash. But that was the extent of my tidying up. Most adult children would probably go into overdrive trying to clean when their parent was going to visit. But I had neither the energy nor the inclination to do anything in order to impress my mother. She was going to judge me whether I had streak-free windows or not.

"You didn't have to come," I replied as I took the seat across from her.

"That's not what you said when you called me. In fact, I think your exact words were 'Please come.'"

Damn wine.

"Well, I was just having a bad night. I'm fine now."

"You know I can always tell when you're lying."

I sat back and folded my arms. "I'm not saying everything is perfect. Obviously. But me and Maya are getting through it."

Gloria looked behind me. "Where is my beautiful granddaughter, anyway?"

I tried not to roll my eyes at her question. In order to have a granddaughter, you had to be a grandmother. Biologically, yes, she was. But Maya had only seen the woman two times in her life, and she was way too young to probably even remember. My daughter had had more conversations with the lady who cut her hair than with Gloria.

"She'll be home from school in a few minutes."

"You're not picking her up?" she said.

"Her friend's mom is dropping her off."

"Oh," Gloria said. It was one word, but her tone seemed to be saying a lot more.

"Oh, what?" I accused.

She shrugged and got up from the table. "Oh, nothing," she said.

"I can also tell when you're lying, you know." Her tell was a subtle flare of her nostrils. I hadn't seen the woman in years, but I was quickly seeing that she hadn't changed that much. That's how I knew there was more to the story as to why she'd suddenly appeared on my doorstep. Eventually, I'd get it out of her.

"Fine. I just thought you'd be picking her up. That was one of the reasons you said you could never come to Florida. You said you didn't trust any other parent to take her to school or pick her up. And you were also way too busy during the summer taking her to all of her activities."

God, I hated that she had the memory of an elephant.

"That might have been true last year. But I've gotten to know Valerie, the friend's mom, and she offered to help me out. It's not that big of a deal."

It actually had been kind of a big deal. I'd barely gotten Maya to school on time on the first day. Which meant I'd left the house wearing two different slippers, pajama pants, and a wrinkled gray New Kids on the Block T-shirt. So when Valerie ran into me in the school parking lot and asked if I wanted to join her and a few other moms for coffee, I had to decline. And when she asked me again the following day, I turned her down. Again. Finally, she asked if everything was okay, which was when I told her David had gotten a new job in San Francisco and that

I wasn't coping very well with him being away. It was as much of the truth as I was willing to share without running the risk of becoming hysterical. She'd very kindly let me know that she could take and pick up Maya for as long as I needed, since she only lived around the corner.

Gloria was right, though. The old me would've balked at the offer. The old me would've insisted all was okay and that I could handle anything I needed to.

This new me? Well, she barely had the energy these days to comb her hair.

My mother's raised eyebrows let me know she was suspicious. "If you say so," she replied.

"I do say so."

Instead of saying anything else, she walked over to the sink and turned on the water.

"What are you doing?" I asked.

"A load of dishes. Do you have any gloves?"

I jumped up from the table. "Mom, you are not doing my dishes. Besides, I have a dishwasher."

"Fine. I'll fill up the dishwasher." But before she could open the door, I stopped her.

"I don't need you to do my dishes. Period." I hadn't meant to sound so . . . harsh.

"I told you I was here to help," she said.

This time her voice was soft. It immediately made me feel guilty.

I let out a long sigh. "I appreciate that. I do. But . . ."

"But what?"

How could I tell her that having her here and seeing me like this was embarrassing enough? I didn't need her to witness the full extent of the current disaster my life had become. And I especially didn't want her to see me failing as a mother—something I couldn't bear to see myself.

"Look, Maya is going to be here soon. We can go to an early dinner, and then we can look at flights for Florida. I bet you can find something out of LAX in the morning."

Gloria opened her mouth to say something, but before she could, we both heard the front door open.

"Mommy, I'm home!"

"In the kitchen," I yelled. Then I met Gloria's eyes. "Let me do the talking, okay?"

She nodded, and I turned and began walking toward the living room. I wanted to meet Maya before she entered the kitchen.

"Hi, baby! Cómo te fue en la escuela?"

Over the summer, Maya had started watching a bilingual kids' show on YouTube and asked me to start teaching her more Spanish. I wasn't exactly fluent, but I knew enough from spending lots of time with my abuela. Although David's grandparents were from Mexico, his parents were born in the States and had never taught him the language. I was proud that Maya wanted to learn and was also ashamed I hadn't tried to teach her as a toddler.

So I welcomed the chance to also practice the language for myself.

My daughter nodded and said, "Bien, gracias." Her face scrunched into thought, and I knew she was trying to think of the words. She opted for English ones. "We painted boxes today, and when they're dry, we get to use them for our pencils and stuff. Can I have some cereal? Tengo hambre."

I cleared my throat as I took her backpack from her. "Maybe. I have to see if we have any. But before we go into the kitchen, I wanted to tell you that we have a visitor today."

Her small face immediately lit up, and she squealed, "Daddy? Is Daddy here?"

And before I could stop her, she ran toward the kitchen.

"Maya, wait!" I called as I followed her.

She stopped in her tracks when she saw Gloria. "Who are you?"

My mother smiled and held out her arms. "I'm your grandma. Can I get a hug?"

My incessant lectures about stranger danger apparently had made an impression because Maya shook her head, ran toward me, and promptly attached herself to my side.

Gloria's face fell in disappointment, and I almost felt bad for her. Almost.

"It's okay, baby," I said, and I bent down so I could look her in the eye. "This is my mom, Gloria. She's your grandma. You haven't seen her in a long time, so that's why you don't remember her. Say hello."

Maya nodded and slowly walked over to Gloria. She held out her hand. "Hola. Me llamo Maya. Mucho gusto."

My mother arched her eyebrow in what I recognized as both amusement and confusion. Then she smiled and shook her hand. "So nice to meet you, Maya."

Maya smiled back and then tilted her head. "Do I call you 'Grandma' or 'Abuela'?"

My mom looked over my daughter's head, met my eyes, and held them for several seconds. I'm not sure what, if anything, she saw in them. Whatever it was, it made her nod at me. Finally, she looked back down at Maya and said, "I think 'Grandma' suits me better. Is that okay?"

We ended up getting dinner delivered about an hour later. Maya was in her picky eating phase, and there were currently only two restaurants she'd eat from. One of them was closed on Mondays, and the other required reservations. So delivery it was.

As we feasted on a meal of spaghetti with meat sauce and delicious garlic bread, Gloria entertained Maya with stories about Florida. My daughter acted both horrified and impressed that an alligator had once crawled across Gloria's street. Even I laughed when she shared how Carlos had wanted to capture it and make it the live mascot at one of his dealerships.

But when Gloria promised Maya that she would take her to Disney World one day, I was done with the Florida tales and decided it was time for Maya to work on some homework and then take her bath. My mother offered to clean up and put the leftovers away. I didn't argue with her this time.

After I'd made sure Maya was in bed, I headed down the hallway to face my mother.

It had been years since we'd had any sort of argument. Well, in person anyway. Although I tried to keep our monthly phone calls superficial, the occasional touchy topic would sneak in, and one of us—usually me—would cut the conversation short after some loud back-and-forth.

That was going to be hard to do if she was standing right in front of me.

I stopped at the door to the guest bedroom when I heard her talking. I hated eavesdropping, especially in my own house. However, Gloria's penchant for not sharing critical information with me made it necessary.

"She wants me to come home tomorrow, but I don't think I should."

Silence.

She had to be talking to Carlos.

"I understand that, but I haven't even been here a full day. And she definitely needs some help around the house. It's such a mess."

I rolled my eyes and continued listening to her side of the conversation.

"She can't physically put me on a plane, Carlos. I'm not leaving until I do what I came here to do."

What she came here to do? I didn't like the way that sounded. But it confirmed my suspicions that there was another reason why she was here.

Because of course there was.

She kept talking, but I'd heard enough and walked into the kitchen. Although the overall space was still cluttered, the table was clear, and I could hear the hum of the dishwasher.

A few minutes later, Gloria walked out. "Where's Maya?"

"In bed," I replied as I poured myself a glass of ice water.

"Oh," she said. "I wanted to say good night. Can I go peek in her bedroom?"

I took a long sip before answering. "I'd rather you didn't. She'll be asleep soon, as long as she's left alone."

"Okay. Well then, I guess I'll go back to the room and unpack."

It was time to set things straight with Gloria. "Not yet, Mom. We need to finish our conversation."

"And which conversation was that?"

"The one where you tell me the real reason why you're here. If you don't, then there will be no need for you to unpack."

Her shoulders stiffened at my harsh tone. I didn't care, though. I knew from experience that you didn't get anything out of Gloria by beating around the bush.

I motioned for her to sit down at the table, and I joined her.

"Spill it," I said.

She shrugged. "I honestly don't know what else I can say. You asked me to come, so I'm here."

Time to be brutally honest. "Look, I was drunk. I was sad. But you and I both know that usually wouldn't be enough to get you on a plane back to California. Besides, that was almost two weeks ago. If you really wanted to help me, then why did you wait so long, and why didn't you tell me you were coming?"

Gloria looked down at her hands before meeting my eyes. Hers looked dimmed with a hint of guilt. "I didn't tell you I was coming because I knew you'd tell me not to. Of course I could tell you were drunk when you started talking to me that night. But when you didn't call the next day to take back what you'd said, I decided I didn't want to give you the chance. And the more days that passed without a call, the more I convinced myself that maybe you had really meant it. So I booked the flight."

Despite my usual suspicions about anything that came out of her mouth, I believed her. Well, I believed she believed her reasoning.

I thought about Maya and how happy she'd been during dinner. It was also the first night in a week that she hadn't cried for her dad. Who, of course, had failed to call her. No doubt it was to punish me for not immediately agreeing to mediation. Maybe having Gloria here for a few days might be a good distraction.

Still, I had my reservations.

"If you stay, you have to agree to some rules when it comes to Maya."

Her face brightened. "Anything."

I took a long, deep breath. "First, you do not talk to her about David. Ever. She misses him, and I can't have you bringing him up and making her upset."

"Of course." I didn't miss the way she pressed her lips into a thin line after answering. A sign she was holding back what she really wanted to say. I knew better than to open the door to that. So I ignored it and continued laying down the law.

"Second, please do not make promises that you can't keep."

"Like what?"

"Like taking her to Disney World. You and I both know that's probably never going to happen, so I don't want her to get her hopes up."

I had a long list of promises broken by Gloria to last a lifetime. There was no way I was going to let my daughter have even one.

"But why wouldn't it happen?" she asked. "I've been inviting you to Florida for years. And she's at the age where I think she'd really enjoy Disney World."

"She's already been to Disneyland. Besides, she doesn't need you to get her hopes up with promises you won't keep."

"And there it is!" she yelled, throwing up her hands. "I've been here less than a day, and you couldn't even wait to throw my mistakes in my face." Her eyes grew big and she covered her mouth, as if she seemed surprised by her own words and the volume of her voice.

I stood up. This was my house. Maya was my daughter. I'd lost control of so much in the past two weeks. Letting my mother know she couldn't talk to me like that anymore was something I could still control. "I knew this wasn't going to work," I told her calmly. "Just go back to Florida, okay? You played grandma for a few hours. I'm guessing that should be enough to last you another couple of years."

I began to walk away, but she jumped in front of me. "I'm sorry, Claudia. I shouldn't have said that or raised my voice. You're right. I shouldn't be making promises to Maya. Not because I don't plan on keeping them, but because I know I haven't earned the right. Please let me stay so I can do that. Please."

Her pleading surprised me. Gloria had never begged me for anything in her life. My anger subsided a little.

"I have enough to deal with," I said truthfully. "I don't need you adding to my stress or Maya's."

Gloria waved her arms. "I won't. I know I don't deserve your trust, but I really do want to get to know Maya. And I want to do what I can for you. I really just want to help."

My thoughts drifted again to my daughter. Her life was never going to be the same, and as much as I wanted to protect her from that, I had to admit I had to fix myself first. Some of my best childhood memories were because of my abuela. She'd stepped up when Gloria couldn't or wouldn't. Although Abuela hadn't been in my life long, I still treasured every moment I'd had with her. I wanted that for Maya. Especially since it was becoming apparent that she might end up losing her father.

Gloria was far from being the world's greatest mother. For Maya's sake, I hoped she was telling the truth about at least trying to be a decent grandmother.

"Fine," I said with a sigh. "You can stay."

For a brief second, I thought Gloria was going to cry, or worse, give me a hug.

Instead, she smiled and nodded. "Thank you. I promise . . ." She stopped herself. "Thank you."

We stayed there looking at each other for a few more seconds. It was awkward.

"I have to take out the trash," I finally said.

Her expression switched from emotional to stoic. "Okay. I will go unpack. See you in the morning?"

"Yeah."

A few minutes later, as I carried the trash bag from the kitchen outside to the backyard, I tried not to panic. Had I really just agreed to let my mother stay with us? I didn't want to think the worst. But experience warned me that it was not going to be all fun and games. I just had to hope the good parts would outweigh the bad ones that were bound to happen.

I lifted the lid of the trash can and threw the bag on top of the remnants of the espresso machine. I was just about to let the lid slam down when a voice from next door made me freeze.

"You can't keep ignoring my calls, Rachel," I heard Nick say. "And I'm going to keep calling. I'm tired of the stupid emails and cryptic texts. We need to talk. Really talk. Call me back."

Praying my mother wouldn't come outside and give me away, I stayed as still as a statue and pressed my lips together in silence. It was quiet for a few more seconds, and then I heard what sounded like the lid of a trash can slamming closed. I waited until I was sure Nick's back door had shut before finally taking a breath. I gently closed my own trash can and ran back inside my house.

Then I made a note to only take out my trash during the day, when I knew he would be at work.

I'd just agreed to let my chaotic mother stay with me. The last thing I needed was to have an uncomfortable conversation with the man married to my husband's mistress.

God, my life had really turned into one of those telenovelas my abuela used to watch.

Drama? Definitely.

Evil villain? Rachel, of course.

Scheming mother? Obviously.

All I was missing was a long-lost twin. Which I wouldn't totally put past Gloria.

It would've been funny if it wasn't so depressing.

At least with telenovelas, their improbable twists and turns always worked themselves out into one thrilling yet satisfying ending.

I couldn't say the same about my life.

CHAPTER SEVEN

THINGS I NEVER KNEW #112: CABRONAS DON'T ALWAYS HAVE TO WIN

Dear Diary,

Today was the best day ever! That two-faced cabrona Melanie Beck has finally met her match. Her name is Rachel Martinez, and she just transferred here from Arizona.

Remember how I told you how Melanie, the queen of the eighth grade cabronas club, decided she didn't like me and forbid any of her friends from talking to me? It got so bad that I've been eating lunch by myself by the basketball courts instead of the cafeteria because no one wants to sit with me anymore.

Well, Melanie got assigned by Mrs. Shelley to show Rachel around the school today. They looked like they were getting along pretty well, and I figured Melanie had found a new member for her stuck-up club. Then Mrs. Shelley asked me to explain our history project to Rachel, and that meant we got to go to the library together so I could help her pick out her topic and the books she would need.

I found out that Rachel's dad is in the military, and she has lived all over the country. She's an only child just like me. She's Mexican too but doesn't really speak Spanish. Well, except for the bad words. And we both love sour gummy worms and the same TV shows. I was having the best time with her, but then the bell rang for lunch. My stomach got upset as I walked with her to the cafeteria. She stayed with me as we got our food. Then Melanie spotted us and waved at Rachel to come sit with her group. When I didn't move, she told me to come with her. That's when I told her that I wasn't allowed to sit with those girls.

Rachel laughed, so I guess she thought I was joking because she tugged on my sleeve and pulled me with her. But I nearly threw up when Melanie told Rachel, "Just you. Not her."

I don't think Rachel still understood because she said, "Are you serious?"

That's when Melanie let her true colors show and said, "If you want to be friends with us, you can't be friends with Claudia."

My heart sank and I bit my lip so I wouldn't cry. I thought for sure Rachel was going to turn to me and say sorry or something and then sit down. But my mouth dropped open when she told Melanie in a really loud voice so the other girls at the table would hear, "Well, good thing I don't want to be friends with you. Let's go eat somewhere else, Claudia."

Diary, you should've seen that cow's face. I don't think anyone has ever told Melanie that they didn't want to be friends with her. I wish someone would've taken a picture so I could frame it and keep it by my bed forever.

Later, when we'd finished eating lunch at the basketball courts, I told Rachel that it was okay if she wanted to eat lunch with Melanie and her friends tomorrow. But Rachel said she didn't want to because she didn't need to hang around those kinds of girls. Then she invited me to go over to her house this weekend so we could work on the history project together.

I don't know if she really wants to be my friend or not. Or maybe she's just being nice so I can help her with the project. But I guess I'll worry about that later.

I decided I'd let myself be happy, at least for today, that Rachel Martinez came into my life.

CHAPTER EIGHT

"Mommy, don't forget that tomorrow is the party for all the September birthdays in my class," Maya said as she finished the last bite of her mashed potatoes.

I'd made her grilled chicken strips for dinner, and she'd only touched one of the three, yet she'd devoured the potatoes. At least the mashed potatoes weren't the boxed ones. I knew technically they weren't vegetables, but I was still going to count tonight's dinner as a win.

I stood up from the table to take my dishes to the sink. "I thought the birthday parties were on Fridays."

"Miss Lima isn't going to be here on Friday, so the party is tomorrow. I promised I would bring cookies."

"Ooh, I love cookies!" my mother said. She was still seated at the table and picked up one of Maya's uneaten chicken strips off her plate with a fork. "Except for peanut butter ones. My favorite are the ones from the store with the pink frosting and sprinkles."

"I wanna take cookies with pink frosting and sprinkles," Maya exclaimed.

I walked back to the table to clean up the rest of the plates. "Maybe for the next party. I can make some sugar cookies, and I think we even have some sprinkles."

Both Gloria's and Maya's mouths turned into identical frowns. Maybe it was just my imagination—or paranoia—but my daughter was starting to look more and more like her. It had only been two days.

"Por favor, Mommy. Please can I bring cookies with pink frosting to the party?"

Gloria met my eyes. "Por favor."

God, I hated when they double-teamed me.

Any reservations I'd had about my daughter accepting Gloria as her grandmother had been thrown out the window basically overnight. My mother and Maya were practically best friends now.

Not only did Maya ask Gloria to do her hair before school that first morning, but she even agreed to let Gloria pack her a lunch. And when Gloria asked if she could include some slices of turkey and a couple of crackers in her turquoise bag, I explained that Maya didn't like turkey.

"It's okay, Mommy. I can try to like it today," my daughter said, as if I hadn't tried to send her with turkey in her lunch box numerous times before. I was shocked.

I tried not to let it bother me. I knew I should be happy that they were getting along and that Gloria was giving Maya the extra attention she needed right now.

Still, part of me felt like I needed to step up my mom game.

And that's how I ended up at the store right before closing time on a Wednesday in search of cookies with pink frosting and sprinkles.

Luckily, I found them right near the entrance to the store and picked up two cartons. I was about to leave when I remembered we were out of milk and only had two rolls of toilet paper in the hallway closet.

I hadn't stepped into a market since the day David left. My grocery delivery app had been working overtime ever since. Besides, it wasn't like I was planning meals for the week like I had before. Instead, I'd order whatever we needed for dinner and do the same thing the next day if we didn't do takeout or drive-through. Amazon or Target curbside took care of everything else. It wasn't the most cost-efficient way to live. I knew that. It was easy, though. And easy was the priority for me right now.

While I'm here, might as well get some other things I need.

I put the cookies down, went back outside, and grabbed a cart.

Aimlessly, I pushed it through the produce section, looking for inspiration on how to get Maya to eat more vegetables. She refused to even taste carrots, no matter if I boiled them, roasted them, or gave them to her raw with a side of ranch. I thought about trying mashed cauliflower, since she loved potatoes, but I wasn't sure if I could pull off a bait and switch.

Remembering I'd saved a recipe on my Pinterest board a few weeks ago, I pulled out my phone. I was just about to open the app when I recognized a man's voice behind me. He was asking someone if they had any more bags of Caesar salad mix in the back.

I froze.

Without even turning, I knew it was Nick.

The employee told him everything they had was out on the shelf and that they might get some more with their delivery in the morning. He apparently must have been satisfied with the answer because I didn't hear him say anything else. I dared not move in case he pushed his cart past me.

After waiting a few minutes, I figured the coast was clear and I slowly turned around to search for him. But I was the only person left in the produce section.

I wanted to leave right then and there, but I remembered I still needed coffee creamer. The store was about to close, and I really didn't want to have to come back in the morning. So I quickly headed to the dairy refrigerators located in the back of the store. Just as I turned the corner, though, there was Nick, studying the assortment of coffee creamers.

He was wearing a faded black T-shirt, wrinkled khaki cargo shorts, white ankle socks, and dark-blue tennis shoes. Definitely not the usual working attire I'd seen him wear hundreds of times before. I assumed then that he'd stopped at home before coming to the store. Had he already eaten dinner, or was he there because he hadn't?

Why do you care, though?

He'd left his basket behind him unattended, and I couldn't help but take a peek. It was only about a quarter of the way full. Besides a box of Keurig coffee pods and a bag of red apples, the only items inside were frozen dinners and bags of salad mixes. I remembered Rachel complaining once how Nick didn't know how to cook, so that meant she was responsible for making dinner during the week, even though she usually got home from work later than he did.

My snooping was cut short when Nick opened the door of the refrigerator and reached for a bottle of coffee creamer. I made a U-turn in the aisle and headed for the register. Gloria and I would just have to make do with the powdered stuff we had in our pantry until I placed an Instacart order.

When I got home, I put away the things I did buy and then told Maya it was time for her bath and bed. She whined a little because Gloria had let her look through the jewelry she'd brought with her, and she wasn't done trying on every bracelet and necklace.

Before I could say anything else, though, my phone rang. I looked down and nearly dropped it. I didn't answer it until I was back in the hallway outside the guest bedroom.

"Sorry I didn't call the other night. Is she still awake?"

I cleared my throat. "Yes, but she's just about to take her bath," I told David.

"Okay. How about I just tell her good night then?"

I looked back inside the bedroom and saw Gloria putting one of her bracelets on Maya's wrist. Then they both laughed when it fell right off because it was too big for her tiny wrist. I knew talking to David would change Maya's mood. But how could I deny him when I'd practically begged him to call?

"Fine, but be quick."

"I will."

Two hours later, I'd finally gotten Maya to stop crying, and she'd fallen asleep in my arms. Carefully, I laid her back onto her bed, covered her with her comforter, and then tiptoed out of her bedroom. Gloria was sitting on the couch when I walked into the family room.

"That was awful," she said, rubbing her temples.

"It was," I agreed as I sat down in the armchair next to her.

"Why did he have to call her so late?"

I laid my head back on the couch cushion and closed my eyes. "I don't know why David does what he does these days."

"You should've told him to call back tomorrow."

I bristled at the accusation. "He's her father," I said, lifting my head so I could face her. "I'm not going to not let him talk to her when he wants to. Plus, Maya misses him."

"I understand that. What I don't understand is how he could put her through this. Or you."

My chest tightened with familiar sadness. I didn't want to have this conversation with Gloria. I was physically and emotionally exhausted from trying not to break down in front of my daughter after she'd kept asking me why her daddy had gone away.

"Yeah, well, join the club. It's late, Mom. I want to go to bed."

"So go," she said, waving her hand toward the hallway.

I hesitated. "Um, I usually try to relax here on the couch first. It's how I wind down." I didn't add that the couch was also where I slept these days. Although if she hadn't figured that out by now, she would eventually.

If she thought I was lying, she didn't say. Instead, she stood up and nodded. Before she walked away, though, she said, "None of this is your fault. I'm sure Maya knows you're doing the best you can."

I didn't let myself cry until I heard the bedroom door close.

CHAPTER NINE

THINGS I NEVER KNEW #125: THE CRIMINAL LIFE IS NOT FOR ME

Dear Diary,

I cheated.

My hand is shaking even writing those two words. I feel horrible. It's been three days, and I can't stop thinking about what I did.

We had our first semester finals this week. As I've told you before, freshman year has been a lot harder than I thought it would be. Especially Biology. And I'm not the only one who thinks so. Even Rachel, who usually loves anything to do with science, was barely getting a C. Since she wants to try out for the dance team next year, she couldn't risk failing the final and bringing down her GPA. I'm not trying out, but I was going into the final with a solid D. Which meant if I failed it, then I would fail the class. And I couldn't let that happen.

So when Rachel found out that old Mr. Bautista uses the same multiple-choice test every year, she got a copy from Lyle Thomas, a sophomore who's tried asking her out a few times. She told him she'd go out with him and even kiss him in exchange for the test. Then the night before the final, we wrote down the answers for each multiple-choice question on a tiny piece of paper that we then taped to the inside of our matching bangle bracelets. We purposely made sure to get at least three answers wrong (we each chose different questions so our tests wouldn't be exactly the same, though). We weren't trying to be greedy or dumb. We both just wanted to get at least a B.

Well, it worked. Mr. Bautista graded them in front of us as soon as we turned in our tests. I nearly peed my pants, though, when he congratulated me and said he was proud of me for studying so hard.

Ever since then, I can't shake this feeling of awfulness. I'm officially on winter break now, but I can't eat and all I want to do is sleep.

It got so bad that earlier today, when Gloria yelled at me after she came home from work because I was still in bed, I just started crying and confessed my crime.

Silly me thought she'd understand why I did what I did.

Instead, she yelled at me all over again. "Are you fucking kidding me? I can't believe you would do that. You could get kicked out of school, Claudia!"

I told her that failing the class was not an option. I told her I was desperate.

Then she told me how disappointed she was because she thought I was better than that. And, of course, she blamed Rachel. "If that girl told you to jump off a cliff then you'd do it, wouldn't you?"

That's when I got mad. I defended my best friend and said she was only trying to help me. But when she kept going on about what a bad influence Rachel was, I lost it and yelled back, "You're the bad influence, Mom! You break the rules all the time! If anyone taught me how to be a cheater, then it was you!"

I still can't forget the expression on Gloria's face when I said that. For a second I almost flinched because I thought she was going to slap me. Instead, her eyes grew big and wide and her bottom lip trembled. She actually looked like she was going to cry. But then she kind of shook it off and put her hands on her hips and told me very calmly:

"Sneaking into a movie after only paying to see one or not driving back to the store because a cashier forgot to charge me for a second twelve-pack of Diet Coke is not the same as purposefully cheating on a test that could get you expelled. Also, you are not me. You've been moping around this apartment for days, which means you obviously don't have the stomach for doing the wrong thing, so I think you're punishing yourself way more than I could ever punish you. So I'm only going to say one more thing about this, and then we're never going to speak about it again, okay? Nothing can change what happened. But you have to learn to live with your mistakes and then the next time you do better. So get over it and move on."

Why does she think it's that easy?

CHAPTER TEN

"Time to get up!"

Gloria's voice startled me awake. My eyes opened, but I didn't move.

"Okay, okay," I grumbled.

Just when I thought I could try to get a few minutes more of sleep, the comforter covering me was cruelly ripped away. That made me uncurl and yell, "What the hell!"

My mother walked over to the side of the couch and bent down. "I told you it was time to get up."

I was too tired to argue back. Instead, I sat up and rubbed the lagañas out of my eyes.

Then she shoved a folded green towel in my face. "Here. Go take a shower. You stink."

"I do not stink," I said with a roll of my eyes. "Stop exaggerating."

"You haven't left the house or changed out of those clothes in three days."

"That's not true," I said. "Remember, I went to the store to get the cookies."

"That was Wednesday, Claudia. Today is Saturday."

I opened my mouth to argue that that couldn't possibly be right. But since Maya hadn't woken me up to get her ready for school, then it had to be. I took the towel from her and got off the couch.

"Where's Maya?" I said after a big yawn.

"She's in her room making her bed, and then she's going to help me clean up a little in here. That's why you need to get up and get off that couch. I told her we could walk to the park after."

"She doesn't need to help you clean anything. And I'll take her to the park."

Nearly every Saturday morning of my childhood was spent mopping floors or vacuuming. I hated it. Maya was responsible for keeping her room tidy, and that was it. There was no way Gloria was going to give my daughter chores without talking to me first. And she didn't even know where the park was!

I was about to walk to the bathroom when Gloria said, "What's wrong with you? Why aren't you sleeping in your own bed?"

"Um, you know what's wrong. Or did you already forget the whole 'husband abandoning me and my child' thing?" I scoffed.

She took a few steps closer. "Of course I didn't forget. But something happened that night you went to the store. You've been a zombie ever since. You get Maya ready for school, you help her with her homework, you give her a bath and then put her to bed. But that's it. The rest of the day and night, your ass is on this couch asleep or watching TV. So I know for a fact that something else happened. Tell me."

What I wanted to tell her was that she was wrong and didn't know a damn thing. But, again, no energy to argue. Instead, I grabbed my phone from the coffee table, scrolled to the Instagram post, and handed it over.

I plopped back on the couch, still clutching the towel, and waited.

She looked at the screen for less than a minute and then set the phone back on the table.

Then she let out a long sigh. "Why haven't you blocked her?"

I was impressed my mom knew about blocking people on social media, since she had no presence on it at all. But I was too embarrassed to tell her that. Instead, I shrugged and said, "I did block her. On everything. But that night after Maya's crying episode, I decided to try to reach out to her. I figured I'd message her through Instagram, since I know she for sure blocked my phone number."

Gloria sat down next to me. "But why?"

That was the billion-dollar question. Because I'm stupid. Because I'm stubborn. Because I obviously needed another punch in the gut.

I didn't say all that, of course. Instead, I let out a long sigh and said, "Because I wanted to tell her that she didn't have to worry about me trying to get David back. And all I wanted was for him to regularly call Maya and let her know that he still loved her. I thought maybe if I could make her understand that, then at least I could help give my little girl some peace. She's in so much pain, Mom. And I hate that I can't make it better."

Tears streamed down my face, and my throat was thick with grief. I covered my mouth in an attempt to stop any sobs from escaping, since I knew Maya was in her room. When I was able to take a few breaths, I said softly, "Then I saw the post. And I knew."

"Knew what?" Gloria asked.

"David is happy."

Rachel's Instagram page had been wiped clear of all pictures except for one. It was of her and David standing on some rocks with the Golden Gate Bridge in the background. She was half kissing him on the lips, and they were both looking at the camera. He had this huge, almost laughing smile.

The fact that he was obviously deliriously happy in San Francisco with Rachel while Maya and I were here at home miserable and crying had been just too much to bear.

It was like I was at the bottom of a big hole trying to claw myself out of it. And anytime I'd make any progress, these thoughts of David and Rachel laughing at how they'd managed to fool me for months just kicked me back down the hole. It overwhelmed me and made me too exhausted to do anything more than just make sure Maya was dressed and fed.

But my worst fear was that one day I wouldn't even be able to do that.

After a few minutes of silence, Gloria sighed.

Then she reached out, grabbed me by my chin, and turned my head to face her.

"Why are you punishing yourself for something that wasn't your fault? You're not the one who cheated, so why are you still letting them win?"

"Win what, Mom?" I said, blowing the wayward strands of hair out of my face.

She let go. "The fight. You're acting like it's over, and they get to walk away and be happy while you don't get anything. It's not over, Claudia. Yeah, maybe they've knocked you down. But you can still get up and fight. Their happiness isn't the prize. Yours is. And so is Maya's. That's what you need to focus on winning."

"What if I don't have it in me?" I asked, my voice cracking again.

"You're my daughter. You're Abuela's granddaughter. Of course you do."

CHAPTER ELEVEN

THINGS I NEVER KNEW #134: EVEN GOOD MOMS AREN'T PERFECT

Dear Diary,

One of the worst things in the world happened. Rachel told me last night that her parents are getting a divorce.

Her dad was in town for two weeks on leave. She said at first everything was good and she was happy to have him home. But then she started hearing her parents arguing more and more. During the last fight, she overheard her dad tell her mom that he knew she'd been cheating on him and had followed her to the guy's house earlier in the day.

I was shocked. Mrs. Martinez is the nicest woman. She knows Gloria isn't around much, so she said I could come over whenever I wanted to have dinner with them or stay the night. I couldn't believe she would cheat on Mr. Martinez. I've only met him a few times, but he seems like a good husband and I know Rachel loves him a lot. She loves her mom a lot too. Which is why it made me sad when Rachel called her mom lots of names and said she hated her for what she had done. I tried to tell her that maybe they wouldn't get a divorce because her dad might forgive her mom. I told her Gloria had gone back to a few boyfriends even after she found out they were cheating on her. So it was possible. But Rachel said her dad had already left to go back to his base.

She told me we were the same because we both were going to be raised by single moms. I didn't argue because she was so sad. But it's not the same. Even though Rachel's parents are going to get a divorce, her dad is still going to be in her life. Maybe she isn't going to see him as much, but it's not like he's living with them full time anyway.

I've never even met my dad. All I know is that his name is Andy, and my mom only went out with him a few times. She never even told him she was pregnant. And the one time I asked my abuela about him, I was told to never mention his name in her house again.

So, no, it wasn't the same.

I would give anything to have a mom like Mrs. Martinez. But even I felt a little hurt and betrayed by what she'd done. It wasn't like I thought she was perfect. No adult is. But she seemed like the kind of person that would put her family first and never do anything to destroy it.

How could I have been so wrong about someone?

CHAPTER TWELVE

A week after Gloria arrived on my doorstep, my house was somewhat back to normal. Well, the look of it anyway.

Despite my initial protests about not wanting her to clean it, she'd slowly tackled little pockets. I wasn't surprised. She'd always been a tidy person. Growing up, our refrigerator might have been empty or the electricity might have been turned off for a day because she'd forgotten to pay the bill, but damn our floors and counters sparkled. Abuela had cleaned houses for the rich people in Beverly Hills and had taught my mother how to clean. *Really* clean. It was probably the only lesson Gloria had ever learned from her.

I had to admit that the clutter and mess mostly being gone did make me feel like I could breathe again. The anxiety and sadness still overwhelmed me at times, though. The difference was that they overwhelmed me in a clean space—which made it easier for me to calm myself before another panic attack could hit.

I still couldn't see the light at the end of the tunnel, but at least I'd taken a few steps toward it.

And not only had I blocked Rachel on Instagram, but I'd also deleted my entire account and the app itself. Now I wouldn't be tempted to snoop after a few glasses of wine.

Gloria was right. The fight for my and Maya's happiness wasn't over. I couldn't let other people dictate how I felt twenty-four hours a day, seven days a week. I had to get off my ass and take back control of my life.

Which meant it was time to tackle another challenge.

"Maybe I need to start looking for a job," I told Gloria after Maya had left for school on Thursday morning.

She put down her cup of coffee. "Why?" she asked. "Isn't David still paying the bills?"

"He is. But he let me know it wasn't going to be forever."

"Did you get a divorce lawyer already?"

"He wants us to do mediation," I explained. He'd asked me again the other night after talking to Maya. I told him I still needed to think about it. Obviously he wasn't happy. He probably thought I was being difficult on purpose. The truth was the pit in my stomach seemed to grow every time I thought about having to face David eventually—whether that was going to be in front of a judge or a mediator didn't really matter. Even though I probably would've jumped at the chance in that first week to talk to him or see him, that wasn't the case anymore. Because I knew now the only reason he was willing to come see me was to get the divorce finalized. I couldn't help it if I wasn't in a rush to give him that satisfaction. Especially since I knew he was going to try to control things for his benefit. He'd already proven that he couldn't care less about my feelings or my wants. He'd pulled the trigger on this divorce on his own terms. Of course he was going to do whatever it took to see it through. Even if it came at my expense. And Maya would just be the casualty of it all.

"Why?" Gloria said, her eyebrows raised so high her forehead was indented with parallel lines of wrinkles.

I shrugged before taking a sip of my own coffee. I'd dug out our Keurig coffee maker from the pantry the day after Gloria arrived. The woman needed her dose of caffeine at least three times a day.

"Probably because he doesn't want to spend the money," I said a few seconds later. "I'm sure it's Rachel's idea."

It had to be. David grew up with wealth. He rarely looked at price tags and didn't even know how to budget. That was always my job. So the fact that he all of sudden cared about how much a lawyer was going to cost him was out of character.

It had to be because of her.

"And what do you want?" Gloria asked, taking me out of my disturbing assumptions.

It was a loaded question. I opened my mouth and then closed it. I almost said I didn't want a divorce, period. That I didn't want this new reality, and I wanted everything to go back to the way it was. But did I really?

I'd always told myself that I wouldn't want someone who didn't want me. I was too proud. Or at least I used to be. However, my newfound pettiness would make sure I never ever let a person make a fool out of me a second time.

I thought again about Gloria's question. What I wanted was what I'd always wanted. To be a good mother.

I let out a long sigh and told her the truth. "I guess I just want whatever is going to be easiest on my daughter. None of this is her fault, and she shouldn't be punished for the mistakes he made . . . the mistakes we both made."

It was the first time I'd said what I'd been thinking since finding out about the affair. I wasn't naive enough to believe I'd been the perfect wife. I definitely didn't deserve what David—and Rachel—had done to me. There had to be a reason why it was so easy for the both of them to leave me. Because you didn't hurt someone you loved the way that they had hurt me.

"I'll never understand why you quit your job in the first place," Gloria said after a few moments.

I tried not to get defensive. "I wanted to stay home and take care of Maya."

And as much as I wished I could still be a stay-at-home mom, circumstances had changed. Now, in order to take care of Maya, I needed a job. I needed my own money.

Gloria stood up to refill her mug. "I get that," she said as she put a new pod into the Keurig. "But you used to be so . . ."

"What, Mother? Less pathetic?" Okay, the defenses were definitely up now.

Her eyes grew big, as if I'd just offended her and not the other way around. "I was going to say 'independent.'"

"What on earth are you talking about?"

"You had a great career as a business . . . person."

"I was a business manager," I reminded her.

I'd handled all project accounting and budgeting for a large construction firm based in Pasadena. I'd been there for four years and was making well over six figures. Before that, I'd worked for a different company for five years. In fact, I'd been working steadily ever since getting my degree. And I was damn good at all of my jobs too. I'd almost forgotten that.

Gloria waved away my correction. "My point is, I didn't even graduate from high school, so my options were limited, and the easiest one was to find a man who would take care of me. But you were different. You have a college degree. You were supposed to do something with your life. You were supposed to *be* something."

My fingers gripped my mug so tight I thought I might actually break it. "I *am* something. I'm a mother. But I guess you wouldn't know what that looks like."

To her credit, she ignored the dig. "Yes, you are a great mother. But what are you outside of that? You were a wife. You're not going to be one for much longer. I'm just disappointed that you would give up all of your independence for a ring and a nice house in the suburbs."

That was it. I couldn't bite my tongue anymore. "You are seriously going to sit there and judge me for wanting to be married and have a family? You? The woman who has picked up and moved countless times just to follow a man? Or had to change jobs because you slept with your boss? You have no right to judge me for my choices. Especially since I made them all because of you."

Gloria's eyes widened in shock as she sat back down at the table. "Me? I didn't tell you to marry David. In fact, I distinctly remember telling you the night before your wedding to leave him."

As if I could forget that special Gloria moment. But I wasn't about to let her throw that in my face.

I could no longer contain the years of frustration and sadness I'd kept bottled up inside. As much as Gloria had shown she was trying to do better and be better, some scars never heal and never forget. My emotional barriers had been decimated by what seemed like a constant barrage of what I would describe as daily mini bombs of pain. From David's insistence on only communicating with me via email or text to out-of-the-blue reminders that I no longer had a best friend, my tolerance for pain and bullshit was at an all-time low.

"Do you really want to know why I wanted to marry David?" I yelled at Gloria. "Do you want to know why it was so easy for me to give up my career?"

"I do," she said as she sat back in her chair with folded arms.

"Because I had to spend nearly my entire childhood, teenage, and college years taking care of myself! So yeah, it was nice not worrying about how I was going to make rent or tuition. It was nice going to a store—any store—and knowing that if there was something in there I wanted, then I could buy it. After a lifetime of relying on only myself to survive, I was happy to let someone else take care of me for once. But don't think for a second that I let David control me. Yes, I made sacrifices along the way. But they were my choice. And I don't know why I'm even listening to you right now. You have no idea how a marriage works."

"I was married . . . once," Gloria said.

"For two weeks!" It turned out her and Simon's marriage lasted just a few days longer than those carnation and pink rose bouquets. I laughed bitterly and shook my head. "I thought we could actually have a real conversation without you making it all about yourself. I was wrong. Again."

"Claudia . . . I . . ."

"Save it," I told her, and I held up my hand. "I have to run some errands. I'll be back later."

Gloria called my name again, but I ignored her. I grabbed my purse and keys and walked out the door.

I didn't really have any errands to run. I just needed to put as much distance between us as possible. For about fifteen minutes, I drove around the streets of South Pasadena aimlessly. It was after nine on a weekday morning and schools were already in session, so traffic wasn't too bad.

I loved where we lived. Although a suburb less than fifteen minutes from Los Angeles, South Pasadena felt like a small town with its tree-lined streets, historic homes, film-ready neighborhoods, the hundred-year-old soda fountain at the Fair Oaks Pharmacy, and a variety of other quaint mom-and-pop shops.

Deciding I'd rather walk than drive, I pulled into a public lot and parked. I made my way down the main sidewalk, looking in store windows at everything and nothing. I turned a corner and thought about heading back to the car. That is, until something colorful caught my eye. I stepped closer to the window of a store I'd never been in before. It was a beautiful table runner that seemed to be handwoven. I had been looking for something exactly like it for the long table in my entryway. It was hanging off a rack in the middle of the small shop's large bay window. The glare from the sun and my own reflection made it a little difficult to see all the details. The sign above the door read *Tesoro*, which I knew meant "treasure." My interest was definitely piqued, and I went inside.

A bell announced my arrival, and I heard a woman's voice from the back say, "Welcome in."

"Thank you," I answered as I walked to the window to examine the table runner. I pinched the fabric between my left index finger and thumb, and I was surprised by how thick it felt despite its delicate appearance.

"It's beautiful, isn't it?" someone said behind me. "And it's one of a kind."

I turned around to face a woman I had never seen before. She looked to be a little older than me, with salt-and-pepper hair twisted into a tight bun. She wore minimal makeup and small gold hoop earrings. Short but stout, she wore a traditional Mexican peasant blouse, black capri pants that fell just below her bare knees, and a pair of all-black Nike running shoes.

"I love the craftmanship," I told her.

She nodded and reached to pull the textile from the display. The woman draped it across both of her outstretched arms. "The unique fabric is woven by a process called telar de cintura, and it was made by a woman who lives in the Santo Tomás Jalieza community in Oaxaca, Mexico."

I gingerly traced the colorful threads that made up the design of crisscrossed lines and diamond shapes. "My abuela used to have one very similar to this. Although she probably got hers from the swap meet or a thrift shop in downtown LA. How much?" I asked, even though I already knew I was going to buy it. The sensible part of my brain told me I should be careful with my spending, but the other part ignored the warning. Maybe it was silly to be so drawn to a piece of fabric. But the instant I'd seen it, I was transported back to my abuela's small two-bedroom house in East LA. I knew this table runner wasn't the one she'd had. Yet it was as close as I'd ever come to finding one just like it. I had to have it. Budget be damned.

"It's usually one hundred twenty. But we're having a sale for the beginning of Latine Heritage Month, so right now it's ninety."

"I'll take it," I said, and I gave her a smile.

She nodded and began to fold the runner. "I can ring you up at the register. Unless you'd like to look around some more?"

"Yes, please. I've never been in here before. Did you just open?"

"In June. But I used to have a shop just like this one back in San Antonio. I actually grew up in South Pasadena and just moved back to town last year. Please take your time and look around. Most of my inventory is handcrafted by artisans in Oaxaca that I source and pick up myself. Other items I get from trusted vendors in Tijuana and downtown LA or international partners that are certified fair trade or support schools and orphanages in Mexico."

The woman then left me to wander around the small shop. For about fifteen more minutes, I explored each corner, looking at the pottery, textiles, and other items. Every time I found something I had to have, I'd find something else I had to have more. By the time I made it to the register, my arms were full with all sorts of treasures. The name of the shop was definitely accurate. I'd found a ceramic water pitcher and pot holders for the kitchen, scented soaps for the guest bathroom, a cookbook of authentic Mexican recipes, and a children's book for Maya written in both English and Spanish.

"I see you found some things you liked," the store's owner lightly teased.

I couldn't help but laugh. "I did. Honestly, I had to put some things back, only because I couldn't carry them all."

She handed me a card and a pen. "If you're interested, I can add you to our newsletter that I mail out at least once a month. I share our new arrivals and upcoming sales."

"Definitely," I answered and began to fill out my contact information.

"I'm Mercedes, by the way," she said as she began to ring up my items.

"I'm Claudia. I'm so glad I found your store today."

And I *was* glad. Happy even.

But that happiness was short lived when my credit card declined the nearly $300 charge. I asked the friendly woman to try charging it two more times, only for it to have the same result. Embarrassment heated the back of my neck and zoomed directly to my cheeks.

"I'm so sorry. I'll just have to take the children's book today, I guess," I rushed as I handed her the ATM card linked to the account I knew for certain was still open and had at least enough to cover the new total.

"No te preocupes," Mercedes said in a kind voice. Even though she told me not to be worried, I very much was. I had just made a payment on that credit card last month, so I knew thousands of dollars were still available on it. So why had it been declined?

A sinking realization began to churn inside my stomach.

It had to have been David. It wasn't enough for him to cut me off emotionally and physically. Now, he was doing it financially. And Rachel was probably all for it.

I couldn't stop the rush of tears that flooded my eyes and began to spill down my cheeks. I attempted a smile before Mercedes might regret being so nice to me. I'm sure she wasn't used to customers breaking down inside her store.

I dared not meet her eyes as she handed me a bag with Maya's book inside. Instead, I croaked out a whispered thank-you and nearly sprinted to the front door.

Shame kept me inside my car for several long minutes, even after I'd gotten back to the house. I couldn't risk Gloria noticing how embarrassed I felt. The last thing I wanted was to face an interrogation, or worse, a tirade about how awful David was being—even if such a tirade was well deserved.

Although I knew the credit card declining had to be his doing, I still couldn't help but feel partly responsible. I'd managed our money for most of our marriage. Why was I suddenly acting like I didn't know how to check account balances or follow a budget?

San Diego State might as well revoke my degree at this point.

Because the version of me in the store had felt helpless. And hopeless.

I didn't recognize her.

I was embarrassed to be her.

The worst part of it all was that I was afraid she was here to stay.

And just like that, I felt like I was back in that hole again.

It wasn't until later that night, after Maya and I had read her new book at least three times, that I realized I'd left both my dignity and my wallet back at Tesoro.

CHAPTER THIRTEEN

THINGS I NEVER KNEW #242: I ACTUALLY DON'T LIKE LIVING ON MY OWN

Dear Diary,

Today was my first day at San Diego State. Although I love my dorm and all my classes, I miss Rachel. She was supposed to be here doing this with me. And I hate that she's not.

We had been so close to moving out of our moms' places and getting our own little studio off campus. The dream we'd had since we were sixteen had almost come true. Almost.

But Rachel didn't get accepted like we both thought she would. Instead, she's going to take one year of general education at the community college and try to transfer here next year. I told her I would do the same, but then our college counselor said I shouldn't—that I could risk my financial aid status if I declined the acceptance for this semester. I could tell Rachel was hurt that I decided to come here without her, even though she told me she was happy for me.

Truth is, I never believed I'd get accepted or even be able to go to college. God knows Gloria could never afford

to send me. If it wasn't for Rachel, I wouldn't have even applied. San Diego State was her dream school, and she insisted I had to go here too.

I couldn't help but feel guilty. And a little scared.

Although I like to think I've basically taken care of myself since my abuela died, I've never lived on my own before. It's weird not having to ask someone else what they want to eat for dinner or worry about someone else (Gloria) using up my favorite shampoo or eating the last ice cream sandwich.

For the first time in my life, I'm the only person I have to answer to.

I'm free. Truly free.

Even still, I'd give it all up if Rachel could be here with me.

She's supposed to drive down for a weekend visit soon, and I can't wait for her to see the campus. I want her to know that our dream is still going to happen.

I promised her that nothing was going to change and I was going to do everything I could to help her get to San Diego State.

Because that's what best friends do. We take care of each other. Always.

CHAPTER FOURTEEN

The bell on Tesoro's door announced my arrival, although I would have preferred to sneak inside, grab my wallet, and escape back home, never to return again.

"Welcome in."

Mercedes's voice carried through the small shop, although I didn't immediately see her. I didn't reply as I walked to the cash register, hoping against hope my wallet would just be sitting there. But it wasn't. I'm sure Mercedes had done what she had promised when I'd called her earlier that morning: to keep my wallet safe until I got there.

I'd arrived just a few minutes after the store opened at 10:00 a.m. I wasn't sure what kind of foot traffic Tesoro usually got on a Friday morning. But I wanted to be the first person inside so I wouldn't have to wait around for Mercedes to give me what I had come for.

"Good morning, Claudia," Mercedes said as she appeared from the back of the store. Today, she wore white huarache sandals and a bright-pink off-the-shoulder dress with colorful embroidered flowers.

I gave her a small wave. "Hello."

She walked behind the register counter, took out a set of keys from the pocket of her apron, and unlocked a drawer in the cabinet behind her. Then she handed me my wallet. "I told you I would keep it safe."

"Thank you," I said as I stuffed it inside my purse. "Have a good day."

Before I could turn to leave, she said, "Can I say something before you go?"

I resisted the urge to run. Experience had taught me that when someone asked if they could ask you a question, it was usually going to be a question you didn't want to answer. But Mercedes had only shown me kindness, and I didn't want to be rude. So I shrugged and said, "Sure."

"I know you don't know me. But some of my friends say that I have this gift. Or maybe it's a curse, who knows? Anyway, I can usually tell when someone is in pain. No, that's the wrong word. I can *feel* when someone else is in pain. My husband used to say that's why I was so nosy and in other people's business. I can't help it, honestly. So whatever pain you are in, Claudia, if it helps, you can tell me because I know it's more than just your credit card declining."

It was as if her words had unlatched the lock of a gate I'd been using to hold back my emotions around strangers for fear of being judged or pitied. The gate swung open, and everything came spilling out.

I told her everything. From the first email, to checking my Ring camera before leaving my house so I wouldn't run into Nick in the driveway, to not being able to sleep in my bedroom, to still not trusting that my mother was telling me the truth about why she was really here, to what I'd learned that morning before arriving at the store.

David had indeed canceled the credit card without telling me. The bank had confirmed it.

"I've emailed and texted him, but he hasn't responded," I said through tears. "Why would he do that? I was using that card for groceries and things Maya, our daughter, needed. Yes, he's paying the mortgage and utilities, but what about everything else? I have no income coming in right now. I'm going to start looking for a job, but that's not going to happen overnight. What am I supposed to do in the meantime?"

Mercedes came out from around the counter and wrapped me in a hug. She let me cry on her shoulder until the bell signaled another customer had walked inside.

I jumped back and quickly wiped my tears. The shame from yesterday was back. All I wanted was to go hide in a hole somewhere for the rest of the year. I had become such a crybaby. I hated it. "God, I'm so sorry," I blurted out. "I'll leave so you can help your customer."

She grabbed my hand. "I have a bathroom in the back. Go clean yourself up, then wait for me in my office. Help yourself to a bottle of water or just sit awhile. I'll be right there."

I nodded and walked away.

Mercedes found me a few minutes later, sitting on one of the folding chairs in her office. I'd just opened a water bottle and was fishing through my purse for some aspirin. My head was throbbing.

"Feel any better?" she said as she pulled open another folding chair next to me.

"A little," I said after popping two pills and taking a swig of water. "Hopefully this aspirin will help."

She nodded and put her hand on one of mine. "You're going to be okay, Claudia," she said softly.

"You don't know that." I knew she was trying to be nice, but sugarcoating my situation wasn't what I needed.

"I do know because you've made it this far. You could've given up. But you're still standing and trying to figure out how to fix things for you and your daughter. I know you're going to get through this because I can tell you want to do it for her."

Tears clouded my vision again. "I get up every day because of her."

I felt her pat the back of my hand. "And eventually you'll get up because of you."

This woman I'd only known for a day had more faith in me than I did. Or maybe she was just saying these things to get me out of her store. Either way, it was what I needed to hear in that moment. "I appreciate your kindness, Mercedes. I feel so embarrassed."

"You have nothing to be embarrassed about."

"Yeah right," I replied with a shake of my head. "I was practically hysterical out there. Not to mention that I couldn't pay for anything except for a book yesterday. As a former business manager, I am absolutely appalled by the state of my personal finances at the moment."

Mercedes pulled her hand away. "Did you say you used to be a business manager?"

"I was. I quit to become a stay-at-home mom when my daughter was born."

Her face brightened. "It's your lucky day, Mija. Because it just so happens that I'm in need of a business manager for the store."

I froze. "You want me to apply to be your business manager?"

"I do!"

Mercedes went on to explain that her husband, Joseph, used to manage the financial side of her store when they lived in San Antonio. But he died two years ago, and she closed that shop and moved back to her parents' home here, which she'd rented out after they'd passed away.

"I thought I could manage the financials on my own, but I'm quickly learning that I don't know as much as I thought I did," she said. "I was just about to post a business manager position online. But I have a good feeling about you. So how about you come work for me?"

I was flabbergasted. "But, but all you know about me is that I'm getting a divorce and that I cry easily in front of strangers," I said, not quite believing what she was saying.

She looked me in the eye and explained, "I told you I can sense things. And I sense that you're a good person. That's all I need to know."

We spent the next few hours going over her books. We agreed the position would be part time to start so I could work a few hours in the morning while Maya was at school. It was the perfect job, and all I'd had to do to get it was spill my guts and gallons of tears.

Two hours later, I walked into my kitchen carrying a box full of paperwork.

"There you are," Gloria said, looking up from the book she'd been reading at the table. "What's all that?"

"I got a job today," I announced happily as I walked past her and headed toward the room that used to be David's office. On the drive home, I'd decided it was now going to be my office.

After setting the box down on the desk, I began to pick up and sort papers David had left behind. Gloria walked in. "Did you say you got a job? Doing what?"

I didn't even look at her as I continued cleaning up. "I'm the new business manager for this small shop off of Fair Oaks. I don't start until Monday, but I wanted to start organizing old invoices and bank statements for Mercedes this weekend. That's the owner."

I still couldn't believe that she'd hired me. I knew it wasn't going to magically fix my life, but at least it was a step toward climbing out of the hole.

"You don't think it's a little too soon to go back to work?" Gloria asked.

I stopped what I was doing and finally looked at her. "David canceled all the credit cards."

Her eyes widened. "He did what?"

"Yeah. So it's not too soon. He's paying the bills for now. But maybe tomorrow he'll decide not to do that either. I can't rely on him to be fair or even considerate. I need to do this in order to take care of Maya."

She walked closer to the desk. "If you need money, Claudia, I can help."

I shook my head. "I'm not taking money from you. Correction: I'm not taking money from Carlos."

"Why not?" my mother asked and threw up her hands. "He has a lot, and he's happy to give it. All I need to do is ask."

"I said no," I said more forcefully than I'd expected. I took a breath and tried to explain myself in a gentler tone. "I appreciate the offer, but I need to do this on my own. I'm tired of letting other people dictate what happens to me next. I need to take control of my life."

"You can take control, and you can also ask for help when you need it," she said.

"Weren't you just telling me yesterday that I needed to be more independent? Well, this job is the first step. I'm not going to rely on anyone else anymore."

Something flashed behind Gloria's eyes. Something I hadn't seen very much of growing up.

I think it was pride.

CHAPTER FIFTEEN

THINGS I NEVER KNEW #299: MY DAD IS A MECHANIC

Dear Diary,

Today I met my dad for the first time. Well, I met the man I think is my dad.

I'm home right now on Christmas break, and of course Gloria hasn't put up the tree or any decorations yet. After bugging her for the past two days, she finally brought down the boxes last night from her bedroom closet. Told me to "knock yourself out" and then left to go to her friend's bar.

The torn and tattered brown cardboard boxes held a mixture of our own ornaments and my abuela's Christmas things that I insisted on keeping after she passed away. First, I set up the figures from the nacimiento she'd brought with her from Mexico. I carefully arranged the 8-inch-tall ceramic statues of Mary and Joseph on top of a card table in our living room. Then I placed the wooden makeshift crib for the baby Jesus between them. I'd learned from Abuela that the baby Jesus himself shouldn't be added until Christmas Eve. Next came the two wise men (the third had an unfortunate accident a few years back). The set didn't have any shepherds, but it did have one cow and one donkey. My next project was to put up our 3-foot artificial tree. I actually hate it. When I have my own house and family, I'm going to always buy a real fresh tree.

Anyway, after I set up the tree I realized I was missing the box with Abuela's ornaments. So I went to my mom's closet and brought out what I thought was the box. But once I opened it, I realized there was nothing Christmassy inside. Instead, it was a disorganized mess of papers, books, and loose photos. One of the photos of my abuela caught my eye, so I started going through everything. And that's when I found it. It was a picture of my mom with a man, and they were sitting on the hood of a blue sedan in front of a mechanic's shop. The sign above read "Andy and Sons Garage." I turned the photo around, and someone had scribbled "Gloria and Andy 1984."

1984. The year before I was born.

Of course, I immediately called Rachel. And she remembered there was still an Andy and Sons Garage near the trade school she was attending in East LA.

So that's where we ended up today. Luckily, Rachel's mom's car was due for an oil change. I was so nervous when we walked into the tiny office to see if someone could check out the car. But I nearly threw up in my mouth once I saw the man behind the counter. I immediately knew he was the one from the photo. The name "Andy" emblazoned on his dark-blue uniform shirt confirmed it.

As Rachel talked with him about the car, I studied his face. His hair and mustache were fully white now, and he'd gained a few pounds since the picture was taken. And maybe it was just because I wanted it to be true, but I could've sworn he and I have the same light-brown eyes and the same long, thick eyelashes. I heard Rachel tell him that she grew up in the area (she didn't) and remembered the shop from when she was a little girl. That's when the man—Andy—said the shop used to belong to his dad, Andre Sr., and that he'd worked there since high school.

Rachel, who had the gift of gab and was also wearing a tight green sweater that accentuated her D cups, spent the next ten minutes getting Andy's life story. He was married and had two sons who also worked at the shop. I wasn't sure when it happened, but it soon became clear that he was flirting with Rachel. I shouldn't have been surprised. Rachel was the type of girl that attracted attention from all kinds of men. But this man who could've been the same age as her father—and was most likely my father—asked my friend if she had a boyfriend and said that he was going to give her a deal on the oil change because she was so pretty. He had just told her he was married, yet that didn't seem to stop him.

Disgust and disappointment twisted my stomach into knots. I couldn't stand to be in his vicinity a minute longer. So I blurted out that I'd forgotten I needed to pick up my mom from work and told Rachel we had to leave. She gave me the "what the hell is wrong with you" look, but when I grabbed her hand to pull her out of the office, Rachel told Andy she'd come back another day.

Rachel thought it was funny that Andy was flirting with her. "I wouldn't be surprised if he would've just given me the oil change for free." She had been enjoying their banter, but I was creeped out. I didn't know the man, but something in my gut told me I shouldn't try to get to know him. Ever. Just another reason why I should've listened to my abuela.

CHAPTER SIXTEEN

By now, there wasn't much my mother could tell me that would render me speechless.

The woman dropped bombshells so often I was pretty much immune.

Like the time she announced she was pulling me out of the eleventh grade because we were going to move to Alaska for a man she'd met through some prison pen pal program. He'd been released the week before and was going to go work on an oil rig for the rest of the year and wanted her to be close for the days he came ashore.

It wasn't surprising that Gloria had decided to uproot her life—my life—for a man she barely knew. In fact, based on her track record, it was inevitable that it would happen. Again. I was so sure of it that I'd already had a conversation with Rachel's mom to ask if I could stay with them in the likelihood of such an event.

And just like I wasn't shocked when she announced the move, I also wasn't the least surprised when she told me the day before she was supposed to leave that the guy had ghosted her, so she wasn't going after all.

But I can honestly say that I was at a loss for words when Gloria asked me over dinner if I knew of a good church she could attend while she was in town.

My entire body froze. The mashed potatoes I'd just spooned into my mouth began to dissolve and slide down my throat on their own.

Eventually, I was forced to swallow the rest, took a big gulp of my iced tea, and tried to figure out if I had actually heard my mother correctly.

"You want to go to church?" I asked incredulously. "Like a real church?"

Gloria smiled and nodded. "I do. Maya, do you know what church is?"

"It's where you go to pray to God," my daughter answered. "But Mommy says we can pray to God from anywhere. We like to pray at night before I go to bed."

"Yes, that's true, sweetie," Gloria said. "You can pray to God anywhere, but sometimes he hears you better if you're in church."

I still couldn't wrap my head around this conversation. "I'm sorry. I need to be clear about this. Did you just say you want to go to a church while you're here?"

"I do. But not a Catholic one, of course," she said.

Although Abuela had raised Gloria as Catholic, she'd never really gone to Mass.

My mother judges me enough. I don't need an entire religion to do it too, she'd once told me when I asked her why.

"Are you really serious?" I still couldn't believe what I'd heard.

"I am. Any Christian church will work. Baptist. Methodist. Even Lutheran. It doesn't matter to me."

I shook my head in disbelief. Okay, that was enough of that. "Maya, it looks like you're done with dinner, so why don't you go get your pajamas ready so you can take your bath soon?"

She agreed and disappeared down the hall after a minute or so.

"What's going on with you, Mom?" I asked in a low voice. "Since when do you go to church?"

She shrugged and took a drink of her tea before answering. "Well, honestly, I was just going to start before I came here. I just hadn't found a church that felt right. I figured I could keep looking while I was here."

"Why? You never went to church with me and Abuela when she was alive. And you never took me on your own. What's with this sudden interest in talking to God?"

"It's not sudden," Gloria said with a shrug. "I talk to God all the time. But lately I've just been wondering if it would be helpful, spiritually, to find something more . . . official. And I'm actually surprised you haven't taken Maya to church before."

I leaned back into my chair. "David and I both decided that we weren't going to force a religion on her. If she decides she wants to go to church when she gets older, then it will be up to her. But as you can see, she knows about God and praying. For right now, that's enough."

The only reason I was baptized in the Catholic church and had my First Communion there was because of my abuela's connections and deep ties to her church. And while I didn't mind attending Mass with her, I never had the interest to keep going once she'd passed. Especially since Gloria didn't seem to care if I went or not.

Truth was, I had complicated feelings about religion that had nothing to do with Gloria's indifference and everything to do with the fact that God had taken my abuela from me in one of the worst ways possible.

It wasn't until after she'd died that I'd realized just how sick and in pain she was in her final days. And if God couldn't help her when she'd needed him the most, then why on earth had she spent so much of her life inside a church? Even at the age of fourteen, I couldn't understand how God would allow someone so devout and religious to die all alone in a hospital bed.

"Well, I guess that's the same for me then," my mom said. "I've come to the decision that I want to try out going to church on a regular basis. So is there one you recommend, or should I just google it?"

I rolled my eyes and stood up to start clearing the table.

Gloria did the same. She brought me Maya's plate. "Mashed potatoes are all gone, but she barely touched the meat loaf."

And just like that, the conversation about church was finished. I was relieved.

"I know," I said. "I thought that if I could sneak in some veggies and then drench it all in ketchup, she'd at least eat half. But she's still not a fan of beef, I guess."

"I ordered a cookbook from Amazon with kid-friendly recipes for picky eaters. I'm sure I can find a few to try."

I couldn't help but be surprised by my mom's proactiveness. "Thanks. That would be helpful."

"That's why I'm here, remember?"

"I know. And I appreciate it."

I really did. I could admit Gloria had been trying. But I still had my reservations. It was going to take more than just trying out a few kid-friendly recipes before she won any Grandma of the Year awards.

After both Maya and Gloria had gone to bed, I tried to do the same. Since I was going to start my new job in the morning, that meant I needed to get a good night's sleep. But by 1:00 a.m., I was still wide awake. I thought about watching something on Netflix. When I couldn't find something that interested me, I grabbed my phone and began scrolling through social media. I still hadn't reactivated Instagram, but I'd kept my Facebook account since I knew neither Rachel nor David were on there anymore. That's when I saw I'd missed a few private messages from Becca—Maya's former Girl Scouts troop leader. Maya had been devastated when I told her she couldn't rejoin her Brownie troop this school year. I just couldn't face everyone knowing what a mess my life had become. Thankfully, Becca had easily accepted my simple explanation that I needed to cut back on Maya's extracurricular activities, and she let me know she could rejoin at any time. She'd also promised to keep me in the loop in case we ever wanted to come to one of their events. Becca had reached out last week to invite me and David and a few other parents to her home for a back-to-school grown-up dinner. It was for this upcoming Saturday, and she'd sent another message earlier that day asking if we were going to make it.

Quickly I typed, Sorry, can't come. Thanks for the invite!

Then I threw my phone back on the coffee table, grabbed a nearby throw pillow, and screamed into it.

There was a time when I would've made sure David and I were at every single parent function. Whether it was the end-of-the-year carnival or a spring run fundraiser, if I wasn't in charge of it, then I made sure we both were at least supporting it.

I wondered if there would ever be a time when I would be comfortable showing my face again at a school event.

I probably should've been more relieved that news of David leaving me hadn't yet made it to the carpool rumor network. But since I knew I wouldn't be able to escape the whispering or pity looks once it became obvious David wasn't around anymore, it wasn't the comfort it should've been.

That's why I'd only told Valerie, Leila's mom, that David had accepted a new job out of town, and we were still figuring things out, which was when she'd offered to bring Maya to and from school. I'm sure she could sense there was more to the story, but I appreciated the fact that she hadn't pried. And I especially appreciated that it seemed like she hadn't been sharing her assumptions with other moms, since no one else had messaged or texted asking why I hadn't shown my face at school or any other places Maya and I used to go to. Like Girl Scouts.

But just like I couldn't stop the divorce, I couldn't stop the news from getting out eventually. Then I wouldn't just be Maya's mom anymore. I'd be Maya's *divorced* mom. I knew I shouldn't be ashamed. Yet I still couldn't help it. Maybe the PTA or Girl Scouts moms would never know all the sordid details about why my marriage had broken up, but it didn't matter. And every time I had to explain why David wasn't around, *I* would remember I was the woman whose best friend had stolen her husband.

It wasn't fair. None of what was happening was my fault. I wasn't the one who'd literally fucked around. So why did I have to be the one to find out? In other words, why had I been left behind to deal with the consequences of David and Rachel's affair?

That's when I thought of Nick. It was true we were in the same boat. He was lucky, though. He didn't have to eventually face the elementary school gossip girlies.

Here I thought my life was finally going to start getting easier because I'd found a job. In reality, things were only going to get worse before they could get better.

I'd survived the initial explosion. Eventually, though, I was going to have to deal with the fallout.

And I knew it was going to be hell.

I had no idea what kind of answers Gloria was hoping to find by going to church. But if it was true that God could hear your prayers better from there, then maybe I'd tell her to ask if he could stop making my life so damn hard.

CHAPTER SEVENTEEN

THINGS I NEVER KNEW #302: NEW YORK WILL BE FUN TO VISIT IN THE SUMMER

Dear Diary,

Today was date number two with David Flores, the cute guy from my English class.

Of course, I already called Rachel to tell her all about it. He'd taken me to the local theater to see the new Iron Man movie, and then we had dinner at this fun pub by campus. We both got cheeseburgers and shared a basket of fries. I found out his parents are dead and he barely speaks to his brother. I thought that was sad. Even though Gloria and I have our issues, at least I try to call her every other week.

David is in his third year like me and majoring in advertising. He already has a really good internship lined up for the summer in New York. When I told him I had never been there, he casually mentioned that maybe I could visit him while he was there. That's three months from now. Does that mean he thinks we're still going to be seeing each other then?

Rachel had already told me I had to play it cool, though. So I just said, "We'll see."

LOL.

After we ate, he drove me back to my apartment and we made out on my couch for a while. He was very respectful and asked me permission before he touched me anywhere. Rachel thought for sure he'd want to have sex tonight, but he didn't even bring it up. She thinks that means he might have some other girl on the side and that she's the one he uses for sex and I'm the nice girl—the one he can take out on dates.

I hope not because I really like him.

But if it turns out that Rachel is right, then I'll just stop seeing him.

If Gloria taught me anything, it's that men never change. And once a two-timer, always a two-timer.

It might be silly to think this since we've only been on two dates. But in my heart, I think David Flores is one of the good ones.

CHAPTER EIGHTEEN

"You know it's only been three minutes since the last time you checked your watch, right?"

I looked up from my laptop to see Mercedes's raised eyebrows judging me. I was standing at the register counter while she was dusting some nearby shelves.

"Technically, it's been four," I answered as I tried to focus on the email I'd just opened with a new pending invoice. But all I could think about was the fact that Gloria was exactly ten minutes late.

It was only my second day working at Tesoro, and I was already a disorganized mess. Well, as a mom anyway. I'd completely forgotten it was an early-release day for Maya and that Leila wasn't going to school because of a doctor's appointment. That meant Leila's mom wasn't going to be able to bring Maya home. But before I could call Mercedes to let her know I couldn't come in, Gloria had said she could pick up Maya for me.

"It's not going to look good to your new boss if you can't come in on your second day," she'd said.

"You don't have a car," I reminded her.

"You have a second car just sitting in the garage, collecting dust."

I hadn't driven David's car since he'd left. Part of me didn't want to risk doing something to it and then having to deal with the repercussions later. Another part of me was a little afraid of the emotions that might be triggered by just sitting in it.

I'd been proud of myself the night before for handing the phone directly to Maya so she could answer his call instead of me. And when Maya told me about fifteen minutes later that her daddy wanted to talk to me, I took the phone back and said, "Sorry, can't talk right now. Goodbye."

He sent a few texts immediately after. One about the mediator question and then two others asking me to call him later or the next day. I left them all on "read."

But when Gloria mentioned helping me pack away the rest of his clothes from our bedroom closet, I balked. I didn't trust that I wouldn't break down, thanks to any items that still carried the scent of his cologne or evoked memories of places or things we'd done together.

Maybe it was just me being a coward. Either way, I had to protect myself and my heart if I'd have any chance of getting stronger mentally and emotionally.

Gloria had said I needed to fight. Well, this was how I was training for that fight.

In the end, David's car stayed where it was. Instead, Gloria drove my car to drop me off at Tesoro in the morning and used it to get Maya from school at noon. Then they were both going to come pick me up at three so they could see where I was working and meet Mercedes. Gloria had texted that they were leaving the house twenty minutes ago, and I knew it should only take her ten to get here.

So where were they?

"It's not like you live far away," Mercedes said, interrupting my panicky thoughts. "They'll be here soon. Why are you so . . . nervous?"

The poor woman had no idea what can of worms she had just opened.

"Let's just say Gloria . . . my mom . . . is not the most reliable person in this world. She also isn't the best when it comes to following directions, or boundaries, or common sense."

"I thought you two have been getting along."

I gave up on the invoice and closed my laptop to look at Mercedes. "For the most part, we have. But having her around has brought up some old feelings. Like, every day I can't help waiting for her to drop some sort of bombshell on me . . . or disappear without a word. That's what living with my mom was like for most of my life. I honestly don't know how she ended up convincing me to let her pick up Maya today."

Mercedes walked over to the counter. "Maybe it's because, despite what you say, you still want to trust her."

"Maybe? But I trusted two people who had never really done anything to betray that trust before and look what happened. It's kind of sad that I want to trust the one woman in my life who has disappointed me over and over again. Isn't that kind of pathetic?"

"Not at all. You have a good heart, Claudia. You want to believe that people in your life also have good hearts. That's not pathetic. That's beautiful."

I let out a long sigh. No matter how nice that sounded, I didn't believe her.

I checked my watch again. Gloria was officially twelve minutes late now.

Just as I was about to call her, the bell over Tesoro's front door jingled.

"Mommy, we're here!"

I heard Maya, although I couldn't see her immediately beyond the tall display of candles. But she soon appeared just a few seconds later, and Gloria was right behind her.

Maya stopped in her tracks when she saw Mercedes. Then she held out her hand. "Hola, mi nombre es Maya. Mucho gusto."

Mercedes beamed at her as she replied, "Mucho gusto, Maya. Mi nombre es Mercedes."

"Mommy says it's not polite to call adults by their first name unless they give me permission," she said after they shook hands.

"Well, I give you permission," Mercedes said.

"Gracias." Maya then came around the counter to give me a hug. I bent down to kiss the top of her head.

"Hello. You must be Claudia's mother."

I looked over to see my mom acknowledge Mercedes with a slight nod. "Yes, I'm Gloria."

"So good to meet you, Gloria," my boss said as she held out her hand.

Gloria took it, but then Mercedes did something unusual. She sandwiched Gloria's hand with both of hers and just held it for several seconds. Then she let it go without another word.

"Why don't you two look around while I gather my things?" I said in an attempt to break the awkward silence.

"Can I get another book, Mommy?" Maya asked before leaving my side.

"Sure. But don't touch anything on the shelves. Some things are breakable."

"Come on, Maya," Gloria said as she took my daughter's hand. "Let's go find the books."

The two walked toward the back of the store, and I began picking up the files I'd left on the counter.

"Maya is adorable," Mercedes said.

"Thank you," I replied with a smile.

"And your mother . . ." she began but then trailed off.

"Not what you were expecting, right?" I said with a chuckle. When she didn't respond, I looked up. Her furrowed eyebrows surprised me. "What?" I asked.

"I, uh, nothing. Never mind."

"Well, now I absolutely cannot never mind. Tell me."

Mercedes looked over her shoulder as if to check to make sure Gloria and Maya were still on the other side of the store. Then she moved closer. "You know, I can sense things about people, right?"

I nodded. I didn't really know, other than she'd told me so.

"Well, when I took your mom's hand, I just felt a sense that she was very guarded."

"That tracks," I said with a nod. "I told you I think she's not being entirely truthful about why she left Florida."

My boss nodded, but I could tell by her furrowed brows and tight lips that she seemed concerned.

"Was there something else?" I asked her.

Mercedes looked over her shoulder again before answering. "Whatever it is, it's weighing on her. Hopefully you can help her release whatever load she's carrying."

"Yeah right," I scoffed. "I'm the last person my mother would ever confide in. If she has something to tell me, then she's only going to tell me when she's ready. Not a second before."

From the corner of my eye, I spotted Maya coming back down the aisle toward the counter. I quickly picked up my folders and stuffed them and my laptop into my bag. I didn't know if Mercedes had more to say, but it would have to wait for another day.

"Did you find a book?" I asked my daughter.

She presented me with two. "Can I get these? Grandma says it's up to you."

I glanced at Gloria, who was over by the jewelry rack examining a pair of earrings. Whatever Mercedes saw in her, I didn't. The woman looked like she didn't have a care in the world, as usual.

Before I could answer Maya, Mercedes said, "How about I let you take them home as a special gift from me to you?"

Maya's hazel eyes opened wide. "Really?"

"Oh, that's not necessary. I'll buy them," I told Mercedes.

But Mercedes wouldn't hear of it. "They're not for sale anymore."

I shook my head and couldn't help but chuckle.

"Can I take them home, Mommy?"

"Yes, you can. What do you say to Mercedes?"

"Gracias."

Mercedes's face brightened with a big smile. "De nada."

The three of us made it to the car about ten minutes later. Maya was anxious to get home and start reading. And Gloria had also left with a pair of earrings—Mercedes did not offer them as a gift, though.

"It's a cute store," Gloria said as I pulled away from the curb. I noticed she'd taken her glasses off and was rubbing one closed eye.

"What's wrong?" I asked. "Do you have one of your headaches?"

She moved her hand away from her eye. "No, I'm fine. I got these new bifocals right before I left Florida, and it's just taking me some time to adjust to them."

"Okay," I replied, still not quite sure if she was telling me the truth. I ignored the doubt and changed the subject back to Tesoro. "And, yes, Mercedes has a good eye for design and art. She personally curates everything she sells."

"She seems nice."

I glanced over at my mom again. Despite the compliment, her tone was flat. "She *is* nice. I don't know what I would've done if she hadn't given me this job."

"That's kind of dramatic, isn't it? I'm sure you would've found something eventually."

I scoffed. "I've been out of the corporate world for nearly a decade. Getting a job in my field would've been hard, to say the least. I'm lucky that what I'm doing for Mercedes is pretty basic. I actually feel a little guilty that she wants to pay me for it."

"She should pay you. Your time is valuable, Claudia. You don't give that away for free, no matter how nice someone is, okay?"

Gloria's little rant took me by surprise. Another pep talk? She'd given me more of those in the past week and a half than in the past twenty years of my life.

My suspicions were growing stronger every day. Something was definitely off with her. But since Maya was in the car, it was neither the time nor place to confront her about it again.

"Okay," I said. "Speaking of my time being valuable, what took you so long to get to the store today?"

"What do you mean?"

"You texted that you were getting ready to leave the house, and then you didn't show up until over twenty minutes later."

"Did you have a stopwatch going or something?" she scoffed.

I could tell she was annoyed, but I didn't care. If she wanted to assume the responsibility of taking care of Maya, then I needed her to know she couldn't change plans just like that.

"No, but it would've been nice if you'd let me know you were running late. That's all I'm saying."

She blew out a long breath. But before she could speak again, I heard a small voice from the back seat say, "We were late picking you up because we stopped to talk to Uncle Nick."

My shoulders immediately tensed at Maya's comment. I didn't realize she'd been paying so close attention to our conversation. I also braced myself because I wasn't sure if I wanted to know what Gloria and Nick had discussed in front of her.

"You did?" I said, trying to sound nonchalant as I looked over again at my mother.

She met my eyes and shrugged. "He was just getting out of his truck when we walked outside. Maya ran over to give him a hug, so I walked over to say hello. I was surprised he remembered me, since I haven't seen him in years."

"And what did he say?" I asked slowly.

"Nothing really. Just that it was nice that I'd come to visit you and Maya."

"He said Auntie Rachel is on a trip," my daughter added.

My hands gripped the steering wheel in rising panic. My heart rate escalated in anticipation of what else Nick had shared.

"Maya asked if they could come over for dinner this week, so that's when Nick let her know Rachel was out of town," Gloria explained in a reassuring and soft tone.

"I told him they can come over when she gets back."

I looked at Maya's reflection in the rearview mirror. My throat tightened at her innocent invitation. She had no idea that there was zero chance of Rachel coming over to our house for dinner ever again.

When we got home, I told Maya she could go read her new books in her room for an hour, and then we'd get started on homework. On any other day, I would've used the new books as a reward for doing her homework. But I wanted to interrogate my mom further about the conversation with Nick.

"So, tell me everything," I said as I followed Gloria into the guest bedroom.

She walked over to her dresser and took out her new earrings from the white tissue paper that Mercedes had wrapped them in. "About what?"

"You know what. About what really happened with Nick." I sat on the edge of the bed. My right leg began to quiver in anticipation and agitation.

Without looking at me, Gloria said, "I already told you everything."

"I'm sure you left stuff out because of Maya. So spill."

I heard her sigh, and then she turned around to face me. "Claudia, there is nothing else. It was a simple hello, and then Maya mentioned dinner. That's all."

Doubt and my mother's history of leaving out important shit wouldn't let me drop the subject. "Did my name get brought up? Did David's?"

"No and no."

"So Nick didn't mention the fact that David and Rachel were out of town together?"

Gloria arched an eyebrow. "Of course not. I've only met the man a handful of times, but he doesn't strike me as stupid or cruel."

I ignored her assessment of Nick. "And how was he with Maya? Did he act weird or annoyed by her?"

"Not at all. In fact, I'd even say he was happy to see her."

"Really?" I asked.

"Really. Why wouldn't he be?"

I guess I shouldn't have been surprised. Nick had always seemed to genuinely care for Maya. He endured her constant requests for piggyback rides and for him to be a guest at her dolls' tea parties. If anything, he always seemed more willing to spend time with her than even Rachel. Especially over the last few months.

When they'd first moved to South Pasadena, Maya had asked me if she could call him "uncle," since she already called Rachel "auntie." Since David and I really had no other close relatives around, I figured it was okay. Although I did ask him permission first. He said he would be honored.

I felt a twinge of guilt for thinking Nick would transfer his negative feelings toward David—and even me—to Maya. After all, it wasn't her fault that her dad and her auntie had turned out to be terrible people.

"Well, now I feel bad," I said as I threw myself backward onto the bed.

"For what? For automatically assuming I'd run off with your daughter instead of picking you up at work?"

"No, not that." I purposefully didn't deny her accusation. "Nick is a good guy, and he was—is—a good uncle to Maya. I hate that it will never be the same between them."

The bed dipped as Gloria sat next to me. "Why does it have to change? He obviously still cares about her."

"Everything has changed now, Mom!" I yelled. I hadn't meant to. I braced myself for Maya to run into the room to find out what was going on. But when she didn't appear for several seconds, I continued. This time in a lower voice. "Maya is never going to stop asking for him and Rachel to come to dinner. It's not like he can keep saying she's out of town forever. Nick will always be connected to Rachel. And Nick was only my friend because of her. How can I be his friend now?"

She gave me a disappointed shake of her head. "Why do you always overthink or automatically assume the worst?"

"Because usually I'm right, and I like to be prepared for the most traumatic situation possible," I said. "Although my husband running off with my best friend was not even in my top ten worst things in the world that could happen. I hate being blindsided. Loathe it. Despise it—"

"All right, all right. I get it. But I still don't see why you can't be Nick's friend and he can continue to be Maya's uncle. I'm not saying it's going to be like it was before. But your and Maya's relationship with him doesn't have to end just because Rachel's no longer in the picture."

Gloria's words seemed sensible. Even comforting. Then, like it always did, my imagination and anxiety conjured up the very worst possible scenario.

What if Rachel *was* still in the picture down the line? Oh God, what if she became Maya's stepmother?

I gasped as if someone had punched me in the gut. Pain squeezed my chest, making it hard for me to catch a breath. I sat up and jumped off the bed. I still couldn't get any air in my lungs, so I ran outside to the backyard.

I didn't realize Gloria had followed until she grabbed me by the shoulders. "What's wrong? Tell me, Claudia, please." Even in my panicked state, I could hear the fear in her voice.

But I couldn't get it out. I was afraid of speaking it into existence. It was one thing to *think* about the possibility of David marrying Rachel. It was quite another to say it out loud.

I shrugged out of her grasp and ran to the end of the yard. Now I was gulping for oxygen, and my heart was pounding hard against my chest as if it, too, wanted to escape from my body in order to get as far away as possible from the ugly thoughts in my head.

Gloria was at my side in a matter of seconds. This time she grabbed me harder and shook. "Listen to me. Unless you want me to call 911 and scare the shit out of Maya, you need to calm yourself down. Take a slow, deep breath. Inhale. Exhale. Do it, Claudia."

The thought of Maya watching me get taken away in an ambulance was enough to make me listen to my mom. I held my hand against my chest as if to slow down my heart and slowly breathed in and then out. I closed my eyes and tried to think of somewhere serene and quiet. A place where I felt safe and protected.

And then I was back in my abuela's church. The wooden pews, stained glass windows, and smell of incense enveloped me in a shroud of peacefulness.

I took another deep breath. In. Then out.

My eyes opened and met Gloria's frantic ones. She began taking breaths right along with me. "In," she instructed. "Out."

I had no idea how much time had passed, but eventually my breathing and heart rate steadied.

"How do you feel?" my mother finally asked.

"Horrible," I admitted. "But better than a few minutes ago."

"Do you want to talk about it?"

"No."

Her face fell in disappointment. So I added, "Thank you for helping me."

"You're welcome. Why don't you stay out here a little longer and get yourself together? I'll go check on Maya."

I offered her a small smile and nodded. I didn't want Maya to see me until I knew for sure I wouldn't have another panic attack.

Especially since I had no strength left to fight the tears that were now breaking through the barrier I relied on to keep my most desperate emotions at bay.

All I could do was cover my face with my hands and let the sobs out.

CHAPTER NINETEEN

THINGS I NEVER KNEW #313: SOMETIMES IMPERFECTION IS PERFECTION

Dear Diary,

Well, I'm officially engaged! David popped the question tonight and I said yes, of course. I'm so happy. My face hurts because I've been smiling for hours.

He went all out for the proposal too. Apparently, he and Rachel have been planning this for weeks. She came to stay with us for the weekend, and I'd made all sorts of plans for us to do things since it had been a while since we'd seen each other. She agreed to all of it, but then said she wanted us to go to dinner on Coronado Island at a restaurant a friend had told her about.

We spent the day shopping and getting manis and pedis and facials. David said he was going to go hang out with his own friends and he'd see me after dinner. Rachel said our reservation was at eight, but she wanted to walk along the beach before heading over. I hesitated since we were both in cocktail dresses and heels, but I knew how much Rachel loved the beach, so I agreed.

As we walked along the sidewalk, I began noticing sand sculptures. The first ones were simple and generic.

One was made to look like a bucket with seashells. Another looked like a fish lying on its side. But the farther we walked, the more detailed and familiar they became. The logo for San Diego State and a figure that resembled Iron Man. When we came upon a heart with my name and David's, that's when I knew.

I was so shocked that I stopped walking, and it was Rachel who had to pull me a few more feet until we came to a path in the sand lined with rose petals. Up until that point, I'd been holding in my tears. But that all went away when I saw David standing at the end of the rose petal path dressed in a suit. Rachel pushed me forward as a crowd of strangers began gathering. Part of me wanted to run in the other direction to get away from all the stares. But I knew I couldn't do that to David. And as much as I wished he would've asked me to marry him in private, I began walking toward him.

It felt like I had taken a thousand steps, so I actually ran the rest of the way. He laughed when I finally reached him. Then he pointed to the sand sculpture behind him and cursed. Some of the details had already crumbled, so instead of saying "Will You Marry Me?" it said "Will You Mar Me?"

The crowd cheered when I said yes, and we kissed to seal the deal. Then David, Rachel, and I walked to a nearby restaurant to meet friends for a surprise engagement party on a patio with a spectacular view of the ocean. I found out during the party, after Rachel had had a few drinks, that there was supposed to be a quartet playing when I walked down the sand. Apparently, their car had broken down on the freeway, so they'd texted her to let her know they weren't going to show up in time. She'd also wanted fireworks to go off when we kissed, but fireworks aren't allowed on the beach. She seemed on the verge of tears when she explained she'd worked so hard to pull off the perfect proposal for me and was so upset that it didn't go the way she'd wanted it to. I tried to reassure her that it was perfect, and I thanked her for helping David pull it off.

In the end, it didn't matter anyway. All that matters is that I'm going to marry David Flores, and right now that makes me the happiest woman on earth!

CHAPTER TWENTY

"Please don't be dead."

I repeat the same four words over and over again as I drive like a maniac through the streets of downtown Los Angeles. Red lights became suggestions. Speed limits only recommendations.

When I have no choice but to come to a screeching halt because of a stupid construction truck trying to maneuver itself into a seemingly too-tiny driveway, those same words morph into one strangled, desperate prayer.

"God, please don't let him be dead!"

I choke back on the tears I've been holding in ever since I received the call less than twenty minutes before from a nurse at Los Angeles General Medical Center. David had been brought in by ambulance and was being prepped for emergency surgery.

At first, I was sure the nurse had called the wrong number. As far as I knew, David was at our house in South Pasadena, in our bed watching the Dodgers game. That's what he told me he'd planned on doing when I spoke to him on the phone earlier tonight.

"It's Saturday. He shouldn't even be driving in downtown," I told the nurse, as if that proved the call was some horrible mistake.

The nurse's voice was gentle when she dropped the final bombshell. "Your husband's business associate, the woman he was having dinner with, is the one who gave us your name and number. I'm sorry, but it is him."

How I managed to find my purse and my keys after that is a complete blur. Because the only thing I could focus on—the only thing I could think of—were those four words.

Please don't be dead.

The truck finally manages to pull into the driveway, clearing a path for traffic to start moving again. I wipe my eyes with my fingers and take a long, deep breath. The influx of new oxygen into my brain dissipates the cloud of panic, and I hear Gloria's voice echo into the darkness of the car.

"Tears don't help anyone, Claudia. Especially when they're shed over something that can't be changed."

To outsiders, Gloria's words may have seemed harsh to say to a teenager who had just lost her beloved abuela. But even at that age, I hadn't been hurt by them. Instead, they'd only made me stronger.

So I take another extended breath, push away my fear, and focus on being strong. Then I press the gas pedal down to the floor and continue my race to the hospital.

Minutes later, I walk through the doors of the emergency room. But my knees buckle when I see Rachel already sitting there among the crowd of the sick and injured. And she's smiling.

Like always, I scream, "Wake up! Wake up, Claudia!"

My subconscious eventually cooperated, forcing me to leave the darkness behind by slowly raising one eyelid. It took a few seconds for the swirl of colors to come into focus. A pale-yellow wall. A sparse white bookshelf. Something gray right below my right eye.

But I couldn't take a breath. Or swallow.

Dryness, not saliva, coated my tongue and the roof of my mouth. My lips were glued together like two pieces of paper, and as hard as I tried, I couldn't peel them apart. That meant I couldn't scream out loud either.

As the rest of my body and senses came alive, I finally realized where I actually was.

Mercedes's back office at Tesoro. Well, more specifically, the right side of my face was attached to the top of the desk in the office.

Slowly, I lifted my head off the cool gray laminate and blinked. A long, deep yawn tore apart my parched lips, allowing me to finally take the breath I'd been starved for just a few seconds earlier. I searched for my Hydro Flask and took another gulp. I drank and drank until I was sure any remnants of desiccated panic and dread had been washed away.

I yawned again as I rubbed my eyes. A dull pain vibrated from my neck to my shoulders, so I stretched muscles and cracked bones until it went away. A quick glance at the display on my rose gold Apple Watch squeezed a gasp out of me. I'd been asleep for nearly an hour.

I nodded in surprise appreciation. Last night had been particularly hard. David had called Maya, but before I handed the phone to her, he'd pressed me about his mediation idea. The asshole had no apologies for canceling the credit cards. His excuse was that he had to pay them off since they were in both of our names, and he needed to start establishing credit on his own.

From the corner of my eye, I saw the tiny white envelope icon pop onto my computer screen. It was an email from him. And even though I didn't open it, I knew it was going to be information about mediators.

Part of me still couldn't believe our interactions had been reduced to emails and texts. How could someone who had professed his love to me every day for nearly thirteen years now barely want to talk to me? Based on my dream, it was obvious that deep down, I still loved him. My heart just had to catch up to my brain, I guess. Because the only feeling I got while looking at his email was loathing.

The email can wait until tonight, I told myself. *Get up and go home.*

I tried to listen to the voice in my head—for about ten seconds. Then I straightened my back, let out another yawn, and reached for my mouse. But before I could open the newly arrived email, the door to the office opened.

"Oh good, you're awake!"

Whatever excuse had been rumbling around in my brain as soon as I saw Mercedes walk in disappeared when I met her worried eyes.

So I told her the truth. "I'm so sorry I fell asleep. It was a long night. It won't happen again, though."

Mercedes walked over and stood in front of her desk. "Don't worry about it. If you need sleep then you need sleep. You're no good to anyone, even me, if you're exhausted."

I nodded and offered her a small smile. "Thank you. I do feel better. I was going to stay a little longer and finish sorting these invoices, but I think maybe I should head home."

She nodded back. "I agree. Now go home and take another nap before Maya gets home from school. But make sure you eat something first."

"I will. Again, I'm so sorry for falling asleep. My insomnia seems to be getting worse."

Mercedes looked at me with concern. "Maybe you need to try some yoga or meditation. Or maybe you should try sleeping in your bed instead of on the couch."

A familiar anxiety bristled over my skin. "I already told you I'm not ready for that," I said.

"I know," she said, and she raised her palm as if to stop me from unraveling. "And I'm not pushing. I'm just . . . trying to help," she said after a long sigh.

Guilt settled in my chest. I knew Mercedes meant well and was worried about me. And I hated that I was doing that to her. I was a grown woman. My boss shouldn't be worried about whether I was eating and sleeping when I was supposed to.

The thought of food elicited a loud grumble from my stomach.

"Don't forget to take the molé home with you. There's enough for the three of you for the next two days," Mercedes said, confirming that she had indeed heard the embarrassing noise.

I couldn't help but smile. "I still can't believe you made that much."

She shrugged. "Molé isn't something you can make a little of. Besides, I'm glad to share it. It gives me an excuse to make it more often." Besides the beautifully crafted items in her store, Mercedes had picked up another thing throughout her travels to Mexico: a love of cooking.

"Well, feel free to make it whenever, along with any other dishes you've been wanting to try out."

Mercedes laughed. "You know, Joseph and I were foodies before the term was even a thing. We actually met in a Mexican cooking class. That was over twenty-five years ago."

She went on to share that Joseph, the son of Irish immigrants, had never been outside of the United States before they met. She said he fell in love with Mexico during their very first trip to the country. And she fell in love with him. They married only six months after meeting and bought their house in San Antonio.

"He was the one who suggested I open my first shop. He knew how much I wished I could bring home everything I'd find during my trips and how important it was for me to support the local artisans. Opening Tesoro was also my way of bringing a taste of Mexican culture to our city. He was the one who came up with the name. I was going to call it 'Mercedes's Mexican Treasures.' Then Joseph asked what the Spanish word was for 'treasure.' And it was like a light bulb came on."

Mercedes went on to explain that during their biannual trips to Mexico, they'd not only visit local artisans to find treasures, but also make sure to ask for recommendations on where to eat and what foods were popular in the area. From cabrito in Monterrey to pozole rojo in Jalisco, Mercedes and Joseph were willing to try anything and everything.

"But it was the molé negro in Oaxaca that was Joseph's favorite. Over the years, I tried to replicate the recipe and would make it for him on his birthday. The one I use now is the closest to the original as I could get without using some of the ingredients native to Oaxaca that I couldn't find in the States."

From our previous conversations, I knew that Joseph had passed away two years ago from a heart attack, and this was the first time she had made molé since.

This batch was special in more ways than one.

When we were done chatting about what I should work on tomorrow, I packed up the files I needed to review later and slipped my laptop into my backpack. Then I stopped at the small fridge inside the office and grabbed the large container of molé.

I found Mercedes restocking some stickers on the counter and thanked her again for the food.

"Any big plans for tonight?" I asked.

"Nope. Just catching up on some shows I recorded. What about you?"

"Actually, I have a parent-teacher conference later this afternoon. That's going to take all my energy. Especially since Gloria wants to go with me."

Mercedes laughed. She had yet to see my mother for a second time, but she'd heard enough stories to know that was not the best idea.

"Exactly. She says she wants to know what she can be doing to help Maya with her homework. The woman probably only went to a handful of teacher meetings when I was a kid. I don't understand her sometimes."

Mercedes walked with me to the front door. "Maybe it's her way of making up for what she didn't do all those years ago. Instead of questioning her motive, maybe just give her the chance to make it right."

"I don't know. I'll think about it."

She gave me a hug. But before I could pull away, she squeezed me tighter for another hug. "You're going to get through this, Mija," she whispered. "You'll see. Things are going to be better soon."

A knot of emotion gripped my entire body, and I couldn't speak. Tears pooled in the corner of my eyes, and I internally screamed at them to go away. I'd been trying so hard to not cry or break down in front of Mercedes anymore. I didn't want her to see that, although I always said I was doing fine when she asked, there were parts of me that were still broken. Might always be broken.

I wanted so desperately to be like how I was before. I'd wished many times that Mercedes could've met the old me. It wasn't like she didn't understand what I was going through—if anything, she was the one person in my life who did. Not because her husband had cheated on her with her best friend, but because he was lost to her. Just like David was lost to me. Maybe that's why she'd taken a vested interest in helping me.

I'd needed a job—and she'd given me one at her store.

She knew I didn't always want to cook or eat—she brought me molé and enchiladas and chile relleno casseroles to take home for dinner.

She knew I couldn't sleep—she let me take naps in her office and encouraged me to meditate or take up yoga.

And it tore me to pieces every day that as hard as Mercedes wanted to help me, I still wasn't fixed. At least not in the way I thought I should be by now.

The dream I'd had during my nap was proof of it.

Because as much as David had hurt me, it was seeing Rachel in it that always made me wake up. That was something I wasn't ready to face.

What I never said, never admitted, was that on more than one night, I had sobbed in the shower after looking through old photos of us. There was a time in my life when I believed Rachel was the one person in this world who would never betray me. When I couldn't rely on my own mother to be there for me, Rachel was. When I was afraid to believe I was better than what others had always told me, Rachel had no doubts.

And when I thought David was cheating on me six months ago with a coworker, Rachel was the one who held my hand and told me I was being ridiculous.

So that's why I smiled and nodded whenever Mercedes or Gloria told me I'd get over David eventually.

Because I'd rather do that than admit to them that sometimes the boogeyman in my nightmares—the one who wouldn't let me sleep—wasn't a man at all.

It was a woman.

CHAPTER TWENTY-ONE

THINGS I NEVER KNEW #371: THE REAL REASON WHY COUPLES ELOPE

Dear Diary,

In less than twenty-four hours, I will officially be Mrs. David Flores.

I'm writing this as I lie in bed in the hotel's bridal suite. Rachel is taking a shower, and we'll probably be going to sleep soon. Although I doubt I'll be able to even close my eyes. I am exhausted. But I'm also excited and can't wait for my wedding day to finally get here.

I have to admit the road was kind of rocky there for a minute. Maybe that's why I just want to hurry up and get married already. I don't want anything else to go wrong.

Thankfully, the rehearsal dinner tonight went off without any major hiccups. Well, except for the fact that Gloria drank one too many beers and decided it was okay to pull me into the ladies' room at the restaurant and try to convince me not to marry David. Of course she didn't have any good reason, other than he was acting suspicious all night. She hinted that maybe she'd seen him do something but wouldn't give me specifics. She just said it was strange that he seemed to disappear, and different people had come up to her to ask where he'd gone. Gloria added that at one point even she went to go look for him. I asked her where she'd found him, and she ignored the question. She just kept repeating the same thing over and over again: If I only listened to her once in my life, then this was the time.

Luckily, Rachel came looking for me and chased Gloria away. She reminded me that my mom had had a lot to drink and was probably jealous that I was about to have the wedding of my dreams. I didn't tell Rachel that I didn't think jealousy had anything to do with it. Gloria actually seemed panicked or even a little hysterical when she was begging me to call the wedding off. I honestly don't know why my mother was acting the way she was tonight. But I can't worry about it anymore.

I'm getting married in the morning. And nothing and no one is going to stop that.

CHAPTER TWENTY-TWO

As I waited outside Maya's classroom for her teacher to finish her meeting with a set of parents, my stomach churned with a little anxiety. I was a grown-ass adult, and talking to teachers still made me nervous.

I'd always been a good student. In fact, I was usually one of the top performers. Yet I always dreaded parent-teacher conference season. Mostly because I would never know until the day of if Gloria would remember to go—or even want to go.

But it was different with Maya. South Pasadena had some of the best schools in the country. When we were looking for houses in the area, I created an entire spreadsheet about which neighborhoods had the best kindergartens—and I wasn't even pregnant yet!

Eventually, David basically threw up his hands and told me he was done looking and that I needed to just pick a house already. When I complained to Rachel one day about his attitude, I was surprised when she ended up agreeing with him.

She told me I was being ridiculous. I brushed it off like I always did when she thought I was overthinking something. She didn't understand because she'd always hated school, and good grades seemed to come harder for her than they had for me. Even after she got accepted to San Diego State after two years of community college, Rachel decided she didn't want to go to a four-year university. So she enrolled in a trade school and graduated from their ultrasound tech program.

I gathered that she liked what she did for a living. For the most part. But deep down I knew Rachel only went to school because she had to. Of course she wouldn't understand why it was so important for me to make sure Maya had the best education possible from the get-go.

Maya had been in this school district for almost three years now. Luckily, she'd had some wonderful teachers who encouraged her inquisitive mind and kind spirit. So why did I always feel like these conferences were more about judging me as a parent? Because of what had happened right before school started, I hadn't talked that much to Miss Lima. By now I usually would've signed up as a classroom volunteer, attended the open house, and rallied other parents to start planning the end of the school year party. Perhaps that was why I was feeling extra nervous. I didn't know Miss Lima, and she didn't know me.

A man and a woman walked out the door, and Miss Lima followed. "Hello, Mrs. Flores. Come on in."

I almost corrected her. But technically I was still a Mrs. I took a seat on one of the folding chairs set up next to her desk. She opened a folder and began explaining what her goals for the first semester were and what she'd been focusing on these first few months of school. Then she went into how Maya was performing specifically.

"Maya is doing very well. She does all her work and is a great helper. She's very curious and interested in learning, which is so good to see."

"And how are her grades?" I asked nervously.

Miss Lima picked up a folded paper and opened it. "As you can see, she has either E's and G's in every subject. Her report card reflects her progress to date. And, honestly, I really have no academic concerns about her at all."

The comments from Maya's teacher were all good, and I began to relax a little.

"She's even been teaching me some Spanish words so I can teach them to the class," Miss Lima said with a laugh.

I was both embarrassed and proud. "Yeah, that's her thing right now. I've bought her a couple of bilingual books, and she's been absorbing the language pretty quickly."

"Well, that's amazing. Studies have shown that learning a second language as a child can boost critical thinking, reading skills, and creativity. Even more importantly, it gives them a connection to a different culture, which in turn will make them even more of a well-rounded human."

"Thank you for saying that and for allowing Maya to express herself this way."

Miss Lima nodded. "Of course. Now, while she has been doing extremely well with her work and listening, I feel like I must bring up that I have noticed a change in her overall demeanor. I know I haven't known her that long, but I've noticed a difference just in the past few weeks. She seems to get more upset easily if I have to correct her behavior or if she can't grasp learning something new. It's not a huge issue right now, but I wanted you to be aware in case it becomes something more than what it is."

My heart dropped into my stomach and made it lurch. "Oh, okay."

Miss Lima folded her hands together and set them on top of her desk. "Some children her age can regress into having more toddler-like reactions because they can't vocalize their emotions. I have to ask. Is this something you've noticed at home, or do you think it's just isolated to school?"

Now I was the one having trouble vocalizing my emotions. I cleared my throat. "Um, yes, I have noticed it at home. She's definitely had more crying episodes lately at night before bed. And I probably should've talked to you about this sooner, but Maya's father and I just recently separated. He's moved to San Francisco, and she hasn't seen him for a few weeks. I've noticed that she's more emotional after their phone calls. I know it's because she misses him."

Miss Lima looked at me with sympathy in her eyes. "I'm so sorry to hear that. Does Maya understand what's happening?"

"We've talked," I said with a shrug. "She knows that he got a new job and had to move somewhere else. But I haven't really gone into details or even brought up the word 'divorce.' Honestly, I'm just not ready to have that conversation."

"Maya is a very bright and intuitive little girl. She may not know the specifics of what's happening, but I'm sure she can see that something has changed beyond just her dad moving away for a new job. My suggestion is to encourage her to ask questions and express her feelings about the situation. Maybe she could even talk to a counselor?"

"Maybe," I answered. I knew Maya was having difficulty with everything. But I hadn't considered that she might need therapy.

"You know, I do have a few students in this class with divorced parents and stepparents. I know things can get complicated, but I want you to know that I'm here to help you and Maya navigate this. I really do want to help."

My anxiety about being judged for my parenting was back. Was Miss Lima insinuating that I wasn't helping Maya enough, so I should get someone else to help? I'd never felt like I could talk to Gloria about what I was feeling. I never wanted Maya to feel that way about me.

I thought about my journal and how that had helped me cope with things. I got my first one when I was about Maya's age. The first few entries were simple, basically just a rehash of my day. Then one day my abuela asked me what I was learning, and I told her math and reading and writing.

No, I don't mean your school subjects, she'd said. *I mean what new things are you learning that will help you in life. You can't know everything. You have to learn in order to grow. Because if you don't learn, then you die.*

So I decided I'd write down the things I learned so I would never forget them. As I got older, the lessons got harder.

Even though I'd never shared them with anyone else, writing did give me an outlet.

So why hadn't I written in it since *that* day?

After I got home, I was still feeling uneasy about what Miss Lima had said. I had planned on texting David to let him know how the conference had gone, but I debated on whether to share everything.

"You need to go next door," my mother announced as I entered the kitchen. She and Maya were both sitting at the table snacking on apple slices.

"Um, no I don't." The last thing I needed to do was go see Nick.

"You have to because he brought those," she said, pointing.

I looked at the bag of apples sitting on the counter. Gloria explained that Nick had stopped by and told her that his tree had doubled its fruit this season, and since he knew Maya liked apples, he wanted to bring some for her. I didn't want to think about the fact that Rachel was probably the only person in the world who could've told him that, since I knew I hadn't.

Still, it was enough to impress my mother. And because she was most likely still annoyed with me because I'd told her she couldn't come to the conference, she laid on the guilt trip.

"Pobrecito looks so skinny. You should take some of Mercedes's molé to him as a thank-you for bringing the apples."

"What's a pobrecito?" Maya asked.

"A poor little guy," Gloria answered.

"I didn't know Uncle Nick was poor," my daughter said.

I glared at my mother. "Maya, baby, why don't you take your plate of apples into the family room? You can watch TV for thirty minutes, and then it's time for homework."

She happily agreed and walked out of the kitchen. I sat down in the chair she'd just left. "I am not taking food to Nick," I said in a low voice.

"But why not? It's not like he's the one who had the affair with David," she explained as she nibbled on some apple slices. "He's a victim just like you."

"I'm not a victim," I said, bristling at the label.

"You know what I mean. Besides, didn't you tell me his grocery cart was full of frozen dinners the other night? It's probably been weeks since he's had a home-cooked meal."

"That's not my problem. I told you what he accused me of that day. Why on earth would I care what he's been eating?"

"Because before all of this, weren't you two friends?"

I thought about it for a minute. Sure, we'd spent lots of time together going out to dinner or to the movies or to a concert. But we'd never hung out just the two of us. "We were friendly. I wouldn't say that we were friends."

"Well, it's still a neighborly thing to do."

"It's not like he's checked on me to see how I'm doing," I said. I didn't care that I sounded whiny. "When you ran into him the other day, he didn't even ask about me, right? So why should I be the one who has to be the good neighbor?"

"Because you get what you give."

Recibes lo que das.

Even though she'd been gone for years, I could still hear the saying in Abuela's voice. And that was all it took. For the first time in my life, Gloria had repeated what her mother had always told us. I could never argue with Abuela, and I wasn't about to start now.

So I poured some of Mercedes's molé into a disposable container—that way there was no risk of having him feel obligated to return it—and walked next door.

"Okay," I told myself on the short trip over. "Let's get this over with."

I put on my best fake smile, took a deep breath, and knocked on Nick's front door.

He opened it after only a few seconds.

"Claudia?" It was almost more of a question than a greeting.

I cleared my throat. "I, um, I came to thank you for the apples. And to give you this."

Nick looked down at the container I held in front of me. But he didn't take it.

"It's molé. My boss made it, and she gave us way too much, so I thought maybe you would like some for your dinner." I rushed the explanation in the hopes our interaction would be over sooner rather than later.

"Oh," he said, taking the container. "Thank you."

"You're welcome. Have a good night." I turned to leave, but I stopped after he said my name.

"I, uh, wanted to apologize for what I said to you that . . . day. I wasn't thinking straight. I didn't mean it."

A big knot of emotion tightened my throat. "Thank you," I managed to squeak out.

"So, how are you doing?" he asked.

I relaxed a little and shrugged. "Okay. How about you?"

"Okay too. Have you talked to . . . her?"

"No," I said immediately.

"Would you tell me if you had?"

The question threw me. "Why would I lie about something like that?"

"Because she's your friend."

My shoulders straightened, bracing for an argument.

"*Was* my friend," I corrected, the irritation in my voice pretty clear.

"I just figured she'd call you to explain or something," he continued.

"Yeah, well, she hasn't. Not that there's anything she could explain, anyway."

Knowing Rachel like I did, I was sure she'd already convinced herself that what she'd done wasn't that bad. Maybe she could even justify it in her own warped way. No, I didn't need to hear anything from her, nor did I want to. At least not anymore.

"I'm just having a hard time processing everything," he said with a sigh. "Like I have so many questions. Is there anything at all you can tell me?"

I was done with the conversation. I hadn't come over to try to help Nick figure things out.

"No, there isn't. And I honestly don't appreciate you asking me these kinds of questions. I'm not the one who left. The only one who can give you answers is Rachel."

"David can."

That's when I realized what he'd been after all along. "You really think David is calling and telling me all the sordid details of their affair?"

Nick shrugged. "Maybe? All I know is that no one is telling me anything, and I think I have the right to know. So if you know something . . ."

My face grew hot. "I already told you I didn't. I have to get back to Maya."

"Fine, if you say so. Thanks for the molé anyway," he said, raising the container in my direction.

His pinched smile and rude tone rubbed me the wrong way. I immediately snatched it from his hands. "I changed my mind," I told him. "You're not molé-worthy."

His shocked expression turned into a confused one. "Molé-worthy?"

"Do you know how long it takes to make molé?" I didn't even wait for him to answer. "Of course you don't. It takes days, Nick. Days. There are three different dried chiles in here. Mercedes, that's my boss, had to rehydrate them. Then puree them. Then combine them with all the other ingredients and let them simmer for hours until they joined together to make this beautiful, complex sauce."

He cleared his throat. "My grandma used to make it for me when I was little. I didn't realize how—"

I wasn't done. "And she didn't just boil the chicken; she developed a flavorful broth from it that she also combined with the molé sauce to give it this rich and hearty depth. Mercedes put so much care and hard work and love into this molé because it was her dead husband's favorite thing to eat in this world. That's why it's such a very special dish, and it's not something she's made in a long time. So, no, Nick. You are not molé-worthy."

And with one final disappointed sigh, I turned around and headed home.

CHAPTER TWENTY-THREE

THINGS I NEVER KNEW #515: DOUBLE DATES CAN BE AWKWARD—EVEN WHEN YOU'RE NOT IN HIGH SCHOOL

Dear Diary,

Today I met the man my best friend is going to marry. And I don't like him.

Let me explain. I don't like him for Rachel. I mean, he seems nice enough and he seems to really love her. But there's just something odd about him.

They met six months ago on a dating app. Rachel says he's some sort of environmental engineer, and their first date actually went terrible. She thought he was boring and unfunny. She told me she was about to ditch him and excused herself to go to the restroom. But before she could get there, she was stopped by an ex of hers, and he was drunk. He got all handsy and began telling her all kinds of crude things. Rachel says Nick, that's her fiancé's name, showed up out of nowhere and confronted the guy. They all nearly got thrown out of the bar because the guy was yelling at Nick and threatening him. But Nick remained calm, and eventually her ex backed down. Rachel was so impressed that they didn't leave each other's sides for the next three days.

Typical Rachel.

Anyway, I'd heard good things about him and was genuinely happy for Rachel. We're both going to turn thirty-two next year, and she still didn't seem any closer to settling down. Not that she needs a man, really. She has a good job working as an ultrasound tech at a clinic over in Thousand Oaks and lives by herself in a one-bedroom apartment. Since I live about an hour away, it's hard to get together, especially since Rachel insisted she wanted the first time I met Nick to be on a double date, "so it could be like we're in high school all over again."

So tonight was the night David and I were finally going to meet Nick.

The four of us went to dinner at an Italian restaurant. As Nick was looking at the menu, he made a comment about how there weren't a lot of non-pasta choices on the menu! Rachel showed him that they did have a steak entrée and a pasta dish where you could add chicken. He said something like, "Well, I guess that's all I'm allowed then as a meat eater."

She laughed it off, but I gave David a look like "What's up with this guy?"

The rest of the night went fine until it was time to pay the check. He made a really big deal about making sure David didn't pay for their food. It was a little awkward the way he kept insisting that even though he didn't like his steak that he always pays his bills. Poor David didn't really know what to say, so we had to flag down the waiter and ask him to itemize. The waiter was obviously annoyed, and I could tell poor Rachel was embarrassed.

God, I hate to write it, but I kind of hope they break up.

CHAPTER TWENTY-FOUR

I usually loved fall in South Pasadena.

But not when it was my responsibility to rake up the millions of leaves that kept piling up in my front yard.

It was already mid-October, and Gloria had been with us for over a month. Although she'd proven to be helpful with Maya and the house, I was ready for her to go back home to Florida. But every time I brought the subject up, she'd just say she was going to start looking for flights soon.

My initial suspicions about why she was here were beginning to creep back into my head.

A prick, followed by a pinch of pain, zapped me from my thoughts.

"Dammit!" I yelled, and I dropped the rake I'd been using to corral leaves into a trash bag.

My right index finger throbbed, and I could make out the small outline of a splinter.

"Are you okay?"

I whipped around to see Nick standing in his driveway.

"I'm fine," I yelled.

Despite my words, he walked over to see for himself. "What happened?"

"Nothing. I just got a splinter in my finger from this old rake, that's all. It's not a big deal."

"Let me see," he said, and he began to reach for my hand.

I pulled it closer to me. "No. I told you it's nothing."

"For God's sake, Claudia. Let me see your finger." Nick grabbed my hand and pulled it up to his face. "Yeah, that's really deep in there. You're going to need tweezers."

I resisted the urge to call him Captain Obvious and snatched my hand back. "Good thing I have some, then."

Without looking at him, I went back inside.

It took Gloria three attempts before she was finally able to extricate the invader from under my skin. She said it was because it was wedged in deeper than she thought. To me, it looked like she was having a hard time seeing it, even though she was wearing her glasses.

"You should probably wash it with soap and then put some Neosporin or some other antiseptic on it," she said.

"Yeah, I will."

"You know if Abuela were here, she'd tell you to just pour some tequila on it."

The memory of her actually telling our neighbor to pour some on his infected toe still made me laugh to this day. "She thought tequila was the cure for everything. Even hangovers."

"If only that were true."

Gloria's somber and wistful tone made me look at her. For a second, I thought I saw her eyes get watery. But then she kind of shook it off and jumped up from her chair. "I promised Maya we'd do a puzzle. Do you want to join us?"

"Um, maybe in a little bit. I'm going to clean this, put on a Band-Aid and then finish raking up the leaves."

"Okay," she said, and she gave me a small smile.

As I washed my hands in the guest bathroom, I couldn't stop thinking about Gloria saying she wished tequila could cure all things.

Actually, I couldn't stop hearing the way she'd said it. There was something in her voice that didn't sit right with me, but I had no idea what. I'd never seen her get like that before, even when we'd talk about Abuela.

I decided rather than worry about it, I'd ask her later. First, I needed to go fight with some leaves.

But it turned out, someone else had stepped in to fight in my place. I walked off my porch and stared in stunned silence at three stuffed trash bags sitting in a row on my now nearly leaf-free lawn.

"If you want me to get the ones in the backyard, I can do that too." Nick appeared from the side of my house and held up what I assumed to be his own larger rake.

"No, you don't have to," I said as he got closer.

"I know I don't have to. But I want to. My way of apologizing for acting like a jerk."

I didn't bother disagreeing with his word choice. "I appreciate the apology. And I appreciate you taking care of the leaves today. But I can manage the backyard. Maybe not today, but I'll get to it this week."

Nick set down his rake and then shoved his hands into his jacket. "Look, Claudia. I realize that we've been forced into this awkward situation, and I'm just trying to make it less awkward."

I wanted to tell him it wasn't awkward. But I couldn't get out the lie, so I just nodded.

"How about this?" he asked. "I can help with your lawn and any other things you need done to the house, and, maybe, when you can, you make an extra plate of whatever you're having for dinner, and I'll come by and get it?"

My eyes widened at his proposal. "Are you saying you'll work for food?"

Nick gave me a sheepish grin. "Uh, yeah, I guess I am. Honestly, I kind of haven't stopped thinking about that molé from the other day. I wish I could've at least tasted it."

That made me laugh, and the hesitation I'd felt a few moments ago disappeared. "Well, I can't promise you molé, since I have no idea how to make it. But yeah, I can send you some dinners, even lunches, in exchange for helping me with the lawn."

"And anything else you need. I mean it."

We made plans for Nick to tackle the backyard during the week.

"He raked your leaves?" Mercedes asked me the following Monday. The store was closed to customers, but I'd come in for a few hours to pay some bills and had told her about my weekend and Nick, the leaf elf.

"And get this," I said, looking at her over the screen of my laptop. "He offered to keep doing it in exchange for some home-cooked meals."

Maybe I'd been right about Nick not being "molé-worthy" before. The leaf raking had at least earned him a bowl of spaghetti, though.

"That seems reasonable," she told me.

"But isn't it weird that the husband of my ex–best friend wants to be my lawn guy?"

"It's not weird at all. You are helping each other out. It's neighborly and has nothing to do with Rachel."

That was the problem. It had everything to do with Rachel because I couldn't think of Nick without immediately thinking of her. Not that I was thinking of Nick. At all. But it was just harder to ignore the thoughts of her when I saw him.

"I don't know," I said after a long sigh. "Gloria thinks I'm making a big deal out of nothing. She says I need to learn how to take help when it's offered."

"Amen. I agree."

I didn't like it when Mercedes agreed with Gloria. Maybe it was petty of me, but I liked having someone on my side—someone who wasn't eight years old and couldn't be persuaded to switch loyalties just with the offer of a cookie.

"Speaking of Gloria, has she said yet when she's planning to go back home?"

That was more like it. "No," I said, and I sighed again. "She keeps evading the question. Part of me wants to call Carlos and tell him to get on a plane and come get her himself."

Mercedes laughed. "Oh, I would pay good money to see that."

"Same. I still think she's not telling me something, though."

I hadn't forgotten what Mercedes had said after she met my mother that first day. Gloria was definitely holding something back. I had begun to doubt that she'd ever reveal the truth.

"Whatever it is, it may come out whether she wants it to or not. There's a saying that 'whatever is done in the dark eventually gets brought out into the light.'"

"Yeah, like screwing your best friend's husband behind her back." I couldn't help but say it.

Mercedes nodded at my crass example. "Well, I don't think Gloria did anything like that. Or at least I hope she didn't. Because all I could feel when I touched her hands was pain. But it could be physical pain or emotional pain."

"She does seem to have a lot more migraines than I remember. But she has no problem telling me about them."

Just last night, she'd asked for an ice pack and then complained that I'd put too much ice in it.

"I can sense things, but I can't read minds, so I honestly don't know," Mercedes said. "I just think whatever it is, she may think it will change what you think of her once you find out."

That made me laugh. "Believe me, I thought the worst of the worst of my mother growing up. My expectations of her are so low I highly doubt there's anything she could tell me to make them go any lower."

"Are your feelings toward her really that tainted? She hasn't redeemed herself in the slightest by coming here to help you with Maya?"

"Honestly, she has surprised me in that regard. She helps her with her homework, and she's even gotten her to try some new foods. Maya's new favorite breakfast meals are yogurt smoothies that Gloria secretly blends with carrots. Her banana oatmeal 'cookies' were also a hit." I made air quotes when I said the word "cookies," since they were really just breakfast bars that Gloria had made into the shape of cookies.

"Sounds like it's been good for Maya having her there. And I'll even dare to say—from my perspective as an outsider—it's been good for you too."

"Let's not start exaggerating," I said, holding up my hand. "But yes, I will agree that Maya seems to be doing better since Gloria arrived."

Mercedes gave me a smug smile at my admission. "And what about Maya's crying episodes after David calls her? Is she still having them?"

"Less and less," I answered. "He still only calls her about twice a week. But maybe because he's doing it more regularly, she isn't as sad when he hangs up."

"Probably. I've been told kids feel more safe and secure with a routine. As long as she can count on those calls, then it might get easier and easier for her."

I nodded and then asked Mercedes if I could ask her a personal question. When she told me I could, I said, "Why didn't you and Joseph ever have kids of your own?"

She let out a long sigh. "We tried, but it just wasn't part of God's plan, I guess. We had lots of nieces and nephews that we doted on instead. And we tried to hire as many local high school students as we could at the shop over the summer. They were like our kids. I know it's not the same, but it was enough for us back then."

"I'm sorry." It was all I could think to tell her.

She waved her hand at me. "Don't be."

We stayed quiet for several seconds—long enough for whatever emotion I knew we were both feeling to pass. Then I said, "So I guess this means I have to start cooking more, since apparently I have another mouth to feed."

Both of us laughed, and the heaviness of the earlier topic disappeared.

It wasn't until later that I thought of Mercedes and her husband again. Which then made me think of Nick and Rachel and the fact that they'd never had kids either.

Although I hated that Maya had to go through this whole divorce experience with me, a tiny part of me was glad that I had someone.

Because as far as I could tell, Nick was all alone.

CHAPTER TWENTY-FIVE

THINGS I NEVER KNEW #563: EGGS ARE GROSS

Dear Diary,

I'm pregnant!

I'm only six weeks along, but I already can't stop smiling. David is over the moon, of course. Even Gloria seemed excited when I finally told her today.

But I have to admit that I'm a little surprised, even hurt, by Rachel's reaction. I actually told her as soon as I took the second test. David wanted me to wait until after my first doctor's appointment, but I couldn't lie to my best friend. She knew we'd been trying for the past year. How could I not tell her the truth?

Except now I kind of wished I hadn't.

She said she was happy for me. But even over the phone I could imagine her expressionless face, based on the way she said it. No emotion. No feeling. I don't know how to explain it. When I mentioned it to Gloria, she said it was because Rachel was jealous. My mom always says that about her, though.

I knew it wasn't true, though, because Rachel doesn't want kids. And neither does Nick. She told me a while ago that they'd both agreed not to have any because they enjoyed their freedom too much. She said she didn't want to have to worry about bringing babies on their vacations to Paris or Greece. And because I'm the good friend I am, I've never pressed the issue or reminded her that they've never even traveled outside the country.

The only thing I can think of why Rachel wouldn't be excited for me was because maybe she was worried a baby would come between our friendship. She and Nick still live in Milwaukee because of his job. It's been over a year since the last time we saw each other in person. I don't think having a baby is going to change things too much. I even told her that as soon as he or she was old enough, we'd make a special trip to go visit them.

She seemed to like the idea. Well, at least, that's what she told me.

But I can't worry about Rachel or her feelings right now. I want to concentrate on getting our new house in South Pasadena ready for him or her. Hopefully my morning sickness will eventually go away. Although I highly doubt I will ever eat fried or boiled eggs again! They are definitely not my friends anymore.

Just between us, I hope it's a girl. And if it is, her middle name is going to be Pilar—after my abuela.

I can't wait to be a mom!

CHAPTER TWENTY-SIX

The first thing I remember ever buying at El Mercadito in Los Angeles was a churro.

My abuela had given me a dollar, and I was so excited when the woman at the cart handed me not just one churro, but a whole bag of them. I ate them as Abuela shopped at other stalls inside the enclosed marketplace for cheeses, spices, dried fruits and chiles, and a pair of new outside chanclas.

It was just an ordinary day spent with my abuela. But it was one of my favorite memories as a little girl.

That's why when Mercedes mentioned she was going to El Mercadito later that Monday morning—the only day Tesoro was closed—I asked if I could join her.

Located on First Street, El Mercado of Los Angeles—that was the official name, although locals called it El Mercadito—was the place to find all sorts of housewares, clothing, natural remedies, hot food, and groceries. El Mercadito originally opened as a food market but expanded over the years to include more items. The large warehouse-looking building was designed to resemble traditional Mexican mercados with different sections on three floors featuring a wide variety of vendors and artisans. You never knew what you'd find around the corner. It was almost like a treasure hunt.

I hadn't visited in over a decade, but Mercedes shared that the owners had really done a good job of keeping the market open and popular with the community. Live music and cultural performances were attracting a younger crowd and families, and a regular night market highlighted even more food vendors. I'd already decided to bring Maya back one night. Maybe the experience would even encourage her to try some new foods.

But today, Mercedes and I were on official Tesoro business in search of items she could sell for the upcoming Día de Muertos holiday. I was also helping her plan her very first Día de Muertos celebration. She'd made a list but admitted she was going to get whatever caught her eye and what she knew would be popular with her customer base.

"The prices are marked up compared to Oaxaca and even Tijuana, so I don't make as big of a profit," she'd explained during the car ride over. "But I only go to the stalls where I know they've purchased directly from Mexican artisans. That way I'm still supporting the smaller business instead of a wholesale company. Besides, most of the items are seasonal, so I don't mind spending a little more."

"As your business manager, I'm obligated to tell you that's not a very good business strategy," I said, half joking.

When I first started working for Mercedes, I had to have a serious conversation with her about the store's profit margin and expenses. In the few months Tesoro had been open, she had just barely broken even. Rent was her biggest expense, followed by her inventory costs. I could tell Mercedes had a good eye for design and decor. The problem was she loved buying the items as much as she loved selling them. And she didn't always consider if the cost was going to pay off in profit down the line.

To her credit, she'd cut back on purchases and even postponed her annual buying trip to Oaxaca. But she needed new inventory for Día de Muertos, which was why we'd come to El Mercadito instead.

"After this, we should go to Olvera Street if we don't find enough things here," Mercedes said.

"Olvera Street?" I asked. "Really? Isn't that more for tourists?"

She shrugged. "Yes, I guess. You're definitely going to find toys made in China or T-shirts mass-produced with some celebrity's face. But it's so much more than that. Many of the vendors come from the original families who have been selling their items on Olvera Street from Mexico for generations. You just have to know where to look and who to talk to."

I was going to ask her another question, but we'd arrived at El Mercadito.

The memory of that day with my abuela came rushing back clear as day as soon as I pulled into the busy parking lot.

Per usual, Gloria had left me with her for a few days. I don't remember the reason why, although my mother's reasons never really mattered—or were even the truth most of the time. It was during my spring break, so the days were spent running errands or doing chores, and during the evenings we'd make dinner and then play cards or watch Abuela's telenovelas. On this particular day, we'd taken the bus to El Mercadito, and I remembered being so in awe of how one building could contain so many different things.

As Mercedes and I walked inside to begin our hunt, that awe and wonder returned.

I let Mercedes lead the way. Only she knew what she was looking for. But I was happy to follow along, pointing to the things I thought were beautiful or unique. Sometimes she agreed with me and would pick it up to examine the craftmanship. Then she'd ask the vendor in Spanish how much—even though to Mercedes, it was only a suggestion. I quickly learned my boss was quite the haggler.

Once we reached a certain section of stalls on the first floor, she made a beeline for the space in the middle. The woman setting out ceramic figures for a Nativity scene greeted her with a huge smile and a hug.

"Doña Mercedes," the vendor said. "Cómo estás?"

"Bien, bien, gracias," Mercedes answered, and then introduced me. I learned the woman's name was Azucena Palomar, and she was originally from Oaxaca but had lived in the United States for more than fifteen years. She and her husband had been selling their imported goods at El Mercadito for ten of them.

Mercedes asked her if she had anything for Día de Muertos, and Azucena led her to the other side of her stall. There on two display shelves, she had a line of papier-mâché figurines painted in bright and bold colors. She had several Catrinas—the iconic female skeleton figure—in various designs. All boasted colorful dresses and oversize hats. One rode a bicycle, one seemed to be dancing, and another held a basket of flowers. Next to them were the more traditional skeletons or calaveras, the male version of the Catrina. Many were dressed in top hats and suits, while others wore the traditional traje de charro of a mariachi. There was a wide assortment of candles and sugar skulls and a basket full of artificial bright-orange cempasúchil flowers.

As Mercedes began to pick which items she wanted, I decided I wanted to make an ofrenda of my own at home. I knew Maya would love it, and I thought it would be a good opportunity to teach her some new Spanish words.

"Okay," I said to Mercedes. "I think I want to build an ofrenda at my house. What do I need?"

"You do?" she asked with a touch of surprise in her voice.

My excitement dampened a little. "Should I not? Is that not appropriate because I didn't grow up with the tradition?"

She waved her hand. "No, no, of course not. I think it's wonderful that you want to start the tradition. You just never mentioned it before today."

"I had been thinking about it when you first started talking about all the things you wanted to buy for the store. And now seeing everything that Azucena has, well, I guess that convinced me."

"This makes me so happy," Mercedes said as she gave me a hug. "There's lots more to see, so we better keep moving."

We visited a few more stalls. I picked up some sugar skulls, two prayer candles, and a ceramic Catrina figurine. Mercedes purchased a twelve-pack of candles, a stack of papel picado banners, and a couple of sugar skulls.

We made our way to the second floor and found another vendor, who sold Mercedes a whole case of small red clay cantaritos. "Besides holding flowers, you can also use them to serve your favorite cocktails," she explained after paying for them.

Two stalls down was a case filled with different kinds of cheeses. We stopped so I could get half a pound of queso fresco and a pound of panela. I liked to crumble the queso fresco on my corn and zucchini. The panela was for Gloria and her quesadillas.

Then it was time to grab lunch. Although El Mercadito had lots of food vendors and restaurants on the third floor, we'd decided to wait until we got to Olvera Street.

But as we turned the corner to head out, I jumped up and clapped like a little kid.

"The churro lady is here," I said, and I pointed to an older woman standing behind a white cart.

I knew, of course, it couldn't be the same lady who used to sell churros here when I was a kid. But I was excited just the same and pulled Mercedes with me so I could get my fix.

"Una bolsa, por favor," I told the woman as soon as I arrived at the cart.

"Seis dolares por seis," she replied. I couldn't help but be surprised by the cost. Even churros had become a victim of inflation.

But I could smell the deliciousness and decided they were going to be worth it. I handed her six dollars and then watched as she filled a white paper bag with half a dozen of the fried doughnutlike sticks covered in cinnamon and sugar.

"Gracias," I said after she gave me the bag.

I waited until we'd walked outside to pull out a churro and then offered one to Mercedes. We knocked our churros together, and I bit off my first piece.

The price might have been different, but the taste was almost exactly the same. That one bite brought me back to a time when I still had my abuela and all was right in the world—even if it was only for a few moments.

"We should've bought you your own bag," I said as I pulled out another churro.

"These are so good I might need two bags just for me."

A few minutes later we were back in the car. We took the streets toward downtown LA. More memories of my childhood came flooding back. I might have lived all over when I was young, but my abuela's little house in this city had always been my real home.

Before too long, we were parking in the lot next to La Placita Church.

My abuela once told me that the church—which was really called Iglesia Nuestra Señora Reina de Los Ángeles, or Our Lady Queen of Angels—reminded her of the one she used to attend as a little girl back in Mexico. But since it was easier to just walk to the one in her neighborhood, Abuela only visited La Placita a few times during the year. I had loved going with her. Especially since we always stopped at Olvera Street after Mass to grab something to eat or just visit the vendors.

About a year ago, I had wanted to take Maya there on the Metrolink for a little day trip. I began researching and was surprised to learn just how important La Placita and Olvera Street were to the history of Los Angeles.

I'd read that La Placita was dedicated in the 1800s to replace the first church ever built in Los Angeles and that Olvera Street had come to be known as the "birthplace" of LA. Historians argued about the original exact location, but today it was where the public could still visit the Ávila Adobe, the city's oldest existing house. The street had fallen onto desperate times by the 1920s, with many of the buildings scheduled for demolition. But a wealthy socialite named Christine Sterling, who knew how important it was to preserve the historical area, launched a public campaign to save it and turn it into a thriving marketplace where Mexican American vendors could sell everything from food to pottery to clothing. Besides La Placita and the Ávila Adobe, Olvera Street was also home to LA's first firehouse and theater. And Pico House—the home of California's last Mexican governor, Pío Pico—was the city's first hotel.

The more I read about Olvera Street, the more I wanted for Maya to see the vibrant history of our culture and the city my abuela loved as much as her native Mexico, while at the same time showing her pieces of my own childhood.

But when I'd mentioned to David that I had wanted to take Maya there, he'd balked at the idea of us going by ourselves.

"It's a tourist trap," he'd said. "Plus, the area around it isn't the best. I don't want you taking her there by yourself."

And since he didn't want to go, that meant we didn't either.

Of course, he couldn't say anything about that now. One of the benefits I guess of being a single parent.

"I think I'm going to bring Maya here soon. Maybe in December," I said as we got out of the car.

"You should! Olvera Street is beautiful during Christmastime. I know she would love it."

"Hey, can we stop at La Placita first? I'd like to take a look inside the church."

Mercedes agreed, and we made our way down First Street. We passed a couple of street vendors selling aguas frescas, churros, and fruit cups. I'd already demolished the bag of churros from El Mercadito and figured I didn't need any more sugar, so I politely shook my head at the verbal invitations to stop and buy something.

We entered the church's open courtyard. It was nearly empty since it was a Monday. I remembered it usually being jam-packed with people after Sunday Mass. One weekend, my abuela and I had come on a Saturday and stumbled upon lines of families dressed in their best outfits. When I asked Abuela why some of the babies and little kids wore white dresses or white suits, she'd explained that they were there to get baptized.

Mercedes and I walked into the building just off the courtyard. It held the church's tiny gift shop and was filled with religious artifacts such as crosses, rosaries, and figurines. We went our own ways to go explore.

I was immediately drawn to the display of rosaries, ranging from the simple to the more ornate and in different sizes and assorted colors. Maya would probably want one of each, I thought. My daughter, just like her grandma, loved shiny pretty things.

After several minutes, I met Mercedes at the register. I paid for a children's prayer book I'd picked up for Maya, and she filled one bag with a couple of rosaries and some ceramic crosses.

I was disappointed, though, when the cashier told us the church was closed to visitors that day because of some ongoing repairs.

"I'm sorry, Mija," Mercedes said as we walked out of the shop and headed to Olvera Street.

"It's okay. Hopefully, it will be open when I bring Maya. I'd love to show her the inside. I might even bring Gloria, if she's still in town."

I couldn't help but wonder if Abuela had ever brought my mother to La Placita as a little girl. And if so, would she even want to see it again? For me, I had nothing but lovely memories about the place. But I was learning that growing up with Abuela as a mother had been a very different experience for Gloria.

We used a nearby crosswalk and made our way over to Olvera Street. We strolled through the marketplace, stopping at vendor stalls or inside one of the indoor stores in search of more things for Día de Muertos. Most places had items similar to the ones Mercedes had already purchased at El Mercadito. But she did get excited about finding yards of fabric with a print of calavera skulls and colorful papel picado.

"I can make some beautiful place mats out of this material," she said.

"Place mats? For you or to sell at the store?" I teased.

She shrugged. "Why not both?"

After paying for the fabric, we walked for a few minutes more but didn't really find anything else.

"I'm hungry," Mercedes announced. "Where should we eat?"

There were several restaurants to choose from. But as soon as Mercedes had said we were coming here, I craved only one thing.

"How about Cielito Lindo?" I asked, referencing the historic eatery that sat at the end of Olvera Street and was famous for its freshly made taquitos and avocado sauce.

Mercedes smiled. "Sounds good. But I'm just warning you now. I'm not sharing this time."

I was still laughing when my phone started ringing. When I saw the caller ID, I abruptly stopped.

"Maya is in school," I told David as soon as I answered.

"I know. I called to talk to you. Do you have a few minutes?"

I held up my hand to Mercedes, so she stopped walking. "I have five." My new thing was setting boundaries with him. He needed to know that just because it was his decision to leave, that didn't mean that I had to do whatever he said. Especially now that I had my own money coming in.

"My new agency closes for the week of Thanksgiving, and I want to come down and spend some time with Maya. Plus I think it would be a good time for us to meet with a mediator. So I really need you to decide if that's what we're going to do."

"Why are you in such a rush?"

"Why are you stalling?"

"I'm not stalling, David. I only found out you wanted a divorce less than two months ago. You've apparently been preparing for this for a lot longer. I need to catch up, okay?"

I heard him sigh, and I could imagine him pinching the bridge of his nose in frustration. "I just think the sooner we settle things, the better for all of us."

"You mean Rachel. 'The sooner we're divorced, the better for Rachel' is what you really meant, right?"

"Rachel has nothing to do with this."

The back of my neck heated in anger. "Bullshit. Have you forgotten I've known her for more than twenty years? She's impatient and self-concerned. I'd bet good money that it was her idea to get a mediator in the first place."

"Don't you want to move on with your life?" he asked softly.

My heart dropped. That's what this was all about. David wanted to move on . . . without me. That's why he was so eager to get the divorce. He was right. Why was I stalling?

"Fine. Set up the meeting."

CHAPTER TWENTY-SEVEN

THINGS I NEVER KNEW #803: NO ONE EVER LEAVES SOUTH PASADENA

Dear Diary,

Rachel and Nick are moving to South Pasadena! In fact, they're buying the house next door!

I can't believe it's really happening. Nick found out months ago he was being transferred to the Los Angeles plant, so Rachel and I had already been looking at houses in Pasadena and other surrounding cities. I nearly screamed in excitement when David told me that the Nelsons were moving to Hawaii. South Pasadena is known for its low inventory of homes for sale. The last time we checked Zillow, there were only three houses on the market compared to more than 50 in neighboring—and more expensive—San Marino. David said it's because South Pasadena is very strict when it comes to new homes being constructed. Our house was built in the 1970s, and we had to renovate most of the rooms before we moved in. I don't know if it's because people are living longer in this city or they're just passing on their houses to their kids, but either way, I was resigned to the fact that Rachel would have to find a house in another town.

The fact that the house next door to me was going to be available, well, it was meant to be, right? I couldn't believe our luck, and I immediately called Rachel to tell her the good news.

It took about a month, but they officially entered escrow today.

I'm looking forward to having Rachel close to me again. I have to admit it's been lonely these past few years with her so far away. Maya starts kindergarten in the fall, and I wasn't looking forward to being home by myself. I'm especially happy that Maya will finally get to meet her auntie Rachel in person. I can't wait for my two most favorite girls in the world to become best friends too.

It's going to be just like old times.

CHAPTER TWENTY-EIGHT

Right away I knew something was wrong.

I was excited to show Gloria the items I'd bought at El Mercadito for our home ofrenda, but the kitchen chair where I usually found her after I came home from work was empty.

I set the bag down and went to look in the guest bedroom. It was also empty.

I was about to go to Maya's room when I heard the sliding glass door to the backyard open. "There you are," I said when I saw my mother walk inside. "I want to show you what I bought."

She looked over her shoulder and waved at me. "Later. First I need you to come outside. I made lunch for us."

"I ate already. Mercedes and I had taquitos from Cielito Lindo on Olvera Street and churros from . . ."

Gloria didn't let me finish. Instead she grabbed my hand and dragged me through the open sliding door.

I was confused. And then I was extremely confused when I saw a man sitting at my patio table. The stranger stood up and walked over. He looked vaguely familiar. Then the recognition hit.

"Frankie? Frankie Lora, is that you?"

"It's me," the man laughed. "Although I go by Frank these days."

He gave me a hug and a kiss on the cheek. I was startled by the move. Yes, we'd dated, but I hadn't seen the man or kissed him in decades.

"I ran into Frank and his mom yesterday at the farmers' market," Gloria explained. "He lives in Highland Park now—what are the odds?"

It was kind of a surprise to hear that my former high school boyfriend and ex-neighbor lived just a few miles away from me. "Oh wow," I said as we sat down at the table.

"Anyway, I invited Frank over for lunch so you two could catch up."

Although I was smiling on the outside, I was beginning to feel uneasy on the inside.

"How . . . nice. And what about Sierra? I heard you two got married right after graduation."

Frank shrugged. "We're divorced now."

"And you're getting a divorce," Gloria added. "See, you two have a lot to talk about. So enjoy the sandwiches I made, and I'll be inside."

I tried to silently tell my mother to stay, but of course she wasn't listening—or, most likely, was ignoring my signals.

"It's good to see you, Claudia," Frank said. "I'm sorry to hear you're getting a divorce. I know a good lawyer if you need one. He represented Sierra."

He thought that was hysterical, but I didn't. It turned out Frank was a lot less funny than I remembered. By the time he'd consumed three of Gloria's sandwiches, I was ready for him to leave.

"Well, it's been great catching up. But I'm going to be leaving soon to pick up my daughter from school."

Frank nodded and stood up. I did the same and was completely caught off guard when he went in for another hug. I held out my hand instead.

"We should do this again sometime," he said after shaking it. "I know a great Cuban place over in Pasadena. I know how much you used to love your café Cubano."

"Um, that was just a phase. I'm more of a regular coffee girl now," I said.

"I drink regular coffee too." His eagerness to agree with me was not lost on me. The warning bells were ringing in my head, which confirmed my suspicions that Gloria had set up this lunch as a date with my ex.

"How about next time, I bring some pan dulce to go with our coffee?" Frank asked.

Next time? Oh, yeah. I definitely needed to say something. First to Frankie, then to my scheming mother.

"Look, this was nice and everything, but I'm just barely separated. Plus I have a little girl. I have no interest in dating anyone for the foreseeable future."

He shrugged. "That's fine. But the one thing I did learn during my divorce is that it's good to have as many friends in your corner as possible. How about that? Could you use another friend in your life?"

Guilt ripped through me. Why was I such a mess? "You're a good guy, Frank. I would like to be your friend. And I'm sorry things didn't work out with Sierra. Can I ask what happened?"

"We just grew apart, I guess. We were basically kids when we got together. And she says she grew up and I didn't. Funny thing is, I feel like a grown-up now."

"Yeah, me too."

I walked Frank outside to his truck just as Nick was pulling into his driveway. I don't know why, but I stepped back when Frank tried to hug me again. Instead of shaking my hand this time, he just kind of gave me an awkward salute.

Before heading into the house, I turned to see if Nick was still outside. He wasn't.

When I found my mother on the couch a few minutes later, the annoyance I'd felt earlier came roaring back. If past experience told me anything, it told me that this conversation wasn't going to go so smoothly.

"I think it's time for you to go back to Florida."

My mom looked up from her Kindle and took off her glasses. "I already told you I'm going to start looking for flights."

"When exactly are you going to look?"

"Tonight or maybe tomorrow. You know they say if you wait until Tuesdays, the flights are cheaper."

"Tomorrow then, for sure, okay?"

"What's the rush? Haven't I been helpful?"

"Yes, you have been helpful, and I appreciate everything you've done for me and Maya since you've been here. But don't you miss Carlos and your life back in Florida? Doesn't he want you home?"

"Carlos wants what I want, and I want to stay a little longer. Why are you suddenly anxious for me to leave?"

"Why are you being so weird about this?"

"I'm not being weird. In fact, I was thinking that maybe I should just stay through Christmas."

I swallowed down my panic. It was time to stop treating her with kid gloves.

"I'm sorry, Mom, but that's not going to happen, okay?"

She shrugged. "Why not?"

I walked closer to the back of the couch and set my palms on the edge. "Because you don't know how to mind your own business. What on earth were you thinking inviting over a man I really don't know to my house where I live with my child? Luckily, Frankie seems like he turned out to be a good guy. But what if he wasn't? This is my daughter's safe place, and I won't risk it just because you thought it would be fun to set me up on a blind date in my own backyard!"

To her credit, she did seem surprised by what I'd said. "I . . . I didn't think of it that way. I just thought it would be nice for you to have someone to talk to. Besides, they say the best way to get over a man is to get under a new one."

Blood rushed to my head. "Oh. My. God. Mother."

"What? It's true. It's what I always did whenever some jerk broke my heart. Rebounds are there to help get you back in the game," she said nonchalantly.

My jaw wasn't just on the floor; it was under it.

"Seriously?" I asked. "One, I am not ready to get under anyone. And two, if and when that did ever happen, it would certainly not be with anyone you invited to my house!"

Gloria raised her hands as if to surrender to logic for the first time in her life. "I see now that it was wrong of me to give him your address. I'm sorry. It won't happen again."

My anger subsided a little. "Thank you. I appreciate it. But I still think you need to go home sooner rather than later. I can't deal with everything else if you're here."

"What's everything else?"

I sighed. "Facing David again. I just found out he wants to come into town in late November to see Maya and for our meeting with the mediator, and he's going to freak out if you're still here. He knows you've never liked him, and what if Rachel comes with him? I can't worry about what that will do to Maya and also worry about what you would say to the both of them."

"Isn't that a little dramatic?"

"I don't know, you tell me. The man resigned, accepted a new job, moved into a new place, and decided to cut me off financially without hesitation. I don't know this David. I don't know what he will or won't do anymore. I honestly wouldn't be surprised if he's already decided to put the house on the market without even talking to me about it first."

"All the more reason for me to be here. If that happens, then I'll take you and Maya with me back to Florida. There's no reason why you can't leave South Pasadena behind either."

Whoa. Since when did my mom think that was even an option?

"I'm not uprooting Maya, not if I can help it. Whatever David decides to do when he's here, I will fight for my daughter. You can bet on that."

"I would, actually."

I put my head in my hands. "Mom, I really do appreciate everything you've done for both of us. And you're a grown woman, so I can't make you get on a plane. But the discussion about you going home is something that we will need to revisit soon. Maya and I need to move forward on our own. So whatever it is that you're hiding from, you're going to need to face it eventually. Understood?"

"Understood."

It wasn't a win. But it wasn't a total blowout either. I'd take it.

The conversation with Gloria was still weighing heavily on my mind hours later. She'd skipped dinner because of a headache, so I decided to take some leftover pork chops and salad to Nick.

I hadn't texted him beforehand, so he couldn't hide his surprise once he opened the door.

"Hey," he said with a smile.

"It's pork chop night," I said as I handed him the paper plate wrapped in foil.

Nick took it and nodded. "Thank you. Uh, did you want to come in?"

"Oh no, that's okay," I rushed. I was suddenly regretting my choice to come to Nick's house—Rachel's house. "I have to get back and give Maya her bath. So, yeah, good night."

"Claudia . . . is everything okay?"

I was unsettled by the concern in his eyes. Yet I had this overwhelming urge to talk to someone about Gloria, about David, about everything.

So I told him the truth. "Not really. But I don't want to bother you with my problems. I really just came over to give you some leftovers."

"Give me a second. Don't go just yet." Nick disappeared inside his house and then reappeared a few seconds later minus the paper plate. Then he stepped onto the porch.

"What happened?" he asked softly.

And then all the sadness I'd been fighting all day—from missing my abuela to the realization that David had a new life he wanted to start without me—came pouring out. I kept blinking back the tears, but there were too many of them. And when my bottom lip began to quiver, that's when Nick reached for me and pulled me against his chest.

I resisted for a full five seconds before finally allowing myself to give in and quietly sobbed into Nick's green-and-black-plaid shirt. I was exhausted. Physically, mentally, and definitely emotionally. And as much as I hated to admit it, it felt good to be held.

Rachel used to complain that she wished Nick were more empathetic, more understanding when she was upset over something. This whole time I'd come to believe that he was indifferent, even aloof.

But there was nothing unfeeling about the way he was hugging me.

When the tears finally stopped, I pulled away and wiped my eyes and nose with the sleeve of my sweatshirt.

"I'm sorry. I didn't mean to cry all over you," I said, trying to sound a lot less awkward than I felt.

"No need to apologize. I'm glad my shirt could help."

"God, I'm so embarrassed," I admitted. Heat traveled up my neck and spread across my cheeks. Why on earth had I melted into his arms so easily?

He reached out to touch my arm. "Don't be. Please? I promised I'd help you anyway I could, didn't I?"

"Yeah, with mowing the grass—not with letting me soak your flannel with my pitiful tears."

First Mercedes and now Nick? I really had no qualms about becoming hysterical in front of people these days.

"Well, to be fair, we didn't really get into the specifics," Nick said matter-of-factly.

I had to laugh. "True."

"So are we okay then? Are you okay?"

I was still embarrassed, but the heaviness in my heart had lightened up. "We're okay. And I think I will be too. Thank you. You did help."

"If you still want to talk about it . . ."

Although I was beginning to accept the fact that Nick and I could be friends without Rachel, I wasn't yet ready to share everything with him. Especially when it came to David.

"Thank you for the offer. I just had a bad day and needed to vent, or I guess cry it out. I'm better, really I am. And I do need to get back to Maya."

"Okay. Well, thanks again for the pork chops. You saved me from having to make my last package of instant ramen."

"Oof. Not instant ramen," I teased.

Nick nodded dramatically but then laughed. "Good night, Claudia," he said after a few seconds.

"Good night, Nick. It was nice talking to you."

And no one was more surprised than me when I realized just how much I meant what I'd said.

CHAPTER TWENTY-NINE

THINGS I NEVER KNEW #899: LOVE DOESN'T ALWAYS MEAN LIKE

Dear Diary,

It's been two days since I've talked to Rachel. I hate that I miss her. I hate that I want to call or text her. Even after what she did.

We had a party at the house on Saturday for Maya's seventh birthday. I'd been planning it for months. It was a Disney princess theme, and she was going to dress up as her favorite princess—Cinderella. Rachel had come over earlier in the day to help us set up. I could tell something was bothering her, but all she would say was that Nick had made her mad the night before. I was way too busy to ask more questions and, honestly, I didn't really want to hear it. I had wanted Maya's birthday to be perfect. A pissed-off Rachel was the last thing I needed. So when she announced she was going to go home and would come back later, I was relieved.

The party started off great. All of Maya's classmates showed up and were being entertained by the bouncy house we'd rented. I'd also set up stations for the kids to decorate their own tiaras or crowns. For food, we had a fruit salad and pizza for the kids and one of those long sub sandwiches for the adults. I also ordered a tray of Maya's favorite cheese pasta from a local restaurant.

Everything was going to plan until Rachel returned wearing a very adult version of Maya's Cinderella costume. And she was drunk.

I tried to get her to go home and change after she flashed some of the parents the booty shorts she was wearing underneath her very short dress while trying to pick up a napkin that had flown off her plate. Then she pulled an accusation right out of Gloria's old playbook. She told me—in a very loud voice—how I've always been embarrassed by her, so she was just doing what I expected.

Nick was out of town, so David was the one who had to take her back home. I haven't spoken to her since. But I know Rachel. Sooner or later, she'll text me to ask for something. Then she'll come over here or beg me to go over there. Then she'll have some excuse about why she did what she did or make me feel bad about making such a big deal out of it. She'll want us to go back to normal and pretend like it never happened.

I'm so mad at her, though. Maybe this will be the one time I don't forgive and forget.

CHAPTER THIRTY

I wasn't sure when it had happened, but Nick had become my unofficial handyman.

One day he was raking leaves, and the next he was fixing a broken shelf in my pantry or replacing the batteries in all the smoke alarms.

All I knew was that I was getting more comfortable asking him for stuff, and he was getting more comfortable doing it. He'd come over the night before to try to fix the kitchen faucet, which had been leaking for a few days. After two hours, Nick proclaimed there was no saving it, and it needed to be replaced. That was why he was on his way to Lowe's with me in the driver's seat. Gloria had another migraine and was resting, so that meant Maya was also along for the ride.

"So what kind of faucet are you looking for?" he said.

I shrugged. "I don't know. I just want it to work and look nice in the kitchen. Actually, if they have the exact same one I have now, I'll just get that. Is that . . . silly?"

"No," Nick said. "Not silly at all."

"Mommy, we should get a pink faucet. I love pink!"

I met Maya's eyes in the rearview mirror. "You sure do."

"Uncle Nick, what's your favorite color?" she said.

He twisted in his seat to look at her. "Guess."

"Purple!"

"Burnt sienna," I offered.

Nick laughed. "Wrong. Guess again."

My brain tried to remember the names in Maya's sixty-four-count Crayola crayon box. "Chartreuse," I yelled out like a game show contestant.

"Blue," Maya said in between her giggles.

"Ding, ding, ding. That is correct," he said.

"And do you have a blue sink?" I asked with a hint of teasing.

"No, but I wish I did."

I turned to look at him, and he had the biggest grin on his face. I realized I hadn't seen him smile like that in a long time.

We arrived at Lowe's about five minutes later. The three of us wandered a few aisles until we found the faucets. They did not have the exact same one as mine, which meant I had to pick something different.

Truth was, I had been dreading this. Not because I was especially attached to mine. But because I knew it would bring up the memory of David and me shopping for it after we'd bought the house. I immediately fell in love with the four-bedroom, two-bathroom 1970s craftsman home. It had a large covered porch entry that opened into a living room with newly refinished original hardwood floors, crown moldings, and a gas fireplace. The formal dining room had beautiful built-in cabinets with leaded glass doors and wainscoting. The kitchen opened into a large family room, and even back then I could picture us in there playing games with our kids who hadn't been born yet.

But despite all the older house's desirable features, I knew it would need a lot of work to turn it into our dream home. And so, after we'd bought it, we spent the next three months researching paint colors, pulling up carpet in the bedrooms, picking out new vanities for the bathrooms, and choosing a new kitchen sink and faucet. The point was I had no idea then that I'd be back here husbandless, doing it all over again.

"How about this one?" Nick asked, pointing to a stainless steel faucet with sprayer combo.

"That's nice," I said, looking it over.

"Ooh, Mommy, I like this one," Maya said, and she motioned to the champagne-bronze touchless faucet just beyond her reach. "It's oro."

"Yes, it looks gold to me too." *But it would be out of place in my kitchen,* I thought instead of saying.

"Can I help you folks?" an employee said as he walked up to us.

"Just looking for a new faucet," I answered.

"Any specific style or color?"

"Not really. But I'll know it when I see it. And maybe I just did."

I motioned to Nick to come over to where I was standing and pointed to the faucet on my left. It was stainless steel, with only one handle and a detachable spout with two settings. He studied the box and confirmed it would fit on my sink.

"Your wife has good taste," the employee said.

"Oh, she's not—"

"I'm not—"

Nick and I tried to correct the employee's assumption right away. The man's pale cheeks immediately turned red. "Sorry, I didn't—"

I cut him off. "We'll, I mean, I'll take it. For my kitchen. In my house."

As I paid for my new faucet, I tried not to dwell on how embarrassed I felt for acting so weird about the poor employee assuming we were a family. It was an honest mistake. It was only a big deal if I turned it into a big deal. So I wasn't going to bring it up.

Back in the car, Maya said she was hungry.

"I'll make you something when we get home," I told her after turning on the ignition.

"Why can't we go out to eat?"

"Because we need to get Nick home. We've taken up enough of his Sunday afternoon."

"I don't have any plans, other than to install your faucet. I don't mind stopping to eat."

I looked over at him before pulling my car out of the parking space. "Are you sure?"

"Yeah. I'm hungry too."

A little nudge of anxiety twisted my stomach. Spending fifteen minutes with Nick picking out a kitchen faucet was one thing. Having lunch with me—even with Maya—was another. What if we had nothing to talk about? What if people in the restaurant assumed we were a family, just like the Lowe's employee?

"We don't have to, though, if you'd rather go home?" Nick's question brought me out of my overthinking. I felt a twinge of guilt for being so weird about things. Again.

"No, no, it's fine. But this little kid only likes to eat at two places right now. So it's either Italian or Denny's."

He laughed and looked back at Maya. "What do you say, Maya? Where should we go eat?"

"Denny's!" she yelled.

"Perfect," he said. "That's exactly what I wanted too."

I laughed. "Are you relieved she didn't pick an Italian restaurant?"

"What do you mean?"

"You don't remember? Really?" His blank stare told me that he didn't. "When we first met? We had dinner at an Italian restaurant, and you were upset because they only had a few meat options."

Nick shrugged. "I remember the dinner. I don't remember being upset, though."

"Okay, well, not really upset, I guess. More like annoyed." I tried to laugh to let him know it wasn't a big deal, even though it had left me with a bad first impression of him.

"Oh wow. I didn't realize I came off like that. Honestly, it was probably just the nerves. I mean, Rachel had gone on and on about how important it was for you and David to like me. I'm sure I was trying to act overconfident or something. I actually like Italian food."

And that made me laugh almost the entire way over to Denny's.

CHAPTER THIRTY-ONE

THINGS I NEVER KNEW #900: ONE MISTAKE IS ALL IT TAKES

Dear Diary,

I'm so sad. Rachel's mom died.

She got a call from her aunt this morning that she'd passed away in her sleep. It had been a few years since the last time Rachel had visited her. They had a weird relationship. To me, it really was never the same after her parents' divorce.

Even though I was still angry at her for how she'd acted at the party the other day, I immediately went next door after she called to tell me. Nick's still out of town at some conference, and I asked David to make Maya some breakfast so I could go be with her. But to my surprise, Rachel wasn't even crying when I got there.

"Why would I cry over the woman who broke up my family?"

I was taken aback by the clear bitterness in her voice. I knew Rachel had resented her mom for cheating on her dad. I had no idea she still held on to that resentment.

It made me sad. Donna, Rachel's mom, had always been kind to me. Even after everything that happened, I could see she was trying to make it up to her daughter. I felt bad when Rachel would yell at her or be rude. And Donna never said anything back. Once I mentioned to Gloria how bad I felt for Donna, and even though I would always take Rachel's side, there were times I wanted to yell at my friend for how she'd act. I told Gloria I didn't understand why Donna never said anything.

Gloria had said it was because Donna probably thought she deserved it.

I had asked Rachel if she'd told her dad about her mom, and she hadn't. That's when she admitted to me that she didn't even have his phone number anymore. I had no idea that she hadn't talked to him in so long. She always made it seem like they were still close. The last I'd heard, he was retired from the military and was living in the Philippines with his new wife.

"I guess I'm officially an orphan now because I have no family left," she told me.

And that was all it took. Everything that had happened at Maya's party didn't seem as important anymore compared to what Rachel was going through now. All I wanted to do was comfort her and choose to be her friend in that moment. Just like she'd done for me back in middle school.

That's what friendship is, right? Loving each other but not liking each other sometimes. But true friendship means always holding the door open for forgiveness. No matter what. I told her that Nick is her family and so are Maya, David, and I.

I promised her that as long as I'm alive, she will never be alone.

CHAPTER THIRTY-TWO

"You two are becoming friends."

Mercedes handed me another box of candles to open and gave me a sly smile while doing it. I had just told her how I'd invited Nick to the store's Día de Muertos event.

"I wouldn't say that exactly," I insisted. "He'd come over to replace the kitchen faucet, and Gloria and Maya were making the tissue flowers for our ofrenda. He saw them and asked what they were for. He seemed really interested in learning more about the tradition, so I told him about your event."

We'd been getting ready for the Día de Muertos celebration for the last few days. Besides the items she'd purchased from El Mercadito, Mercedes had also been stocking up on votive candles and small alebrijes figures, so the store was even more colorful than usual. Mercedes also had begun constructing a community ofrenda that she was going to set up on the sidewalk in front of the store. Customers had been invited to stop by and place a photo of a deceased loved one on it on the night of the celebration.

I was excited for the event, but I was especially looking forward to celebrating Día de Muertos with Maya for the first time. Growing up, it wasn't something I knew about. Abuela had a table in her living room with lots of old pictures on it and some of those tall prayer candles.

She'd once explained to me that everyone on the table had passed away. She called it her "altar" and kept it up year round.

In the past few years, Día de Muertos seemed to have become more popular in the United States—probably because of movies like *Coco* and *The Book of Life*. I watched *Coco* for the first time last year to see if it was something Maya would like. Needless to say, I was a sobbing mess for hours later and decided I'd wait before allowing Maya to see it. I knew teaching Maya about Día de Muertos was important, though. I'd bought her a book from Tesoro that explained what the holiday meant as well as its traditions. She'd already learned a few new Spanish terms like "papel picado," "pan de muerto," and "cempasúchil."

"Oh, I forgot," I told Mercedes. "Maya wants to know if pictures of pets are allowed on the ofrenda. Her friend Amy wants to stop by and place a photo of her family's Chihuahua that passed away earlier this year."

"Pues, como que no. All who were loved and now missed are welcome on the ofrenda."

"She'll be so happy to tell Amy that. Thank you."

"And what about you? Are you planning to bring a photo on Saturday?"

I nodded. "I already printed out a copy of my favorite picture of my abuela. My mom actually took it of her at a birthday party for one of her neighbors. She's wearing one of those cone party hats and laughing. I have a bigger one framed in my entryway at home."

"I can't wait to see it," Mercedes said. "You know you talk about your abuela so much, I feel as if I know her. I love how you keep her memory alive. That's what Día de Muertos is all about too."

"You would've loved my abuela. She was quite the character," I said.

"And would she have loved me?"

I considered her question for a few seconds. "Not at first," I replied with a laugh. "My abuela didn't love a lot of people. And she only really liked a handful. But I think she would've grown to like you, even love you, eventually."

"Why do you think that?"

"Because you would've reminded her about all the wonderful things she loved about Mexico."

Mercedes stopped cutting the purple tissue paper for the papel picado banner. "When did she come to the US?"

"When she was eighteen. She and her younger sister came to live with one of their aunts in Los Angeles after their mother died. It was only supposed to be for a year or so—just until they could earn enough money to go back and her sister could finish school here. But then my abuela got pregnant with my mom, so she decided to stay, and her sister went back a few years later."

"So your abuela never went back to Mexico?"

"Just to visit her sister and some other relatives. She used to tell me that she wanted to move there permanently but was going to wait until I went to college. But she never made it. She died when I was fourteen."

My throat tightened with emotion like it always did when I talked about my abuela.

Mercedes squeezed my shoulder. "You were lucky to have her."

I gave her a quick smile. "I was. As you know, Gloria wasn't always the most reliable or responsible mother. So my abuela basically raised me until she passed."

"And how was their relationship, if you don't mind me asking? Were they close?"

"Not really. I mean, my abuela was always there for whatever Gloria needed. But they were both very stubborn, and I think neither of them knew how to say 'I'm sorry.' So they'd get into their arguments, not speak for a few days or a week, and then I was the one who usually had to step in and nudge my mom to go see her, or sometimes Gloria would just drop me off for an afternoon, and when she'd come back, she'd walk inside the house and start talking to my abuela as if nothing had happened. And my abuela would just talk right back."

Mercedes shrugged. "Sounds like they were a lot alike."

"In some ways," I said with a nod. "I still don't understand why they were like that with each other. To me, my abuela was the most loving and caring person in the world. But to my mom . . . I don't know. Gloria really knew how to push her buttons, until my abuela would get so angry and say things she thought were hurtful. I'm not saying Gloria didn't deserve some of the things my abuela said. But sometimes she went too far, and that just made my mom want to stay away for a while. Which meant I couldn't go see her either. That's why we didn't even know she was sick until the hospital called to tell my mom she'd died."

I wiped a tear that had dropped onto my cheek. "I still can't stand the thought that she died all alone. And although I blamed Gloria when it happened, I'm also still angry that my abuela never picked up the phone to tell us just how sick she was."

A few more tears had joined their friend, and I brushed them away with the back of my hand. I hadn't ever told anyone that story. Not even Rachel. I still carried a lot of guilt about not being more adamant with Gloria to get over herself and call my abuela after that last fight. Maybe if I'd whined or yelled more, we could've taken her to the doctor or at least had a chance to say goodbye.

Mercedes patted my hand. "I'm sorry for making you talk about what must have been a very hard time for you. But I'm a believer about things happening for a reason, because they propel us into our next life lesson. That's how we grow as humans."

"Why does it seem like some of us have to learn more than others?"

"That I could not tell you. All I know is that we all end up where we're supposed to be because of the things that happen to us. Even losing the people we love. It's one of the reasons why I celebrate Día de Muertos."

I nodded and gave her a quick smile. "You know I didn't mind helping you get the store ready for the celebration, but I wasn't really sure about whether I wanted to participate in the event when you first told me about it. It just seemed like it would be so sad, and I've kind of had my fill of sad for the year."

Mercedes walked over to where I'd begun sorting tissue paper by color. "I've been wanting to ask you how you've been feeling. But I also don't want to pry."

"Most days I'm okay," I admitted. "Other times, it's like my sadness is the only thing in the room. I can't get away from it."

"I understand, Claudia. Believe me. Some days my grief is so overwhelming that it feels like Joseph just died. I've learned that the best way for me to get through it is to accept it, deal with it, and then allow myself to move on."

"I feel silly that I just can't get over it," I said.

"Honey, it hasn't even been three months. You're allowed to take as much time as you need to grieve the relationship and grieve the loss of the life you used to have."

My chest tightened with a familiar pain. "And how do you grieve someone who's still alive?" I asked.

Mercedes let out a long sigh and shrugged. "I don't know. But no one is expecting you to get over this just like that," she said with a snap of her fingers. "I mean, you two have a child together. Of course—"

"I'm not talking about him. I'm talking about *her*."

It took a minute. Then realization crossed Mercedes's face. "Oh, sweetie. I didn't realize . . ."

I'd finally confessed the secret I'd been holding deep inside my heart. "Is it horrible that some days I miss Rachel more than I miss David?"

She touched my arm and squeezed. "Not at all. You loved her too. You probably still do."

I could only nod. Tears filled my eyes, and I let out a loud sob. Mercedes took me into her arms and let me cry. Just like she had on the first day I met her.

When it was finally quiet again in the store, she handed me a tissue. "Día de Muertos is about honoring our loved ones, but it's also about allowing ourselves to grieve their memory. Because if we do that, then it helps us move on. I think that's what you need to do with Rachel.

You need to grieve the friendship you had with her. Pretending that it never happened will only hold you back."

"So what you're saying is that I can't move on until I talk to Rachel?" I asked, already knowing I wasn't going to like the answer. In the beginning, I had felt like I needed to hear from her. But when I never did, I decided it was better to not have to talk to her. Even if it was through email or a text. And since I'd blocked her anyway, I wasn't expecting a call.

She shrugged. "I think you need answers. No matter how hard it will be to hear them."

"Maybe."

Her eyes widened as if she remembered something. Mercedes clapped her hands. "Wait here. I have something for you."

A few minutes later she returned with something wrapped in yellow tissue paper.

"What's this for?"

"I've been saving it for the perfect time, and I think today is it. Maybe you can even use it for your ofrenda."

I raised my eyebrows at Mercedes's comment. The package she handed me was rectangular, lightweight, and soft. As I peeled the layers of tissue paper back, I began to understand what she'd meant.

Slowly I unfolded the cream-colored fabric until the full length of the table runner was in my hands. It was the one that had brought me into Tesoro that first day.

"I thought you sold it," I said, overcome with emotion.

"I would never. This was meant to be yours. I was just holding it for you."

Warmth spread over me as I looked down at the familiar design. "I don't know what to say except thank you. Thank you so much."

"You're welcome. When you look at this, I want you to always remember how far you've come from that day when you first saw this in my window. Healing from grief is never about the final destination. You're not going to wake up one day and magically be okay. It's a journey just like any other, with stops and starts. The goal is just to always keep moving forward."'

◆ ◆ ◆

That Saturday, the shop was busy all day long. I had offered to help Mercedes run the register, since Gloria had said she could bring Maya later on for the lighting of the candles on the ofrenda. The time flew by, and before I knew it, a crowd had formed outside, ready for the official celebration to start.

I helped Maya place the photo of Abuela on the altar. Unexpected emotion squeezed my chest. What I wouldn't give for my daughter to have known her.

"Is this okay to put here?" Nick was standing next to me, holding a photo.

"Yes, of course. Wherever you can find a spot."

I watched as he placed the frame he'd been holding next to the photo of my abuela.

"It's my dad," he offered, even though I didn't ask. "He passed away a few years ago."

"I remember," I told him softly. He and Rachel had gone to Texas for the funeral. My heart hurt for the pained expression on his face. He wore his grief as heavily as I wore mine.

The ceremony officially began with a welcome from Mercedes. She explained the history behind Día de Muertos.

"Today we mark the beginning of Día de Muertos, or Day of the Dead. We believe that the souls of our loved ones return during this time. We celebrate the holiday by building ofrendas, also known as altars, like this one here. Most ofrendas feature certain important elements, such as photos of our loved ones, prayer candles, water, papel picado, flowers, usually marigolds or cempasúchil, salt, sugar skulls, and food offerings."

I walked over and began placing items on the ofrenda as Mercedes explained the symbolism of each one.

"These items represent the four elements of water, wind, earth, and fire," she said as a solo guitarist strummed a somber melody. "We offer a pitcher of water so the deceased can quench their thirst after their long journey to visit us. We hang this papel picado to represent wind and the fragility of life. Earth is represented by this pan de muerto."

She picked up a container of cempasúchil leaves and sprinkled them on the ground to form two vertical lines leading to the ofrenda. "The cempasúchil will guide our loved ones home, while this bowl of salt will help purify their souls. Finally, we light some candles to represent fire and light the way as they make their way back into this world."

After explaining the symbolism behind the items, Mercedes handed the microphone over to a woman who began to sing a haunting rendition of "La Llorona"—a sad song about the Mexican legend of a woman who weeps for her dead children—followed by the moving "Amor Eterno." Its lyrics about grief and wishing a loved one had never died always broke my heart.

By the time she was done, my cheeks were wet with tears.

"Here," Nick whispered, and he passed me a blue bandanna handkerchief.

I nodded my thanks and dabbed my eyes. I felt Maya grab my hand and pull me down.

"Are you sad, Mommy?" she said as she touched my cheek.

"A little. I'm just missing my abuela."

"Grandma must be missing her too. Look, she's crying just like you."

My eyes moved to my mother, who had been standing next to Maya. Although the sidewalk was illuminated only by streetlights, I could see the tears streaming down her face. It was the first time I had ever seen her cry over my abuela.

I reached out to hand her Nick's bandanna.

She seemed startled by the gesture, almost embarrassed that she'd been caught showing emotions. That didn't stop her from taking it, though.

Later that night, I helped Maya put the last of the items on our home ofrenda. We set it up in our entryway. The long table underneath Abuela's framed photo was covered by the runner gifted to me by Mercedes. We lit two candles, and Maya placed a bowl of pumpkin seeds next to the glass of water and a small container of salt. Mercedes had given us a pan de muerto from her favorite East LA bakery, and I set it on a ceramic plate next to one of the candles. Gloria hung a banner of papel picado along the front of the table. Then I added Abuela's rosary bracelet that I'd kept all these years as the final touch.

"Is that it?" Maya asked.

"Oh, I almost forgot! I'll be right back." Gloria disappeared and came back a few minutes later with a mini bottle of Chivas Regal liqueur.

"Really, Mom?" I said, shaking my head.

"What? You knew your abuela. If you wanted her to come to anything, then there had to be alcohol waiting for her."

I rolled my eyes. But I couldn't argue with her reasoning.

"Mommy, can I stay up and wait for your abuela to come visit us tonight?"

I laughed. "It's not like Christmas Eve, Maya. She's not Santa. If she visits us, then I think we'll know it in our hearts. We don't need to see her to believe."

"So she is like Santa," Gloria said matter-of-factly.

I didn't say anything to my mother. "All right, time for bed. You were up late last night because of Halloween and you're up way too late tonight. You need to get some rest now."

Although she protested at first, it took only about ten minutes for Maya to finally close her eyes. Poor girl, she really was exhausted. My mom intuition signaled that maybe she was coming down with something. I pressed the back of my hand against her forehead, but it was cool.

Since tomorrow was Sunday, I decided to let her sleep in.

After making sure her comforter was covering every part of her except her face, I put away her book and turned on her night-light. Then I crept out of her room. I was going to get ready for bed myself when I remembered I promised Mercedes that I'd take a picture of the ofrenda when it was all done.

I wasn't the only one who'd come back to it.

I watched as my mom stood there staring at my abuela's photo. I thought she didn't know I was there until she said, "You know, she wanted me to give you to her when you were first born."

Surprise made me furrow my brow. "What do you mean?"

She turned to me. "The first time she held you in her arms, she asked if she could raise you."

I walked over and looked at my abuela's photo. "Really? Why?"

"Probably because she knew I'd be a bad mother," Gloria said with a bitter laugh.

"Mom . . ."

"She was so angry at me when I told her I was pregnant that she wouldn't talk to me for a week. Then when she finally decided to speak to me, she said she was going to pray that I had a boy because she didn't want me to know the sadness of having a daughter who was just going to repeat my mistakes."

"I can't believe she would say that to you."

I knew that my abuela and my mother had had their issues. But part of me always believed that Gloria didn't understand her and was just a defiant daughter. It was hard to imagine my abuela ever doing or saying anything purposefully to hurt her.

"Well, she did. I think she knew all along that you deserved better than me. So that's why she said she would raise you as her own daughter."

"I don't think she really meant it like that," I said, becoming a little defensive of my abuela.

Gloria shrugged it off. "Don't get me wrong, I'm glad she loved you the way she did. In a way, you were the best thing that ever came into her life. And I'm so sorry that the two of you didn't have more time together."

When her voice broke, so did the emotion I'd been trying to push down. My abuela had been gone for more than two decades. I'd lived more years without her than I'd lived with her. And I'd been so focused on my own grief that I had never considered my mother's. Especially if she believed my abuela had loved me more than her.

I sometimes forgot that my mom was once a little girl just like Maya and that all she ever wanted was to be loved. When she couldn't get that from her mom, she'd sought it out from any boy or man.

In a way, Gloria and I were a lot alike. The only difference was that I had looked for love and validation from Rachel when I didn't get it from her.

It made me sad.

I walked over and put my arm around her shoulders. "I'm sorry you didn't have more time with her too. But I think she would be happy and proud to know that you're following in her footsteps by showing your granddaughter how much she is loved."

"Maybe," she whispered. "You know that's why I told Maya to call me 'Grandma' instead of 'Abuela.' I didn't think I deserved to be called the same as her," she said with a thick voice.

I shrugged. "That's what I thought. But you're the only abuela Maya will ever have."

"I am, aren't I?" Gloria said as she wiped her tears.

We stood there in silence for a while just looking at my abuela's photo, our grief and sadness filling the air with a heaviness I hadn't felt in a long time.

And maybe it was just the breeze sneaking under the front door, but I could've sworn both of the candle flames seemed to flicker out and then come back.

But just in case it was something else, I smiled at her photo and whispered, "Welcome to my home, Abuela. We've missed you."

CHAPTER THIRTY-THREE

THINGS I NEVER KNEW #907: JEALOUSY IS A LYING BITCH

Dear Diary,

I'm so ashamed of myself. Today I acted like a fool and did something I never thought I would. I told David he couldn't hang out with Rachel without me.

In all our years of marriage, it never occurred to me that something might happen between David and Rachel. If anything, I've always wanted them to be close. I saw Rachel as a sister, and I always told her that David was like her brother-in-law.

But maybe that's why they say to be careful what you wish for?

Maya and I weren't supposed to be home tonight until after six. The Girl Scout meeting ended at five, and I'd texted David that we were going to grab dinner with a few of the troop members and their moms. He'd texted back that he was planning to work later anyway and probably wouldn't be home until seven or eight. But then after eating just a few bites of her mac and cheese, Maya told me she didn't feel well and threw up several minutes later in the restroom.

We left and went straight home. When my garage door opener wouldn't work, we had to use the front door. I was surprised when I saw David appear from the hallway. Poor Maya couldn't even say hi, she ran to the guest bathroom. But as soon as she yelled that the door was locked, I heard her get sick all over again. All over the floor. By the time I got to her, Rachel was coming out of the bathroom. I was so worried about Maya that I didn't have time to ask why she was at my house when I wasn't home or why David wasn't at work like he said he would be. The questions and accusations came out later, after Maya was asleep.

He explained that he'd decided to finish up his work from his home office and ran into Rachel as she was leaving something on the porch. He'd invited her in, offered her some wine, and she'd spilled it on her jeans. She had just been washing out the stain in the bathroom when we'd gotten home.

I have to admit that the story still didn't make sense. Why hadn't he called me to tell me he was going home? Rachel knew I would be at the meeting, so why wouldn't she have waited to bring over the package like she usually does when something of mine is delivered to her house by mistake? But then he showed me the unopened Amazon box on the counter that had apparently been misdelivered next door. He told me he was just being nice and didn't understand why I was getting so upset. And that's when I told him I didn't want him hanging out with Rachel without me. He thought I was being unreasonable, and he stormed out after accusing me of not trusting him. But what he didn't know was it had nothing to do with trust or thinking that something was going on between them. Yes, I'd been jealous. But not of Rachel. I was jealous of David.

The truth was, Rachel was my friend first. And I didn't want David or anyone else to ever steal her away from me.

I know now that was ridiculous. We aren't in junior high anymore. Nobody can steal best friends. Jealousy had whispered ugly untrue things in my ear, and I'd believed them instead of believing that David would never betray me like that.

Never.

CHAPTER THIRTY-FOUR

Gloria left for Florida early on a Wednesday morning.

But promised she'd return Saturday.

She'd let me know only a few days before that she'd forgotten about an important appointment, and Carlos needed her in Florida to sign some documents. After assuring me that she wasn't going to be signing over anything serious, she would only add that she couldn't reschedule, and Carlos was adamant that she keep the appointment.

"Okay," I'd said. "But you really don't have to come back right away, Mom. Maybe instead you come back early next year." I'd hoped that if I left the door open for a future visit, then she'd realize it was okay to stay home.

Instead, she emailed me her itinerary that night, which showed her return flight was booked.

She almost didn't leave for the airport, though. Maya had come down with a fever after battling a yucky cough for nearly a week. Although the temperature on Halloween and the night of the Día de Muertos celebration had been in the high sixties, Gloria was sure she must have caught a cold then. And when the fever came on, my mother debated on whether she should leave at all.

"Mom, I'm taking her to the pediatrician this afternoon. It's not like you can do anything for her that I'm not doing now. Just go to the airport, and I'll call you after her appointment and let you know what the doctor says."

"All right, but you better call me or else I will turn around and get right back on the plane."

I could tell she was absolutely serious, so I agreed.

The rest of the morning I tried to do some work from home, even though Mercedes had told me to take the entire day off. When she wasn't coughing or complaining that her head hurt, Maya would sleep. I tried to keep myself busy and was grateful for the work.

Finally, I took Maya to her appointment that afternoon. I had expected the doctor to write her a prescription for a stronger cough medicine and maybe an inhaler, since she'd told me that morning that it hurt to take a deep breath.

But my mom intuition began to suspect this was more than just a bad cold. For starters, as soon as the nurse took Maya's vitals, she left the room and came back with the doctor within seconds. He started listening to her chest with his stethoscope, and I didn't like the expression on his face—concerned. Even scared.

He sat down on the nearby stool and rolled it closer to me. "So, Mom, I think your daughter might have pneumonia," he began. "It's going around right now. Normally, I would give you a referral to an imaging center so they can x-ray her lungs. But because this type of pneumonia—if it's the one that we've been seeing in our other patients—is a little more pesky, it's better to get it treated as soon as possible. I want you to take her to the emergency room at the children's hospital in LA immediately. I'm going to call ahead so they will take her right away."

My heart started beating as if I were running a marathon. I forced the tears that threatened to spill over to go away. I couldn't show Maya that I was scared.

The doctor had apparently done what he'd promised because as soon as I checked Maya in to the emergency room, a nurse was summoned to take us to a room. I was holding it together pretty well until the room was invaded by a team of more nurses and other staff wearing scrubs. When one of them announced her temperature was 103, my knees couldn't support me any longer, and I fell onto a nearby chair.

I couldn't even see my baby anymore. She had an oxygen mask covering her little face, and the spaces around her not filled with machines were blocked by people. Then one of the nurses explained that I needed to step out of the room so they could take an x-ray. I didn't want to leave Maya, even though I was only going to be a few feet away.

As I watched the team do what they needed to do, I thought about calling Gloria. She'd already texted to let me know she'd landed and wanted an update. But I knew if I told her what was happening, then she really would get on a plane tonight. Instead, I decided to just text her and let her know that the doctor wanted an x-ray done to rule out pneumonia. It was as close to the truth as I could get without sending her into a panic. There was no reason for both of us to be upset.

The next person I thought about calling was David. He'd talked to Maya in the beginning of the week, when she'd only had a stuffy nose and sore throat. He could tell she wasn't feeling well and cut their call short. To his credit, he'd texted the next day to check on her, but we hadn't heard from him since. I made the decision to wait to call him until I knew what was going to happen.

After an agonizing several minutes, the main nurse called me back into the room. The ER doctor was already there.

"Hello, Mrs. Flores," he began. "I'm Dr. Jordan, the attending pediatric physician for the emergency room. So it looks like little Maya might have something called mycoplasma pneumonia. We'll know for sure after we get the lab results back, but I'm pretty confident that's what it is. We've been seeing a lot of cases lately in kids her age and even younger."

"How do you treat it?" I asked, my throat tight with fear.

"We're going to give her some antibiotics and breathing treatments to help her little lungs. She's very dehydrated, so we're going to have to give her an IV and get some fluids going. I'm hoping we can do all of this here. But we may admit her upstairs if we think she's going to need additional meds."

"Admit her?" I croaked.

He nodded. The main nurse then added, "It would be only if necessary and just to make sure she's getting more one-on-one care."

"Do you have any questions?" the doctor said.

I shook my head. I was sure I'd think of some later, but all I could focus on was my Maya and how I hated that I couldn't do anything to help her feel better.

The next few hours were torture. Nurses came and went to check vitals and the IV drip. Thankfully, Maya slept through most of it.

I finally texted both Gloria and David and let them know varying levels of information. I told Gloria not to book a flight until I knew for sure they were going to admit her. All David wrote was to keep him updated.

But I was afraid I wouldn't even be able to do that soon. My phone's battery was down to 12 percent. And my head was throbbing from stress and hunger. I knew it was time to ask for help.

Mercedes picked up on the first ring. With a cracked voice, I told her what was going on.

"Oh honey, I'm so sorry. What do you need?"

Relief spread like a warm comforting blanket across my chest. "My neighbor Nick has a spare key to my house. Could you get it from him and then go inside to grab a few things for me?"

"Of course. I'll leave right now."

"Let me text him first. I'm not sure if he's even home. I'll text you when I know for sure he can give it you."

"Okay. I'll wait to hear from you. In the meantime I'm going to pray that Maya starts to feel better real soon."

I nodded through my tears. "Thank you." Then I hung up because I couldn't say anything else.

Next, I texted Nick:

Can I send my boss to your house to get my spare key? My mom is out of town and Maya is in the emergency room at the children's hospital and they might admit her. I need my phone charger, her stuffed flamingo and some other things.

I held my breath until three small dots appeared.

Yeah. Of course. But I'm not home right now. I'll text you as soon as I get there.

I replied: Okay. Thank you.

More dots appeared as if he was typing something. Then they went away.

I'd considered that Nick probably didn't know I'd given Rachel a spare key to my house, or that he'd even know where she kept it if he did. It sounded like he did know, and I couldn't worry about whether the information would somehow be hard for him. Even though we'd become friends, the subject of Rachel was still touchy for the both of us.

I texted Mercedes to let her know Nick wasn't home. If I'd been thinking clearly, I would've just given her his number so they could coordinate. But the doctor came back into the room just then.

"So I've been talking with the team upstairs, and we all agree it would be best to admit Maya, at least overnight, so we can monitor her fever and fluid intake. We're also going to give her another dose of antibiotics. Once she finishes that, they'll come to take her to a room."

"Is she not improving?" I asked, afraid of the answer.

"A little, but I think we need to be a little more aggressive in our treatment than I originally thought. From the cases I've seen so far, this pneumonia is stubborn, and sometimes it takes a little extra to get rid of it. Typically, the kids just need one night in the hospital, and then they get sent home with a nebulizer and more antibiotics. I just want to make sure that her fever doesn't start climbing again, so it's better that we monitor her here at the hospital. Does that make sense?"

"Yes. Thank you." Even though I said it, none of this made sense to me. How could a simple cold turn into a hospital stay?

"You're welcome. Okay, Jackie is going to get the new antibiotics going, and hopefully we can get Maya in a room soon. And of course you're allowed to stay with her all night. Do you have someone you can call to bring you food or things you need?"

"I already called them."

"Perfect. Don't worry, Mrs. Flores. I know Maya will be back to feeling like herself soon."

An hour later, Maya was still in the emergency room, and I was still without a phone charger. The battery was completely dead, and I had no way of getting in contact with Mercedes or Nick. I had already scolded myself a hundred times for not replacing the charger in my car when it stopped working two weeks ago.

Tears filled my eyes, and I became overwhelmed by a rising sense of panic. I'd never felt so alone. The doubts and fears about being a single parent that I'd been trying to ignore came roaring to the surface. I covered my face with my hands and cried quietly with my face turned away from a sleeping Maya.

When I was done feeling sorry for myself, I scooted closer to the hospital gurney.

"You're going to be okay, my baby," I whispered as I stroked her hair. "And I'm going to be okay too. I promise."

I bent over, crossed my arms in front of me, and laid my head down.

A light tap on my shoulder woke me up from a restless nap. I wasn't sure how long I'd been asleep.

It was one of the nurses. "Sorry to wake you, Mrs. Flores, but there's someone at the front reception desk. He says he's your neighbor and that he brought the things you needed."

My mind was groggy. I thought I'd heard her say my neighbor was here. "My neighbor?"

She nodded. "Yes, he says his name is Nick."

That woke me up.

I walked outside the double doors and saw Nick standing off to the side, holding a tote bag in one hand and a paper bag in the other. He nodded at me when he caught my eye.

"Nick? What are you doing here? Where's Mercedes?"

"When you didn't text me back, I figured your phone had died. I tried calling the shop, but she didn't answer and I don't have another number for her. So I decided to just come myself. I hope that's okay? I also brought you a sandwich."

And because it had been a long horrible day and my nerves and emotions were shot, I teared up and threw my arms around his neck. "Thank you," I whispered.

He stiffened at first. Then he relaxed.

"Sorry," I said with a laugh after I let him go. "It's been a rough day."

I took the bags from him and thanked him again. I expected him to walk away, but he didn't. "Can I see Maya?"

The question surprised me, and I nearly began crying all over again. I nodded.

After getting Nick a visitor's pass, I led him through the double doors and down the hall to Maya's room. She was still asleep. While he walked closer to the gurney, I reached into the tote bag to grab my charger. I touched something soft instead. Warmth spread throughout my chest as I pulled out Maya's stuffed flamingo.

"You brought Felicia," I said out loud as I looked down on the pink and purple flamingo. She'd picked it out herself the first time I'd taken her to the LA Zoo.

"I also found a book by her bed that I figured she might want. I remember you saying once that she loved for you to read her a bedtime story every night."

I spun around to face him. "She's going to be so happy. I really don't know how to thank you."

He shrugged sheepishly. "I wish I could do more. I'm sure this is all very scary for you, especially . . . especially since David isn't here."

It was true. His absence was basically the elephant in the room. I had been trying to ignore it, especially when well-meaning nurses asked when Maya's dad might be showing up.

"Mommy?" a tiny hoarse voice whispered.

I went to Maya and leaned down so she could see me. "I'm here, baby."

"Am I home now?"

My heart broke. "No, baby. Not yet. But look what Uncle Nick brought you." I placed Felicia the Flamingo on her belly, and she smiled.

"Felicia," she said as she pulled her up to snuggle with her. Her eyes closed again, and I knew she'd fall back asleep soon.

"I'll go so she can rest," Nick whispered. "But let me know if you need anything else."

Suddenly, I didn't want him to leave. "Wait. Um, I thought I'd eat the sandwich outside so I don't make a mess in here. Do you want to sit with me for a little?"

"Sure. And I saw a vending machine in the waiting room, if you're thirsty. I wasn't sure what to bring you to drink."

I grabbed the paper bag with my sandwich and stopped at the nurses' station to let them know I'd be right outside. I left my phone charging so it would at least have some juice when I returned.

After I'd bought myself a can of Coke, Nick and I exited the emergency room and found a nearby bench. I didn't think I could eat that much with my nervous stomach, but as soon as I took the first bite, I was ravenous.

"Either this is the best sandwich I've ever had or I'm starving," I said with a mouthful of bread and deli meats.

He laughed and nodded. "Probably a little bit of both. The sandwich is from a shop down the street from here. I remembered it being pretty good, so I was glad it was still open."

"It definitely is." I took another bite and then a drink of my soda. Although my head still throbbed, it wasn't as excruciating. I hoped the caffeine would get rid of it altogether. "What time is it, anyway?"

"It's almost seven."

"Seven? Wow. We've been here almost five hours already. I didn't even realize it was dark outside."

"So are the doctors going to admit Maya?" he asked after several seconds.

I nodded. "They're just waiting for this last bag of antibiotics to finish and to get a room ready. They're hopeful it will just be overnight."

"What's wrong with her?"

"Pneumonia. Apparently it's going around right now and it can get really bad, especially in kids. So they're treating it very aggressively. That's why they want to admit her."

"That's good that they're taking it seriously. I'm sure they're doing everything they can for her."

"I know. I just . . . I just feel so helpless. If I could trade places with her, I would. I hate seeing her so weak."

Nick nodded. "That's what makes you a good mom," he offered.

"I sure don't feel like I am. I should've called the doctor sooner or taken her to urgent care earlier. I don't know what I'd do if the treatments don't start helping her feel better."

"Hey, don't beat yourself up. Obviously, I don't know what you're going through, but I could barely take care of myself after Rachel . . ." His voice trailed off for a few seconds. "The point is, you have a little human that you're responsible for, and I'm sure it hasn't been easy doing it all on your own. If there's anything I'm grateful for out of this whole mess, it's that we don't have any kids. I guess Rachel did me at least one favor by getting the hysterectomy years ago."

I nearly choked on a piece of salami. "Rachel had a hysterectomy? When?"

His face went blank. "Back in Milwaukee. I thought you knew."

"No. No I didn't. Why did she do it?"

"Because of her mom," he said matter-of-factly. "When they diagnosed her with stage one ovarian cancer, she immediately decided to do the surgery. She didn't want to put it off like her mom did."

I put down my sandwich and covered my mouth with my hand. Rachel had had ovarian cancer? She had told me that her mom had died from liver disease, which she attributed to being a longtime alcoholic. Why would she lie to me about both of those things?

"I'm so sorry, Nick. I had no idea. Rachel never told me about any of it."

He dragged his hand over his face. "I'm sorry that you found out this way. I didn't know that you didn't know."

"I'm finding out that I didn't know a lot of things. She had told me that you guys didn't want kids."

His eyes widened in surprise. "Wow. I don't know what to say about that."

"I'm the one that's sorry now for telling you."

"Don't be," he said. "I mean, I was sad for a while about not having kids, but like I said, it worked out in the end, I guess."

I looked at my sandwich. These two revelations about my former best friend had me reeling, and suddenly I wasn't hungry anymore. What else had Rachel lied to me about over the years?

CHAPTER THIRTY-FIVE

THINGS I NEVER KNEW #927: SHOPPING REALLY IS THERAPY

Dear Diary,

I had the best day with my best friend. Rachel called me early this morning and said she was taking me out for a girls' day. We hadn't had one of those in a while, so I was surprised but happy.

She picked me up by ten, and I said goodbye to David and Maya. I still had no idea where we were going or what we were going to do. But I was up for anything.

First we stopped at our favorite day spa. We got massages and facials. Then we went to a nearby salon. Rachel had booked us appointments for manis and pedis. Next we had lunch at this little bistro I had mentioned I'd wanted to try that opened last month. Everything was delicious. Finally, we went shopping at Paseo Colorado in Pasadena.

As we headed back, I couldn't stop thanking Rachel for spending the day with me. I even told her that I missed us. But I was curious as to what made her want to do this.

"I just wanted to thank you for being such a good friend. I think sometimes I don't say that enough."

Her words surprised me. Rachel had never been one to say things so deep or meaningful. If anything, I was the mushy one in our relationship. So it meant a lot to me for her to say that.

When we got back to our houses, she grabbed my hand before I could walk home and pulled me in for hug.

I'll never forget what she told me tonight. But in case I do, I'll write it down here. She said: "Your friendship means the world to me, and I hope I never do anything stupid enough to ruin it."

I tried to tell her that would never happen, but she just kissed my cheek and told me to have a good night.

Her words seemed genuine, yet I can't shake the feeling there was something else behind them. But I'm trying very hard not to overanalyze—something Gloria says I do a lot. So instead I'm just going to be happy and grateful that I got to spend a wonderful day with my best friend.

CHAPTER THIRTY-SIX

Fortunately for me, the universe decided to take at least one worry off my plate the next day. My little girl was awake and fever-free.

I called everyone to tell them the good news. Nick was back at the hospital within the hour.

"How's the patient?" he asked as he walked into the room.

"Ask her yourself," I said with a big smile and pointed to Maya, who opened her eyes.

"Hi, Uncle Nick," she said in a small scratchy voice.

He walked closer to her bed. "Hey there. How are you feeling?"

"Okay, 'cept my throat hurts."

"I'm sorry to hear that. You know what? I hear ice cream is good for yucky throats. How about I bring some over when you get home?"

Maya's face transformed into one big smile, and she nodded excitedly.

Nick stayed until the day shift nurse came in and explained that she was going to check her vitals and replace the antibiotics IV. I told Maya I wanted to walk Uncle Nick to his truck, and she nodded sleepily.

We were quiet on the elevator ride down. But when we stepped outside the hospital, I said, "Thanks for coming to see her."

He shoved his hands into his jacket. "She looks so much better."

"She does. The nurse thinks she'll be able to come home tomorrow. My mom's plane lands tonight, so she says she's going to scrub the germs out of the house to get it ready for Maya."

Nick chuckled. "How long is she planning to stay this time?"

"Who knows?" I said with a shrug. "I don't have the energy to play a million questions with her about it right now. I just want to focus on getting Maya healthy."

We arrived at his truck, and I could tell he was hesitating about saying something.

"What?" I asked.

He cleared his throat. "And David? When is he coming to see her?"

"The week of Thanksgiving," I said.

"Oh. For that whole week?"

I didn't even try to hide my frustration. "Um, no. We have our first meeting with a mediator on Tuesday, and then he wants to come by the house to spend some time with Maya. He's flying back to San Francisco on Wednesday. Apparently, his new agency throws a nice Thanksgiving shindig for all their employees, and he can't miss it."

"Oh," Nick said again. I felt exactly the same way.

I hated that David hadn't dropped everything to come see Maya. His excuse was she was getting better and he was coming back to South Pasadena in less than two weeks anyway. But Nick had already been here twice. He could've waited for her to get discharged and then visit once she was home.

If I'd needed any more evidence that David had checked out of being a dad, this was it.

Just another thing to add to the list of unforgivable acts he'd committed.

But being mad or upset about something I couldn't control wasn't what I needed to be. And at this point, I didn't want to force David to spend time with us. I could only control what I could control. And that was making sure Maya had a nice Thanksgiving.

"By the way," I began. "If you don't have any other plans, you're welcome to come over and have dinner with us. Unless of course, you've been looking forward to spending the holiday with a frozen turkey potpie?"

Nick laughed at my teasing. Then he nodded in appreciation. "Thank you for the invitation. I would like that."

Part of me wanted to ask if he had talked to Rachel. I hadn't dared ask David if she was also coming back to town with him. Nick did seem surprised when I said he'd be in town Thanksgiving week. Maybe he had been wondering the same about Rachel. Even if she was planning to make the trip with David, both of them would be gone by Wednesday, since I assumed that she would be his plus-one at the agency party.

And if I could go those few days without seeing her, then I would be very thankful indeed.

"Can I ask . . . can I ask if you two have talked?"

"Just a few times over the past few weeks," he said. "But she barely says anything or even answers my questions. Typical Rachel, I guess. If she doesn't talk about it, then she doesn't have to deal with it."

That was true. And it explained why she had yet to reach out to me. Not that I really wanted her to anymore.

"I stay up some nights racking my brain thinking of what I missed," I confessed.

"Same. But if I'm honest with myself, I guess I have to admit our marriage had been in trouble for a while. Part of me wishes we'd never moved to South Pasadena, but then part of me knows this was always going to be the result. Not the affair, but her leaving. Apparently she hasn't been happy for a while—she did tell me that little gem during our last call."

As much as I hated to add to Nick's obvious pain, I agreed with him.

But there was one thing he said that raised a flag for me—that David and Rachel wouldn't have had an affair if they hadn't moved next door. It was as if fuzzy memories I'd pushed away began to come into focus. Like the times she'd always compliment David's haircuts or new shirts. Or when she'd laugh a little too loud at his jokes.

My head began to throb again. So much so that I rubbed my eyes.

"You okay?" he asked.

"Just tired."

"Sorry if this conversation is making it worse."

I shook my head. "No need to be sorry. I'm the one who asked about her."

I should've listened to my gut about steering clear of any conversations about Rachel.

"What does David say?"

I ignored my gut yet again and decided to tell Nick the truth. "Not much. We usually keep our calls limited to the topics of Maya and the divorce. Whenever I start to ask questions about the affair, he always has to get back to work. How convenient, right? My mom says I have to find a way to be okay with never getting any answers from either of them. Otherwise, I'll never be able to move on."

Nick rubbed his hand through the hair on the top of his head. "I probably should take that advice myself," he said. "So now what? What's next?"

That was the million-dollar question.

I looked past him as if I could see into the future. But all I could see were cars and an ambulance. The future—at least for today—was beyond my sight.

CHAPTER THIRTY-SEVEN

THINGS I NEVER KNEW #955: EVEN BEST FRIENDS CAN KEEP SECRETS FROM EACH OTHER

Dear Diary,

Something is up with Rachel. I can't quite put my finger on it, but I know something is wrong. She says she's fine whenever I ask if everything is okay. I even asked her today if I'd done something to make her mad at me. She said no, but I don't believe her.

What I do know is that she's been weird lately about coming over to the house and has canceled on me a few times. Today we were supposed to go shopping for the groceries for our Thanksgiving dinner. I was going to make the turkey and stuffing and the rolls. She was in charge of making all the sides and dessert. But when I called to ask if she was ready to go to the market, she told me not only was she not going to cook anything but that her and Nick couldn't come over at all.

I was shocked. Spending Thanksgiving together had become our annual tradition ever since she'd moved next

door. We had been planning this dinner for months. She apologized and said her dad had called her out of the blue last night and said he was in Las Vegas and wanted to spend Thanksgiving with her. They were driving up there in a few hours and were going to meet him for dinner tomorrow at the fancy restaurant at his hotel.

I don't know why it affected me like it did. But I actually started crying when she was explaining. I could barely speak when she was done apologizing for the second time. After managing to get out a "Drive safe," I hung up.

David didn't understand why I was so upset. He told me not to be selfish and I should be happy that Rachel was going to spend Thanksgiving with her dad.

What I didn't tell David or Rachel was that a few years ago, I'd friended Rachel's dad on Facebook. He posted the day before that he and his wife were spending Thanksgiving with friends in Chicago.

So what on earth is Rachel hiding from me?

CHAPTER THIRTY-EIGHT

A week after being discharged from the hospital, I decided we needed to celebrate Maya's complete recovery from pneumonia. She got to pick what was for dinner and she also got to pick who joined us: Nick.

He showed up exactly at 6:00 p.m. on the dot, carrying a tub of chocolate chip ice cream—Maya's favorite.

I was genuinely happy to see him. I was getting used to having him around, and not just to fix things.

"I hope it's okay," he said when I took the tub from him to put it into the freezer. "Can she eat ice cream yet, or will the cold hurt her lungs?"

I smiled. "She can eat it. Thank you for bringing it over. Dinner is almost ready. We're having secret spaghetti."

Nick raised one eyebrow. "Secret spaghetti?"

"It's a recipe that Gloria came up with. She told Maya she hides candy in the sauce. And supposedly I'm not supposed to know that she does it, so that makes it their little secret. Really it's just made with shredded zucchini and carrots."

"That's very clever. I might need the recipe."

"I thought you didn't cook?" I asked without thinking. He had to know that I only knew that information from Rachel. But he didn't seem to mind.

"I don't. Not really. But I'm trying to teach myself a few basic meals, and spaghetti is one of them."

"Good for you," I said, not being able to contain a big smile. His earnestness was endearing.

"Uncle Nick!"

We both turned to see Maya running into the kitchen. Gloria appeared just a few seconds later.

He bent down to give Maya a high five. "Hey there! How are you feeling?"

"Bien, gracias."

"I'm so glad. Thank you for inviting me over for dinner."

"You're welcome," she said and then leaned closer. "Did you bring me ice cream?"

"Maya Pilar!" I said. "It's not polite to ask someone if they brought you something."

Her big smile disappeared. "Lo siento, Nick. It's okay if you didn't."

He laughed and whispered in her ear. The big smile was back, and I knew he'd told her what was waiting for her in the freezer.

"Maya, how do you say 'ice cream' in Spanish?" Gloria asked.

"Nieve," my very smart daughter answered.

I smiled and shook my head. Ever since she'd come back to South Pasadena, my mother had decided that she was also going to help Maya learn Spanish. And she'd brought back two more bilingual children's books to teach her, since Maya wouldn't be going back to school until after the Thanksgiving break.

"Okay, time to set the table," I announced.

Secret spaghetti was a big hit, especially with Nick. I tried not to laugh when he kept asking my mom to tell him what the secret ingredient was.

"Sorry, Nick. I won't even tell Claudia," Gloria said.

When he dramatically feigned disappointment, Maya snickered. She gave a thumbs-up to my mom, proud that their secret was safe. I was happy that the two of them had gotten so close. What I wasn't happy about was that Maya's health scare had renewed my mother's determination to stay in South Pasadena indefinitely.

"So, Nick, did you grow up in Southern California?" Gloria asked.

I rolled my eyes and swallowed the spaghetti I'd been chewing. "Mom, I'm sure Nick didn't come over to be interviewed," I said with a laugh. God, why was she so nosy?

"I'm just making dinner conversation," she said in her fake innocent tone.

"It's okay. I don't mind. Um, no, I didn't grow up here. I actually grew up in Texas."

Gloria clapped. "Ooh, Texas? I love their barbecue. Can you make us some ribs this weekend?"

"Oh my God, Mom." I was so embarrassed.

"Definitely," Nick said, surprising me. "I also make a pretty good brisket." I'd known him for years yet had never known that. I thought the man couldn't cook?

"It's a date then. You bring the meats, and we'll bring everything else."

My mother really had no shame. Especially when it came to food.

The chocolate chip ice cream was the perfect ending to a pretty perfect night. Nick couldn't stop saying thank you after Gloria packed up a container filled with leftover secret spaghetti.

"So do you have anything else around the house you want done?" he asked me as I walked him to the front door.

I thought about it for a few seconds. "No, I don't think so. Why?"

"You just gave me dinner for at least two more nights. It's the least I can do."

"I hope you don't think I invited you over because I wanted something?" I said, half laughing, half worried.

When he didn't answer, guilt made me take a deep breath. "I'm so sorry if I made you feel that way."

"No, you didn't, I promise. It's just me. I guess I'm still getting used to this." Nick motioned to me and then himself. "We've never hung out this much before. You know, without them."

I understood completely. Through Rachel, I'd been so wrong about the kind of man Nick was. And that was the main reason why I'd had no real interest in becoming his friend before—his real friend. He'd been at my side for weeks and proven ten times over that I could trust him.

"You're right," I told him. "And honestly, I think I owe you an apology for not trying to get to know you better as Nick rather than just Rachel's husband. Hell, I didn't even know you made a mean brisket."

"You don't have to apologize, Claudia. I can say the same about you."

"You can? So does that mean there's something you learned about me too?"

"Uh, let's see," he said, and he tapped his chin with his index finger as he thought. "Yeah, I've learned that you are really bad at raking leaves."

I laughed and nodded. He had learned something about me after all. "Then how about we start from scratch as just Nick and Claudia?" I asked.

"Sounds good to me."

"And just so you know, Maya was actually the one who wanted you to come over for dinner. Don't get me wrong—I would've invited you anyway. I just thought you'd like to know that it was her idea. It really meant a lot to her that you came to visit her in the hospital. She's going to remember that for the rest of her life, I think."

"Thank you for saying that," he told me. "And I will totally understand if you don't want her calling me 'Uncle Nick' anymore. I know I was only uncle by association."

I thought about everything Nick had done for Maya and for me the past few weeks. "You have absolutely earned the title of 'uncle.' So that will not be changing."

"Good," he said sheepishly. "I'm happy that she's home."

"Me too," I said with a big smile.

After he headed home, I walked back into the kitchen.

"Nick says he wants the recipe for your secret spaghetti," I told Gloria.

"Of course he does. My spaghetti is delicious," she said as she filled the dishwasher.

I laughed and walked into my office in search of a pack of index cards. Once I'd found what I was looking for, I took two over to Gloria and set the rest on the counter.

"What are those for?" she asked as she pushed buttons on the dishwasher.

"What are you doing?"

"I'm trying to turn on the dishwasher, but these buttons are so confusing."

I waved her away and pressed the clearly marked "start" button. "See? Not complicated at all. And the index cards are so you can write down the recipe."

"You want me to do it tonight?"

I shrugged. "Or in the morning."

"You do it for me, okay?"

"Um, I don't know every ingredient."

"You made it tonight just fine."

"Yeah, but you were over my shoulder telling me what to do step by step. Write it down on one card for me and one card for Nick."

"How about I tell you and you write it? My eyes are tired. Plus you always say you can't read my handwriting."

That was true. She should've been a doctor, based on how illegible her writing was. Still, something was nagging me about her excuses. Then, in typical Gloria fashion, she changed the subject.

"I'm glad Nick was around to help you when Maya was in the hospital," she said.

"Me too."

"I guess this means you two are friends now."

I grabbed the cleaning spray and began to wipe down the counters. "Guess so."

"And who knows? Maybe down the road you can be more than friends."

"Oh my God, Mom. Do *not* go there. I could never think of Nick that way."

Although that wasn't entirely true. Two nights ago, Nick had been the subject of a very sexy dream. But I'd never admit it, especially to Gloria. And especially not when he was quickly becoming someone I liked having around. I didn't want to make things awkward by letting my subconscious become more conscious when it came to him.

Billy Crystal's voice whispered in my ear about men and women not being able to be friends because sex always gets in the way.

When Harry Met Sally . . . was another of my abuela's favorite movies and one she made me watch with her at least once a month. I hadn't seen it in years but did a rewatch late one night last month on Amazon Prime. How many times had I seen the scene where his character explained the risks of taking your significant other to the airport and how not wanting to take them anymore was a sign of bad things to come?

The irony wasn't lost on me.

Was I that lost that I was going to take relationship advice from Billy now?

Before Gloria could argue, I continued: "Have you forgotten the fact that he's still Rachel's husband? I'm sorry to dash your yet again ill-informed matchmaker fantasies, but Nick and I are never going to be together like that."

My mom shrugged and pushed her lips together in a pout. "Okay, fine." I nodded, satisfied that she'd finally gotten the message. Oh, how wrong I was.

"But that doesn't mean you couldn't comfort each other in another way during your time of need. If you ask me, that would be the best revenge," she added.

"Mother!"

CHAPTER THIRTY-NINE

THINGS I NEVER KNEW #1003: MY HUSBAND WANTS TO MOVE TO SAN FRANCISCO

Dear Diary,

I am exhausted and summer's just started. I've signed Maya up for lots of activities, and I think it might be too much. I'm hoping she'll hate at least one of them. Is that awful?

It could also be that I'm just extra stressed. David and I have been fighting lately over his job. A few days ago he dropped a huge bombshell on me. Apparently, he was offered a position with a competing agency. But it's based in San Francisco. I had no idea that he'd even applied!

He says it wasn't something he was looking for, but the more he learned about the job, the better it sounded. It would be more money, and he'd be leading his own team—something he's wanted for a while now. But more responsibility would mean more hours at the office and probably more traveling. I told David that he's barely home these days as it is. When he isn't on a business trip, then he's at the office at work or at the office here in the house. We rarely do things as a family anymore, and it's seemed like I've been running around even more lately.

That said, this is the only home Maya has ever known. I moved around a lot as a kid, and I remember how hard it was for me to make and keep friends. I don't want that for Maya.

So I told him I don't want him to take the job.

We got into a huge fight, and he made a comment about since he was the only one working, then I really shouldn't even get a say. That pissed me off, and I refused to talk to him for the rest of the night. I even slept in the guest room. That's how mad I was.

It's been a couple of days, and things are still tense. We're talking again, but whenever I ask him if he's turned down the other agency, he just tells me not to worry about having to move to San Francisco anymore.

Maybe that's why I went a little overboard with Maya's summer schedule. I wanted to prove to David there were many reasons why we needed to stay in South Pasadena. And for me, one of those reasons is Rachel. We've lived next door to each other now for almost three years, yet I still feel kind of disconnected from her lately. If we moved, I'm afraid that would be the end of our friendship for good.

I'm hoping David just needs some time to get over this and he'll eventually come to see that jobs come and go. What really matters is our family and what's going to be best for all of us.

CHAPTER FORTY

Nick's house was haunted. Well, haunted in the sense that I was afraid of going inside and seeing Rachel everywhere.

Not her ghost, technically. But her presence. I knew I was going to feel it everywhere, even though she hadn't been there for almost three months. It was the main reason I kept telling Nick that my mother had been joking the other day, when she'd told him he had to barbecue for her.

But he'd texted me a bunch of times to let me know he was looking forward to grilling for us and was even going to pick up a kids' mac and cheese from Denny's for Maya.

So I had no choice but to put on my big girl chonies once again and face a ghost.

The three of us arrived on Nick's doorstep at five o'clock on an unseasonably cold Saturday afternoon. We'd all needed jackets just to travel the few feet from my house to his. I'd also made Maya wear a beanie and a scarf. I wasn't taking any chances of having her relapse.

But inside was a different story. It was warm, even cozy, thanks to the central heat and the gas fireplace in the living room. The layout of Nick's house was similar to mine. It was also a craftsman style with a wraparound porch. But instead of four bedrooms, there were only two, and no formal dining room. The previous owners had lived there for nearly forty years and had done little to no updates. Rachel had wanted to at least renovate the kitchen but told me Nick had said they could barely afford the mortgage payment as it was.

So it didn't come as a surprise that Nick hadn't changed a thing since Rachel had left. I hadn't, either, but that was because I was the one who'd handpicked every piece of furniture and knickknack in my home. I'd loved it when David lived there, and there was no reason why I shouldn't love it still. But at Nick's house, from the mystery books on the shelves to the treadmill in the corner of the living room, everything still screamed Rachel.

I wondered if he ever got the urge to just throw everything away.

"I've been smoking the brisket and ribs all day, so they should be ready soon," Nick announced. "I was only going to grill some veggies."

I handed him the containers I was holding. "Sounds good. And we brought a mixed green salad and some cookies for dessert."

We took off our jackets and followed him into the kitchen. Even through the French doors leading to the backyard, I still got a wonderful whiff of charcoal smoke mixed with cooking meats.

"I'm bummed the weather is so cold today," Nick said. "I had hoped we could eat out on the patio. But I guess we'll eat inside."

"I think that's best too," my mom agreed. "As long as the food is good, I can eat anywhere."

"I like that. All right, I'm going to go check on things outside. Make yourselves at home, get something to drink, turn on the TV, whatever you want. Claudia knows where everything is," he said. Nick met my eyes and offered me a small smile. I nodded.

Maya did exactly what Nick suggested and immediately turned on the TV in the family room. Gloria joined her, and I soon heard the familiar dialogue from their favorite Disney show. I decided to make myself useful and set the kitchen table with the paper plates and napkins Nick had set out on the counter. After that was done, I found a serving bowl in one cupboard for the salad and opened another to get glasses for the four of us.

That's when I saw it.

The glass mug was a gift for Rachel's twenty-first birthday. I'd found it at one of those engraving places they used to have in malls. It cost me more than I'd planned to spend, especially since I'd barely started working at my part-time job at a restaurant off campus. It was the engraving that jacked up the price, but I had my heart set on what I wanted it to say, so I bit the bullet and agreed to the price.

Carefully, I pulled the mug from the middle shelf of the cupboard and cradled it in my hands. I outlined the rough lines of both of our names engraved in a cursive font. It was Rachel's go-to beer mug—perfect for pizza nights. I turned it around to look at the other side's writing: *Best Friends Forever*. I don't know why, but part of me had expected it not to be there anymore, as if it would've magically disappeared now that it wasn't true.

My eyes watered, and I quickly put the mug back in its place before Gloria or Nick caught me crying over it. I wiped the tears away with my sleeve and picked out four regular glasses to use for our dinner.

Nick wasn't lying when he'd said he made a good brisket. And judging by Gloria's inappropriate moans on the other side of the table, she was definitely satisfied with what she was tasting.

"I thought you said you couldn't cook," I said after pushing my plate away.

"I can't. But cooking and grilling are two different things," he said.

"Amen to that," Gloria said.

I swear I couldn't take this woman anywhere.

Nick didn't seem to mind. In fact, he looked absolutely entertained by my mother. As usual, Gloria had charmed another member of the opposite sex. I wouldn't be surprised if Nick offered to grill her some meats every weekend.

"Thank you for the mac and cheese, Uncle Nick. It was delicioso," Maya said.

"De nada."

I raised my eyebrows in appreciation of his use of Spanish. Then I turned to my daughter, who was sitting in the chair next to me. "That was very nice of you to say, Maya," I said, impressed that I hadn't had to nudge her to do it.

"Can I have a cookie now, por favor?"

I couldn't help but laugh. The kid knew how to manipulate us all. Sometimes she was too smart for her own good.

When dinner was over, I offered to do the dishes. I thought my mom and Maya would just go back and watch TV while they waited for me to finish. Instead, Gloria announced she was taking Maya home so she could get her ready for bed. They said their goodbyes to Nick before he went back outside to clean his grill and smoker.

"But it's only seven," I said as I followed my mom and Maya to the living room.

She helped Maya with her coat and said, "I know, but she's still recuperating. What if the temperature drops even more? It's better to get her home now rather than later. It's okay. You stay and help Nick, and I'll take care of Maya. No need to rush home."

I didn't miss that little smirk as she wrapped the scarf around Maya's neck. And then it all became crystal clear. If my daughter hadn't been right there, I would've told her where to go with her matchmaking efforts. But Maya didn't need to learn those kinds of Spanish words.

"Fine. You two go home, and I'll be there . . . *soon*." I made sure to emphasize the last word. Then I put the beanie on Maya's head, made sure her ears were covered, and sent them on their way.

After I'd watched them reach our driveway from Nick's living room window, I went back to the kitchen to start cleaning up. He came inside just as I was starting the dishwasher.

"All done," I said.

"Me too."

We looked at each other for a few silent seconds before I said, "Well, I'm going to go. Thanks again for dinner."

"Wait. I . . . if you want . . . you could hang out for a little longer. We could finish that bottle of wine, and I could show you the new firepit outside."

"You added a firepit?"

He nodded enthusiastically. "I actually just finished putting in the rocks around it. I know it's cold, but I think it will be warm enough once the flames get going. But if you need to get home to Maya, then I can show you another time."

I debated for a minute. But as much as I wanted to disappoint Gloria by showing up at home so soon, another glass of wine by a firepit sounded pretty amazing. "I can stay."

After I'd put my coat back on, we went outside.

"Wow. This looks very nice. I can't believe you did it yourself."

"It wasn't as hard as I thought it would be. They actually sell a kit at Lowe's."

"Of course they do," I said with a laugh.

Nick handed me a glass of wine, and I sat in one of the camping chairs he'd set up near the pit. Then he went inside and came back a minute later with a beanie and a blanket. "Just in case," he explained.

He lit the logs inside the pit, and a blaze of red, yellow, and orange flames ignited inside, immediately casting a wind of warmth in my direction. When he seemed satisfied with the fire, he grabbed his wineglass from the nearby patio table and finally sat down.

I could tell he was very pleased with what he'd built. It was nice to see him so happy.

"All right, I know you're dying to share," I said. "So go on. Tell me how you did this."

Nick didn't hesitate. "Since I wanted the pit ring-shaped, I had to get trapezoidal blocks. They're narrower on one side so the edges can fit snugly together to form the circle. I debated on whether to put it on the grass or directly on the patio. I figured the patio was safer . . ."

I listened intently as he spent the next several minutes explaining the process of how he'd built the firepit. When he was done, he apologized for boring me.

"I wasn't bored. In fact, I'm thinking that my backyard might need one too."

"Just say the word, and I'd be happy to do it."

"Great," I said, not being able to contain the huge grin I knew was spreading across my face.

"What?"

"What what?"

"What's with that look?"

I shrugged. "Must be the wine. And the fire."

"Come on. Tell me."

"I don't know. I guess it's nice to see you so excited about something. And I have to admit it's also very nice that you did something new, you know? Something that had no tie to her."

Nick nodded before taking a sip of his wine. "I guess that's why I wanted to do it. I wanted a place in the house—well, technically it's outside—but it's still a place that's all mine."

"Good for you." I meant what I'd said about it being nice to see him so excited about something. It was such a stark difference from the man I'd hidden from in the grocery store all those nights ago.

We sat there without speaking for several minutes. The night air pricked the skin on my face like cold needles, but I didn't care. It was nice sitting here with Nick while the crackling of the wood serenaded us and the embers of the flames kept us warm.

Finally, it was Nick who broke the comfortable silence. "So your mediation hearing is next Tuesday, right?"

"Yep. I can't believe it's already going to happen."

"Are you nervous about seeing him?" he asked softly.

"Yes. I'm also afraid," I admitted.

"Afraid of what?"

I hesitated. As much as Nick and I had grown closer, I wasn't sure how much I should share about David. Or rather, my feelings about David. There were things I knew I couldn't share with Gloria, mainly because she had a tendency to harp on things I'd rather forget.

If I couldn't confess this to her, then maybe I could share it with him.

"This is going to sound silly," I warned.

"Just tell me. What are you afraid of?"

"I'm afraid that when I see him, I'm not going to hate him. I'm afraid that I'm going to realize that I still love him, and I'm afraid that will mean I've been lying to myself this entire time."

Nick didn't say anything. He just nodded. And I knew he felt the same way about Rachel.

CHAPTER FORTY-ONE

THINGS I NEVER KNEW #1018: MY BEST FRIEND AND MY HUSBAND HAVE BEEN HAVING AN AFFAIR!

CHAPTER FORTY-TWO

The moment I saw David walk into the waiting room on his phone, I wanted to slap him.

Not because of the obvious reasons but because of one brand-new one.

The man looked exactly the same.

He didn't look tired. He didn't look skinnier. He didn't look like he'd aged a bit. On the outside, this David looked exactly like the old David.

I guess I'd expected to see someone else. It would explain how he could've done the things he'd done. I was expecting a monster to walk through those doors.

But it was just him.

Which meant it wasn't some demon or evil entity that had somehow transformed my husband into someone so cold and uncaring. It was really just David, and leaving me and Maya behind really had been that easy for him.

Whatever words I'd practiced for this moment went out the window. I couldn't speak. I couldn't move. Hell, I couldn't even stop staring at him.

We'd agreed to meet at the mediator's office building in Pasadena. Since it was our first session, I wasn't quite sure what to expect, but I'd done my research. What I couldn't prepare for was how I'd feel at seeing my husband again.

David finished his call and finally saw me. He walked over to me and bent down as if to give me a hug. I put out my hand to stop him.

He straightened his back and stuck his phone into his jacket pocket. "You look good, Claudia." His tone was friendly. Calm. I hated that. I hated that he didn't seem rattled like I was.

Dammit, Claudia. Stop being ridiculous. Don't let him dictate what you feel or how you act at this meeting.

I allowed my body to slowly untighten, glared at him, and didn't reply to his pitiful compliment.

"You know this whole mediation thing will go a lot smoother if you at least talk to me."

"I'll talk when we're in front of the mediator," I finally said.

I kept my promise. As soon as we were called into the conference room, I was ready to answer questions and had come with my own paperwork.

"All right, let's start by putting everything on the table," the mediator said before passing us water bottles. Her name was Carla Garrett, and she looked to be about the same age as Gloria. She kind of reminded me of a teacher I'd had in the fifth grade. She even wore the same wire-framed glasses.

"Let's start with you, Mrs. Flores," she said.

I took a sip of the water bottle. My heart was running a marathon in my chest, and I willed it to calm down. I had to keep it together. For Maya's sake. And mine.

"I want full custody of Maya," I began.

"Fine."

David's quick reply surprised me. So I added, "And child support."

He didn't say anything, but I could see the outline of his jaw tense.

"I want to keep the house," I continued.

David shook his head. "I want to sell it. And since I've been paying the mortgage, I feel like I should get sixty percent of the proceeds and you can have forty."

Carla cleared her throat. "Please, Mr. Flores. You will have your turn—"

"You moved out," I said, ignoring the mediator. "You abandoned your family and the house. That means you forfeit any claim to either."

"That's not how it works," he replied, and he sat back in his chair as if his words were the final say on the matter.

"Actually, if we take this to court, it will be up to a judge to decide how it works. And some still believe that abandonment should be a factor in deciding property division and even spousal support." It was a veiled threat, and I could see by the shock in David's eyes that he knew exactly what I meant. He opened his mouth, but before he could say anything, Carla told him to let me continue without interruption.

So I did.

Mercedes had come over last night to help me get it all organized. One of Carlos's friends was a divorce attorney and was very helpful about answering questions and offering tips on what to say and how much info to provide. Gloria, of course, wanted me to ask for everything I was entitled to.

It was important to me to prove to David how prepared I was and to show him that he wasn't going to be in control of what happened during the first meeting. I was ready to fight. Especially for full custody of Maya. I didn't care about anything else. It didn't matter if Rachel was going to be in the picture now or in the future. There was no way I was going to let David take Maya away from me. Especially since he'd already proven he wasn't interested in being a full-time father. I knew the only reason he'd fight me for custody was so that he wouldn't have to pay child support. It was an awful thought. But Mercedes, Gloria, and the divorce attorney had pretty much convinced me that I had to be ready.

Since I barely looked at him over the course of that hour, I really couldn't say if David seemed surprised. I did notice, however, that some of his responses toward the end seemed more frustrated. He challenged everything with a raised voice or a sigh, and he couldn't keep still in his chair.

We set a date for the next meeting, which would be over Zoom since David wasn't sure when he'd have time to come back to town. Then I walked out of the office while he was taking another call. I'd bet good money it was Rachel, asking how the meeting went.

But as I entered the parking lot, I heard him calling my name. I debated on whether to break out in a sprint toward my car.

I looked at my heels and decided it wasn't worth breaking an ankle.

I stopped walking and turned around to face David.

"Did I leave something behind?" I asked, making sure I sounded as irritated as possible. I wanted him to know that I was talking to him against my will.

"No, I-I just wanted to—" he began.

I didn't let him finish. "You wanted to what, David?"

"I wanted to make sure you're okay. That's all."

"Really? You didn't seem to care if I was okay when you were telling the mediator all the reasons why you shouldn't have to pay me any spousal support. And you sure didn't seem to care months ago, when you cut off the credit cards or told me I wasn't allowed to talk to you on the phone."

He dragged his hand down his face, and I knew I was getting to him.

Good.

"I know I messed up, and I hope one day you can forgive me for everything."

I let out a bitter laugh. "Why? So you can feel less guilty about destroying our family? Well, guess what? You don't get to get off that easy. And, by the way, no, I am not okay. Not because I miss you or want you back, but because you decided our marriage was over and I had no say. I was completely blindsided. You took away my ability to provide for Maya—our daughter. Again, without warning. What kind of man does that to his family?"

He looked down at the ground. "I thought a clean break would be for the best. I thought it would be easier."

"Yeah, for you. And don't give me this bullshit excuse that you thought it was for the best. You were just being a coward. You basically ran away from home like a child who didn't get his way. Poor baby."

David straightened his shoulders, and his face hardened. "Do you feel better now? How long have you been waiting to say all of that?"

For weeks, I thought. And I wasn't going to hold back.

"Hey, you're the one who came running after me. I thought I'd said everything I needed back in that meeting. But since you asked so nicely, I figured I'd answer your question."

"Fine," he said, and he put up his hands. "I get it. I deserve all the bad things."

I leaned forward a little to make sure he heard me. "Recibes lo que das," I said with a shrug.

He knew enough Spanish to understand me perfectly. "Just make sure Maya is ready. I'll be there in about an hour."

It wasn't until I was back in my car that I let it all out. I sobbed into my hands. The tears were an outlet for me to release all the stress I'd felt for the past few days. I was relieved that the meeting was over. And despite my fury, I was sad that our marriage would soon be over too.

Or at least the marriage I'd *thought* we'd had would be over.

So how could I be so distraught about losing David when it turned out I'd never really had him anyway?

The thought calmed me. Soon enough, it was replaced by new determination to not let David's return ruin what I had planned for Thanksgiving.

When I got home, I put on a smile and told Gloria that everything went great. Then I let Maya know that her daddy would be here in an hour to pick her up and to start getting ready. They were going to the children's museum in Pasadena and then dinner.

Although I'd kept my composure in front of David at the mediator's office, I was worried how I would react to seeing him back in our home.

How in the world was I going to feel knowing he wasn't coming back to stay? How in the hell was I going to pretend I was okay with knowing we would never be a family in this home again?

My mind drifted to the night before he left. Before that last argument, the three of us had had dinner at home and then watched a movie together in the family room. Maya had sat between David and me, holding a bowl of popcorn. It was just another night—nothing special about it, really. Had I known then that it would be our last as a family, I would've savored it more.

But that's the thing about lasts. You don't know they're happening until they're over.

Familiar grief revved my heartbeat, and tears wet my eyes as a new ache bloomed inside my chest. I didn't want Maya to see that I was losing it. I left her in the bedroom to finish getting ready and walked to the kitchen. I'd skipped lunch and could feel a headache coming on. I needed to eat, but my stomach didn't want anything. I still made myself walk into the pantry to look for a can of soup or crackers and spotted some Mexican sweet breads inside a covered container.

I smiled, remembering how excited Maya had been when we'd discovered a panaderia yesterday after her follow-up doctor's appointment. And she was even more thrilled when I said she could get the bread with the chocolate squares on top. It was yet another new food she had tried and enjoyed. It should've been something I could share with David. But when I saw him, it didn't even occur to me. Another reminder that he was not the man I'd married.

My stomach twisted.

I settled on an energy bar and walked back out.

A few minutes later, I put my nervous energy to work by focusing on my prep list for Thanksgiving dinner the day after tomorrow. Mercedes and Nick were going to join us, and I needed to go shopping for the last few items while Maya was out with her dad.

Plates and silverware stacked on the dining room table? Check.

Turkey brining in the fridge? Check.

Vegetables washed and ready to be chopped? Check.

Bottles of wine chilling in the fridge? Check.

Maya ready for her dad?

I sighed and walked back to Maya's bedroom. It was empty.

I found her with Gloria. She was dressed at least. Well, almost.

"I thought you were going to put your shoes on?" I said from the doorway.

"Grandma says my Mary Janes look nicer with my clothes, but I want to wear my sandals."

"Baby, your feet will be cold in sandals."

"Not if I wear socks or tights or socks with tights!"

Gloria laughed. "Your shoes won't fit if you wear both socks and tights."

"Please put on your Mary Janes. Your dad is going to be here soon, and I also need to comb your hair, and you need to wash your hands and face."

"But I took a bath this morning," she whined. "I'm still clean."

After my mom helped Maya with her shoes, I guided her into the guest bathroom.

I smiled as I combed her light-brown hair and placed two pretty barrettes on each side of her head. Her waves were as abundant as mine now. I wondered if she would ever want to straighten them like I did when I was a teenager. Once I became a mom, though, I didn't have time for all that. Now I just accepted their chaos. Some days I even loved them. "You look beautiful, mi amor!" I told Maya once I was done.

"Gracias, Mommy. I mean 'mi amor,'" she said with a smile. "Grandma says I should be a child model. What's that?"

I laughed. "Let's talk about that another day. Right now let's just worry about getting you ready for Daddy."

She nodded and stayed quiet as I finished the job. Just as I reached for a towel, the doorbell rang, and my heart nearly shot out of my chest.

"I'll get it," Gloria yelled from beyond the open bathroom door.

I concentrated on wetting a washcloth with warm water. "Now, let's clean your face," I told Maya as I began to wipe her cheeks and forehead.

A deep male voice traveled into the bathroom.

David was in our living room again. My living room.

"Mommy, why are you shaking? Are you cold?"

"What?" I said in confusion before looking down at my own hands. The tremble was slight, but it was there. God, if I couldn't hide my nerves from my kid, how in the hell was I going to hide them from David?

I tapped the tip of Maya's nose with my right index finger and gave her a quick kiss. "You know what? I am, a little bit. Why don't you go see Daddy, and I'll go find a sweater, okay?"

Maya nodded excitedly and took off. I threw the wet washcloth into the tub and adjusted the shower curtain. Not that David would say anything if he saw a dirty washcloth if he used the bathroom. But hiding it was something I could control, at least in that moment.

Then I did what any normal, emotionally mature adult woman would do when the universe had conspired to bring her face to face with her cheating ex for the second time in one day.

I ran to my bedroom to hyperventilate. Then I put on my big girl chonies and walked out a few minutes later.

Gloria was waiting for me in the hallway. "Where did you go?" she whispered.

"I was cold," I whispered back.

"He looks awful."

"No, he doesn't. Go wait in your room until he leaves." She opened her mouth to argue but stopped when I pointed my finger to her door.

When I found David and Maya, they were in her bedroom, and she was showing him all her new bilingual books.

"I know lots more words, Daddy. Mercedes says when she goes to Mexico next year, she's going to bring me more."

David looked at me. "Mercedes?"

"That's Mommy's boss. She owns this pretty store, and when I get older she says I can work there if I want."

"You guys should get going so you'll have lots of time to spend at the museum," I said, trying not to think of all the information Maya was going to be sharing about me during their visit.

The three of us walked out to the living room. Gloria was there waiting.

Oh dear Lord. Why did that woman never listen to me?

"Gloria, Maya has been telling me all the fun things you've been doing together," David said. "It's nice that you were able to visit. When are you planning to go back to Florida?"

She smiled with her lips when she walked up to him. But her eyes told a different story.

I don't want you here, but I'm going to tolerate your presence for Maya's sake.

"I'm staying as long as I need to," she said.

David nodded and offered her one of his own fake smiles. He'd known—and had accepted—what would be in store for him. I'd warned him after Maya got out of the hospital that Gloria was in town and staying at the house. I didn't offer any further explanation because I didn't owe him one. But the next few hours were all about doing right by Maya. Feelings and ego didn't matter. So everyone had to play nice—even if it killed us.

David put his hands on his hips. "All right, well, I guess we'll be leaving. Say goodbye, sweetheart."

Maya gave Gloria and me kisses, and we waved until David drove away. He'd rented a car instead of taking the Lexus. I'd found out at the mediation hearing, though, that he planned to eventually take it with him to San Francisco.

"He looks skinny," Gloria said once we were back inside the house.

"No, he doesn't," I argued again.

"And I don't remember him being so . . . stiff looking."

"Okay, now you're just being ridiculous. Grab your purse, we have to go to the market."

The day had already been a lot. I was exhausted. But I wasn't going to let David ruin my excitement about hosting Thanksgiving dinner.

I had just walked into the kitchen when I heard something crash behind me. I spun around and saw Gloria bracing herself on the entryway table and one of my candles lying on the tile floor.

"What happened?" I asked after reaching her.

"I . . . I don't know. I just felt a little dizzy. Help me to the couch."

Holding her arm, I walked with my mom to the family room and helped her sit down. Then I sat down next to her. "What's wrong?"

"I've had a headache all day, that's all. And I barely ate, so I guess I'm feeling lightheaded."

My gut told me there was more to the story. There always was when it came to Gloria.

"Mom, what is going on with you? A few weeks ago you couldn't see even with your new prescription and blamed it on the fact that you have to wear bifocals now. When Nick came over for dinner, you refused to write down the recipe because you said your eyes were tired."

She shrugged. "I'm getting old, Claudia. What do you expect? My eyes aren't what they used to be."

"Give me your phone," I said as I held out my hand.

"What? Why?"

"Because I'm going to call Carlos and ask him to tell me the truth."

Her eyes widened. "No, you're not."

"Fine, don't give me your phone. I'll look up his dealership website and start calling every lot until I find him."

I stood up, determined to get answers once and for all. Gloria shot up and then immediately fell back down on the couch. She moaned, and I knew she was in some real pain. That scared me.

"Mother. Please tell me what's wrong with you."

She closed her eyes and put her head back. I gave her a minute.

"Gloria . . ." I began.

"Fine, okay, I'll tell you," she finally said begrudgingly. "Three months ago I went to my eye doctor to get new glasses, and she thought she saw something in one of the scans. She referred me to an ophthalmologist, and he says I have a tumor behind my left eye."

My heart stopped. "A tumor?"

She finally opened her eyes and lifted her head to look at me. "It's called an orbital tumor. When I went back to Florida, it was to see a different doctor and get a second opinion. This doctor agreed with the first. The tumor can be removed, but I'll most likely lose my vision in that eye."

"Oh my God." My shock immediately turned to anger. "I knew there was something. Why didn't you call me when you first found out?"

She shrugged. "I did. I called you that night."

I was confused for a few seconds. Then I knew. "That was the night I got drunk and told you about David and Rachel. And asked you to come." I whispered the last sentence.

"Yeah. Suddenly my little tumor didn't seem like such a big deal anymore. It was the first time you'd asked me for anything in decades. I know I wasn't the best mother, and I didn't always show up when you needed me. I wasn't going to *not* show up for you one last time—tumor be damned."

"What do you mean 'one last time'? Are they worried about it being cancer?"

"Not yet. If I get the surgery soon, the odds are better. But I'm just trying to be a realist about the whole . . . situation."

"Mom, this isn't a situation. You have a tumor!"

Usually Gloria was a drama queen. If there was ever a time to be extra dramatic, now was it. Her almost nonchalant tone made me furious.

"This is just like you!" I yelled.

She looked taken aback. "Why are you so mad?"

"Because I've been asking you for weeks what was wrong. Turns out you were just avoiding dealing with something kind of huge—per usual. What was your endgame, Mom? Were you just going to hide from your doctors and Carlos here and just accept the fact that you could have cancer?"

"I wasn't hiding," she said defiantly. "I'm *not* hiding. I just chose to focus on you and Maya instead of me. Isn't that why you hate me so much? Because I never put you first?"

"I don't hate you," I admitted. "But yes, you have never put what's best for me before what's easier for you."

As soon as I said the words, I knew their implication.

My mother had finally done the one thing I had always wanted. Maybe it wasn't going to cost her her vision or her life, but it had still been a sacrifice.

Tears began to stream down my face. Gloria reached out and grabbed my hands. "I'm sorry I didn't tell you until now. I'll get the surgery. I'll get radiation. I'll do whatever it takes to make sure I have years and years to put you and Maya first. I promise."

She was crying now too.

And for the first time in a long time, my mother hugged me, and I was glad that she did.

CHAPTER FORTY-THREE

It was a perfect Thanksgiving Day in South Pasadena.

The sun was out, but the temperature was in the low seventies. The turkey was in the oven, and the pies were cooling on the counter. I was looking forward to dinner. Especially since I was going to share it with the people who had helped me through one of the hardest seasons of my life.

"I can't find my Día de Gracias book," Maya said as I set the dining room table. She'd been occupied for the past two hours watching the Macy's parade on TV and making colorful cards for each of our guests with hand-printed turkeys on the front. The parade must have been over if she was now looking for the book Mercedes had given her while she was in the hospital.

"Weren't you reading it last night with Grandma? Why don't you go ask her to see if she put it somewhere after you went to sleep?"

"She's taking her shower," Maya whined.

"All right, help me with the forks and napkins, and then we'll go look for it."

I tried not to show Maya that I was worried about Gloria taking a shower. Although she hadn't had another dizzy spell since Tuesday, that didn't mean she wouldn't have one again. As usual, she was being stubborn about my concerns. The one good thing about her trying to prove to me that she was fine was that she helped me all day yesterday with prepping and cooking for today. She'd even offered to make my abuela's special stuffing—a dish I hadn't eaten since I was a teenager. I had no idea that she even knew the recipe.

After locating Maya's Día de Gracias book on a shelf in Gloria's room, I went to work assembling the macaroni and cheese so it could go in the oven just before the turkey came out. Mercedes and Nick were going to arrive at three. She was bringing arroz and calabacita con queso for two additional side dishes, and Nick was bringing the rolls and bottles of sparkling cider.

About two hours later, I emerged from my bedroom dressed with a full face of makeup. I walked into the kitchen and inhaled the most delicious aromas.

"I love the smell of Thanksgiving," I told Gloria, who was standing next to the stove mashing the potatoes I'd cooked before jumping in the shower.

"Me too," she said.

"Did you cook last year, or did you and Carlos go out?"

"I ordered a dinner from one of our favorite restaurants. He worked most of the day, so he came home only to eat and then left again. It was almost just like any other day."

Unexpected sadness swept through my heart. I hadn't ever thought how lonely the holidays must have been for Gloria over the years. We hadn't spent a Christmas together since the one right before I married David. And I couldn't even remember our last Thanksgiving, but I'd bet it was probably just a few years after my abuela had died. I knew I shouldn't feel guilty. The Gloria I knew back then was very different from the Gloria who'd shown up on my doorstep three months ago. For most of my teenage years and adulthood, I'd thought that maybe my life would've been better if Gloria hadn't been in it.

Now I couldn't imagine it without her.

My eyes watered, blurring the bowl of corn I was mixing butter into. I pushed away the grim and regretful thoughts. Today was a day to be thankful for what we had, not what we could lose. I didn't want to be sad. Not today. Not tomorrow. Not anymore.

The doorbell rang, pulling me from my heavy thoughts. Maya yelled that she would answer it. A few seconds later, animated voices traveled down the hallway, signaling that at least one of our dinner guests had arrived.

"Happy Thanksgiving!" Mercedes sang from the doorway. She held two foil-covered pans.

I walked over and took the pans from her. "Happy Thanksgiving," I said and then kissed her on the cheek. She greeted my mom with a big hug.

To my surprise, Gloria hugged her back.

Mercedes had become an important part of my life. I hoped both women would become friends. Or at least friendly acquaintances.

"It smells amazing in here," Mercedes said as she took a seat at the kitchen table. "I'm starving. I barely ate any breakfast and I skipped lunch because I wanted to eat as much as possible tonight."

I laughed as I transferred Mercedes's sides to the serving dishes I had waiting on the counter. "I admit that I might have nibbled on a few things while I was cooking. I couldn't help it."

"Me too," my mom said. "I was hoping the turkey would be done sooner so I could pick off some meat and make me a sandwich."

"Please tell me you didn't?" I said, and I checked the cooked turkey that had been resting on top of the stove.

Gloria waved me off. "Don't worry, I didn't. But that's only because you came out of your room when you did."

The doorbell rang a second time, and Maya yelled again about answering it.

"That must be Nick."

"I'm so glad you invited him, Claudia," Mercedes said softly.

"Me too," I agreed.

Nick walked into the kitchen a few seconds later with two grocery bags. "Happy Thanksgiving, everyone." He wore a brown-and-beige flannel shirt, jeans, and tennis shoes. I smiled as I thought about how many times he'd asked what the dress code was for dinner.

Mercedes and Gloria waved from where they were. I headed over to take the bags from him.

"I wasn't sure what rolls to buy because I didn't know if you wanted the kind you heat up in the oven or not. So I got both kinds."

"You're a smart guy, Nick," Mercedes joked.

"Thank you," I told him. "Either one is going to be fine. And now we have enough for leftover turkey sandwiches too."

Gloria and I served dinner just after three thirty. The conversation was lively, except for when everyone was stuffing their faces. I was so proud of Maya for trying one piece of turkey. She also ate some mashed potatoes and a little bit of the macaroni and cheese I'd made just for her. She was excited to drink cider in what she called a "grown-up glass" and couldn't wait for her dessert of chocolate chip ice cream.

My personal favorite was definitely my abuela's dressing—it tasted just like I'd remembered. The mix of carrots, bell peppers, potatoes, olives, and spices all cooked together in a hearty pork-flavored broth was pure comfort. Mercedes's calabacita was also a hit with everyone. Even Maya seemed intrigued by the dish of diced zucchini, tomatoes, and corn. Most likely because it was topped with layers of melted cheese. While she eventually decided against tasting it, she did say it smelled good, and maybe she'd try it another day. I took that as a win.

"Claudia, the turkey is delicious," Mercedes said. "What's your secret?"

"A two-day brine," I said.

"That's how my mom used to do it," Nick said. Our eyes met, and I could see the realization hitting his brain in real time.

"Yeah. Um, Rachel is the one who told me about it," I said, and I immediately took a gulp of my red wine.

"Who's Auntie Rachel eating Thanksgiving dinner with?" Maya said innocently.

The adults in the room all looked at each other with uneasiness. It was Nick who finally said something. "She's with her friend today."

It was a simple explanation, and luckily it was all Maya needed.

The awkwardness eventually dissipated, and everyone went back to talking about the food and what their plans were for the long holiday weekend. Nick wanted to work on some things at the house that needed fixing. Gloria wanted to do some shopping.

Poor Mercedes had to work. The day after Thanksgiving and the following Saturday were two of Tesoro's busiest days of the year.

"As your business manager, I hope you sell out of every single thing. And as your friend, I hope you sell out of everything," I told her.

"From your lips to God's ears," Mercedes said. I knew she was hoping for a big turnout tomorrow. She'd doubled up on some of the inventory, so she was betting on lots of sales to bring her into the black. I'd encouraged her to switch to an emailed newsletter instead of a paper one. Not only would it save her the expense of paper and postage, but she could also send it out more frequently. As I suspected, her newsletter sign-ups had nearly doubled.

"Well, just make sure there's still some stuff left for me by the time I get there," Gloria added.

We all laughed.

By the time the dishes were cleared and leftovers packed, I was left feeling very satisfied, in more ways than one.

Mercedes and I decided we were still too full for pumpkin pie, but my mom and Nick eagerly cut themselves a piece each, adding a mountain of whipped cream to the top. Maya was content with her ice cream until Nick suggested adding whipped cream to her bowl. Her eyes grew big at her first taste, and she thought it was the most exciting thing ever.

"It tastes like a cloud," she said in amazement. "I love it!"

All I could think was that her daily dairy intake had definitely been met.

It was almost six when Mercedes announced she needed to get home and get to bed. She was planning to get to Tesoro by five in the morning to get everything ready.

"I can still come by and help if you need," I said as I walked her to the front door.

"I'll call you if I need reinforcements, okay?"

We hugged, and she thanked me again for dinner. Then I sent her on her way with a market bag filled with leftovers in disposable containers.

Nick said he was going to head out too. "I don't want to overstay my welcome. Plus, I should probably call my mom and ask her how her dinner at my aunt's house went."

"I'll walk with you," I said, reaching for my sweater.

"No, it's okay. It's kind of chilly out there."

I waved him off. "You carry the extra bottles of wine I'm giving you and the bag of turkey and rice leftovers. I'll carry the containers of everything else, plus the plate with the slices of pumpkin pie."

He agreed and said goodbye to my mom and Maya, and we walked outside.

"I want to thank you again for inviting me," he said once I'd closed my front door. "My mom wanted me to fly to Texas, but I just didn't feel like being around a bunch of relatives. I'm sure all of them know what happened by now, and I couldn't stand to think of people looking at me."

"With pity?" I said.

"Yep."

"I totally understand. I guess that's the good thing about not having any close relatives living nearby. I only have to worry about Gloria, and I'm used to her no-filter comments."

We both laughed because it was true.

Just then a small gust of wind blew past us, sweeping the napkin I'd covered the pumpkin pie plate with onto the ground. We both bent down at the same time to reach for it. Our fingers touched, and we both froze.

Another gust of wind blew the napkin away, but we still didn't move. After a few seconds, I moved to pull my hand away, but Nick grabbed it and held tight.

We stood up, still holding hands. His grasp was firm and warm. And I liked the way his fingers curled around mine. We didn't say anything for a while. Instead, we just kept staring at one another with our hands intertwined.

His hot breath fanned my face, and it sent goose bumps everywhere.

Every sensation in my body seemed to spring to life. Every nerve was heightened. My cheeks flushed. My neck tingled. The hairs on my arms felt as if they'd been zapped by invisible lightning. And a longing I hadn't felt in months made everywhere else ache with need.

But when another gust of air threatened to topple the plate of now-exposed pumpkin pie slices, I let go to hold on to it.

"We probably should get these leftovers into your fridge before we have to chase them down the street," I said.

"Yeah. We better." But he didn't move for a few more seconds.

I waited for Nick to walk down the steps and then followed. We made it to the sidewalk and turned toward his house.

"Oh, and sorry about the whipped cream," he said. "I didn't realize Maya had never tried it. I hope I didn't create a whipped cream monster."

The air between us, in more ways than one, was different now. I told myself that was a good thing. Whatever moment had happened back on my porch was over. I'd overthink it later.

"Don't even worry about it," I replied. "She's a picky eater, so I'm happy when she just tries new foods. Believe me, I'm not above covering veggies or fish in whipped cream if it means she'll at least taste them."

Nick let out a hearty laugh as we turned onto his driveway. I moved behind him as we walked next to his truck. Then I nearly ran into him when he came to a complete stop all of a sudden.

"Hey, I almost lost your pumpkin pie slices again," I said with a laugh as I repositioned the plate and containers in my hands.

His silence finally made me look up, and I saw that he was staring directly at the front of his house. I came around from behind him and followed his gaze. The delicious Thanksgiving dinner I'd spent two days cooking now felt like a pile of rocks in my gut.

Rachel was standing on the porch.

"You changed the locks?" she said.

CHAPTER FORTY-FOUR

When the knock on my door finally came about two hours later, I didn't tense up. In fact, I relaxed a little. I didn't get up, though.

It was as if I'd been waiting for this moment for months, and I was ready for it to be over and done with. I had almost convinced myself that I didn't want to talk to Rachel. But as soon as I'd seen her on Nick's porch, I knew I needed to—for my own peace of mind. I had told Gloria to take Maya to the movies and to not come back until I'd texted her to.

Time to rip off the Band-Aid.

I yelled from where I was sitting on the couch, "It's open!"

The door creaked, and then I heard it softly close.

"Can I talk to you?" I heard Rachel ask from behind me.

"Yes."

She came around the couch and took a seat on the armchair on the other side of the coffee table. My eyes traveled from her head to her toes. Unlike with David, I saw some subtle changes. Her usual light-brown hair also now had salon-provided highlights. The beige cashmere sweater and black leather boots were new—and looked expensive. I couldn't help but wonder if David had canceled my credit card in order to give Rachel one of her own.

"How are you?" she had the nerve to ask.

My glare must have been enough of an answer because she quickly followed up with, "Sorry. That was a dumb question. I'm nervous and not sure what to say to you right now."

It didn't make me feel any better to hear she was nervous. In fact, I didn't want to hear one word about how she was feeling. I didn't care.

"Then why are you here?" I asked bitterly. "Wait, have you been in town this whole week with David?"

She cleared her throat. "No. He came here alone and is already back in San Francisco. We were supposed to go to some party for his work, but I wasn't feeling up to it. So I found a last-minute flight and came straight here from the airport."

"Why?"

"Because I owe you an apology . . . and an explanation."

My eyes narrowed in her direction. "An explanation? Seriously? There is no explaining that would ever justify what you did to me. What you did to Nick."

Rachel slowly nodded and then clasped and unclasped her hands in her lap. "Okay. Then just an apology. I'm sorry."

If there were any two words in the world that could mean less to me, then I had no idea what they were. There was nothing behind them. They sounded hollow. They sounded like a lie.

I scoffed. "No, you're not."

Rachel's eyebrows shot up to her hairline. "Yes, I am."

"You're only saying it because you know that's what you should say. But I can tell when you're saying something just to say it. Did David make you come here and apologize to me or something?"

She hesitated. "No," she finally said after a few seconds.

Her admission stung me unexpectedly because I could tell she wasn't lying. But why was I surprised? Then the realization hit me, and my chest tightened with emotion.

"Nick told you to apologize to me. Didn't he?"

Rachel hesitated again before admitting, "Yes, but I was going to do it anyway. I came back to South Pasadena to apologize to both of you."

The anger I'd been holding on to for weeks would no longer be contained.

"And what exactly are you here to apologize for? Sleeping with my husband for months behind my back? Knowing he was going to leave me out of the blue and not warning me? Telling him to get a mediator, cut me off financially, and not call his daughter?" The last part of that sentence finally got me, and my voice broke. But I was determined to say everything I wanted to say to Rachel because even in this moment I knew I would never speak to her again.

"Or how about apologizing for basically ghosting me for months? We have been in each other's lives for more than twenty years. Even when we lived in different states, we texted or spoke on the phone almost every day," I said through tears. "You were my sister, Rachel. You were my family! And without one word, you were gone. The irony of it all is that you were the one person in the world I needed to help me get through this, and I couldn't pick up the phone to talk to you about it."

Tears ran down her cheeks, and she looked down and nodded. But even now she had no words for me.

I wiped my face with the back of my hand and wiped my nose with the sleeve of my shirt. After a minute, I was able to take a breath and gain back some of my composure.

Rachel looked up and nodded, but she didn't move. My tolerance for her presence had disappeared, and I could no longer be in the same room as her. But before I could get up from the couch, she rushed out, "I swear I never meant to hurt you, Claudia. But I couldn't help it. You know I don't always think of the consequences, I just act. I do things I will eventually regret, especially when I'm drunk. That's why I tried to kiss David on the night of your rehearsal dinner."

It was as if the ground beneath my feet disappeared. I felt as if I'd fallen into a black hole. "You what?"

She seemed surprised that I didn't know. "Gloria never told you? She saw us. Well, technically, David saw her and pushed me away.

Afterward she threatened to tell you so you'd cancel the wedding. This whole time I just assumed you didn't believe her."

The memory of that night came rushing back. She had tried to convince me to call off the wedding, but she never said explicitly why. Rachel was right. I wouldn't have believed her. In the handful of times it had come down to either taking Gloria's side or Rachel's, I would always choose Rachel. Gloria probably knew that. And telling me would only make me mad at her. I might have been mad enough to tell her she couldn't come to the wedding at all.

"That was over ten years ago," I said. "What's your excuse for everything else?"

Rachel opened her mouth. Then seemed to consider what she was about to say carefully. "I don't have one. I know you probably don't want to hear this, but we both tried really hard to stay away from each other. That's why I stopped coming around as much and always wanted to hang out just the two of us."

Another realization hit. "That's why you backed out of Thanksgiving last year?"

She nodded. "But it didn't help. Then the first time it happened, we both swore it would never happen again."

I braced myself. "When was the first time?"

"Earlier this year. Just after my birthday."

I racked my brain thinking about what had happened in February because how could they have managed to be together behind my back? Then I remembered David had been out of town.

"His conference in New York? You went with him?"

She didn't nod. Just explained. "We told each other it would just be those two days. We'd get it out of our system and then go back to the way things had always been."

I couldn't breathe. It was as if Rachel were sucking the oxygen out of the room with her confession. "But you didn't . . . you didn't get it out of your system, did you?" I almost added a not-so-nice name at the end of that comment.

Rachel shook her head. "What can I say? I was unhappy with Nick, and David always seemed like such a good guy. Maybe there was a part of me that had always wanted to be with him, but I never thought I'd actually pursue a relationship with him. But once it became clear he was open to it, then it was like I had the permission I'd always wanted to go through with it."

I couldn't help but scoff. She talked about David as if he was some prize to achieve. But I shouldn't have been surprised. Rachel was always wanting what she couldn't have. Whether it was a Gucci purse or my husband, she just wanted to win.

I was too disgusted to speak. So Rachel continued.

"And once it hit me what I was doing to you, what I was doing to Nick, it was too late. But I'm not a bad person. You have to know that this was the last thing in the world I wanted. I will regret what I did for the rest of my life. Deep down, you know I wouldn't hurt you on purpose. You have to know that because you know me—the real me."

The memory of meeting Rachel that first day flashed before my eyes like a movie and was followed by a million more. Snapshots appeared of all the firsts we'd experienced together—the first time we'd drunk a beer, when we learned how to drive, the first time a boy broke one of our hearts. We'd held each other countless times as we cried until we laughed or laughed until we cried. We had gotten through so much of this life together, and I had never imagined there would be a time when Rachel wouldn't be a part of mine.

She had truly been my person.

Then the pictures disappeared, and old conversations began whispering in my ear—conversations I'd either forgotten or ignored. Her little digs about me being a stay-at-home mom, her sarcastic comments about wishing she'd met someone like David, her hollow explanations about why she could never spend time with just Maya and me.

Gloria had been right all along. I'd had a blind spot when it came to Rachel. Not because I was naive, but because I had wanted to believe that she had loved me as much as I had loved her.

Rachel had been my best friend. But was I ever hers?

Her words still hung in the air. *You know me—the real me.*

I met Rachel's eyes and stood up. "Actually, I don't think I ever knew you at all. You should go," I finally said. "I thought I could sit here and hash it all out. But I can't. More importantly, I don't want to. What you did was unforgiveable. You no longer get to have access to me or to my daughter. Now, get the fuck out of my house."

CHAPTER FORTY-FIVE

The next day I decided I needed to get out of the house myself.

I had no idea if Rachel had stayed with Nick last night. It was none of my business, of course. But I knew I didn't want to stick around to find out or risk her coming back to try to talk some more.

"I'm going over to help Mercedes," I said to Gloria after breakfast.

She took a sip of her coffee before saying anything. "Did she call you?"

"No, but it will be a good distraction."

Gloria nodded in understanding. We'd stayed up until almost two in the morning going over everything Rachel had confessed. She'd been worried that I'd be upset that she hadn't told me what she'd seen the night of my rehearsal dinner. I told her I understood why she hadn't.

Then she'd said something I had begun to believe myself. "I think Rachel has always been jealous of you," she said. "I think you got the life she thought she should have. Maybe she even believed that she deserved it more than you did."

I thought about my mom's words all night, which meant I barely slept. Still, I couldn't sit around waiting for something to happen. What I didn't tell my mom was that I didn't want to wait for Nick to call or come over either. Because if he didn't, then it would confirm something I didn't want to know—that he'd picked Rachel too. For all I knew, she'd convinced him to take her back. Why else had she traveled back to South Pasadena last minute without David?

It felt like junior high all over again. Only this time, Rachel was the mean girl. The ultimate Cabrona.

Tesoro was as busy as I thought it would be. In fact, the entire downtown South Pasadena area was bustling with cars and pedestrians. I had to park in a lot a few blocks away. Mercedes was glad to see me. Part of me knew she wouldn't have called even if she'd needed me. She and Gloria could have a contest to see who was the most stubborn, and it would end up being a tie.

For the next four hours, I stocked shelves and helped customers, while Mercedes rang up their purchases at the register. All the Día de Muertos items were on sale, and most of the inventory was gone even before I arrived. The business manager in me kept seeing profit every time someone left the store with a bagful of merchandise.

"Excuse me, can you tell me what these are used for?"

I stopped folding T-shirts to help the woman standing in front of our pottery and cookware section.

"The small pot is known as a cazuela," I began to explain. "You can use it for cooking or decoration. It's lead-free and made with a traditional terra-cotta clay called barro rojo."

"And this?" she said, raising the item in her right hand.

"That is a mini chiminea burner. It's for incense sticks or incense cones. Some people also like to use them as candleholders. The scent of whatever you're burning travels up through the narrow spout."

The woman seemed to like what I'd said and took the items with her as she continued to shop. I was proud of myself for being able to answer her questions. A few weeks ago, I wouldn't have known the difference between a cazuela and a regular clay pot. Mercedes had taught me so much about Mexican imports, especially how indigenous artisans relied on the income from these handcrafted imports not only to stay in their villages, but to basically survive. It was also a way to protect the legacy and heritage of different groups of indigenous peoples.

Maybe one day I'd even get to meet some of these artisans and see their work firsthand.

When it started to slow down around three in the afternoon, Mercedes ordered me to go home and get something to eat. She'd brought leftovers from last night, but there wasn't enough food for me.

"All right," I said after she'd told me to leave for the third time. "But I can come back if you need me."

"It's just going to get slower. And I know for a fact you were on your feet all day cooking yesterday. You must be exhausted. Go home and don't come back."

I hadn't told Mercedes about Rachel's visit. There hadn't been time, nor was it the place. It could wait until tomorrow or even Monday. And as much as I hadn't wanted to stay at the house that morning, eating some leftovers and then taking a nap was starting to sound like a good idea.

"Okay. I'll call you tomorrow."

She nodded before turning to help a customer who had questions about the Talavera tiles.

I grabbed my purse from the back office and walked outside. I'd only made it about halfway down the block when I recognized the man coming toward me.

Nick.

"Hey," he said when we met on the sidewalk.

I squared my shoulders as if to brace myself for whatever he was going to say next. "Hey. What are you doing here?"

"I tried calling and texted you a few times. When you didn't answer, I went over to the house, and Gloria said you were helping Mercedes at the store. So I decided to stop by to see if you wanted to get lunch or maybe a coffee when you had some time. I think we should talk."

"Yeah," I said, nodding. "Um, there's a café another block or so down this street. Let's go there."

We didn't speak as we made the short trip. Nick ordered himself a regular coffee once we got to the restaurant's counter. Luckily, we'd missed the lunch rush, and there were barely any people inside. I ordered an iced tea and a turkey croissant sandwich, even though I could hear my abuela scolding me in my ear that *You have turkey at home*.

But I was hungrier than I'd realized.

We found a table in the corner and waited for the employee to let us know when our order was ready.

"Was it busy at Tesoro?" he said after a few moments of awkward silence.

"Oh, yeah. The morning especially. I'm happy for Mercedes. She seemed really pleased with the turnout."

"That's good."

"I might help her tomorrow too. The chamber of commerce has been promoting their Small Business Saturday campaign all over town the past few days, so I wouldn't be surprised if tomorrow is just as busy."

The employee came over with our drinks and let me know my sandwich would be ready soon. I waited until he walked away before asking the question I wasn't sure I wanted to know. "So, is Rachel still in town?"

Nick shook his head. "She had an early flight this morning back to San Francisco. I'm assuming she made it."

"Oh, you two didn't talk some more last night?"

"Nah. After she came back from seeing you, she ordered herself an Uber and said she was just going to stay the night at the airport."

Relief swept through me. Followed by guilt. What if Nick had wanted her to stay with him?

"And you were okay with that?" I carefully asked.

He shrugged after taking a sip of his coffee. "I actually don't feel any type of way about it. Whatever Rachel does or doesn't do isn't my concern anymore. What about you?"

Before I could answer, the café employee arrived with my sandwich, and I took a small bite. It was okay, but I knew any sandwich I'd have made at home would've been ten times better.

I finally answered Nick after swallowing. "I couldn't care less about Rachel having to stay overnight at LAX," I said honestly.

A tiny smile escaped his lips. But his eyes were more serious. "I meant, how are you doing after seeing and talking to Rachel again?"

"I'm not sure. Numb? Sad? Angry. I guess I'm feeling everything and nothing at the same time. Does that make sense?"

"Yeah." He nodded. "I was the same way last night."

"Did you get your answers?" I asked.

"I guess so? It's funny. This whole time I kept thinking that the more information I had, the better or more okay I would feel. I thought it was the not knowing that was keeping me angry. After talking with her, though, it's like the details don't even matter, because the ending is still the same."

I thought about that, and it hit me hard. Nick was right. It didn't matter if David and Rachel's affair started this year or at the rehearsal dinner. I was never going to be able to change the fact that they'd both betrayed me. That they'd both hurt me. And now I had lost my husband and my best friend. How I got here wasn't that important anymore. How I moved on from here was what I needed to focus on.

"I think I finally see that too. Obviously I wish what happened never happened. But I'm not going to do myself or Maya any favors with what-ifs or 'Why us?'"

"Exactly," Nick said. "So what's next?"

"A nap, I hope," I said with a chuckle. "After that, who knows? I've always been a big planner and needed to be prepared for whatever was around the corner. This experience has taught me that there are some things in life that you can't ever prepare for. So I'm going to take it easy on myself for a while and just exist in the moment with my daughter. She needs me to be present and help her deal with her emotions. After I know she's going to be okay, then I'll worry about what comes next."

"That sounds like a very good nonplan plan."

"And what about you, Nick? Are you going to be okay?"

He nodded. "I finally think I am. I don't know what's next for me either. But seeing and talking to Rachel let me know that whatever that is, it's not going to be with her. And I wasn't as sad as I thought I'd be to accept that."

"I'm glad to hear it. And for whatever it's worth, I hope your plans include having me as a friend."

That made him smile. "They most definitely do."

Later that night, I was feeling much better. A three-hour nap and a homemade turkey sandwich plus sides definitely helped. Gloria stepped up and handled bath time so I could just rest and watch television. We did the handoff for bedtime. She'd offered, but I told her I wanted to because I had something to give Maya that I'd bought at Tesoro earlier in the day.

"Another book?" she asked excitedly when I handed it to her.

I sat down on the bed next to her. "Sort of. But this is the kind of book that *you* write yourself. It's called a journal, or you could even call it a diary."

Maya touched the cover of the glossy spiral notebook with its whimsical design of hearts and flowers and papel picado. Then she opened it and flipped through the blank lined pages.

"What do I write about?" she asked.

"Anything you want. You can write about your day, things you want to do, or you can write about your feelings. That way you don't keep them inside. You can talk to me about anything, Maya. I hope you know that. But sometimes it might be hard to say the words, so this way you can write them down instead."

"Do you have a diary, Mommy?"

"I do," I said with a smile. "I have lots, actually. I've been writing in them since I was a little girl like you."

Her eyes grew big. "Wow. You must have a hundred diaries!"

I laughed. "Not quite. But yes, I have a lot. And they helped me with my feelings."

"Do you still write in your diary?"

"I haven't in a while. But I think I'm going to start again soon. Now, remember, if there's anything you ever want to talk to me about or ask me and if it's too hard, then you write it down here. Okay?"

She nodded and then closed the journal. "Can I ask you something now, Mommy?"

My mom intuition kicked in, and I knew what was coming. And as much as I wasn't sure if I was ready to have the conversation, I knew I had to face it for Maya's sake. "Yes, of course. Ask me anything."

"Is Daddy ever going to move back home with us?"

I let out a long sigh. I gave myself several seconds before answering. "No, baby. He's not."

Her tiny bottom lip quivered, and her eyes became shiny with tears. "Why?" she said softly. My heart broke as I saw her struggling so hard not to cry. I knew she was trying to be brave, and I hated that my eight-year-old felt like she needed to be.

I pulled her into my arms and held her tight. "Sometimes mommies and daddies decide it would be better if they didn't live together anymore. But that doesn't mean we don't love you, and it absolutely is not because of anything you've done. Remember when you were in the first grade and Caitlyn was your best friend? But now that you're in second grade, your best friend is Amy. It's kind of like that."

"Is Uncle Nick your new best friend?" she asked.

I tried not to laugh. "Uncle Nick is my friend. But I wouldn't call him my best friend."

"Oh. Am I still going to see Daddy?"

"Yes, baby. Daddy is always going to be your daddy. Just because he doesn't live with you doesn't mean he's going to stop being your daddy. He loves you so much. We both do."

"Tommy Estrada says his daddy doesn't live with him anymore, but he's going to go on vacation with him for Christmas."

"That's nice for Tommy," I said.

We stayed there holding each other for a little while. I knew it was what we both needed.

"Thank you for my diary, Mommy," Maya said after a few minutes.

"You're welcome. Is there anything else you want to ask me?" I felt her shake her head against my chest. So I leaned down to kiss her cheek and then tucked her into bed. When I tried to take the journal from her, she held on to it.

"I want to sleep with it, so then I can dream about what I want to write."

"That's a great idea," I said with a smile. "Good night, baby. Te amo."

"Te amo, too, Mommy."

I got up from the bed and turned to leave, and then I saw my mother standing in the doorway. She followed me to the family room, and we both sat on the couch.

"How much did you hear?" I asked after a long sigh.

"Enough," she said with a shrug. "I didn't know you still kept a diary."

"I didn't want you to know. That was the point."

"You know, when I gave that to you, I honestly thought you were just going to color in it."

I laughed. "Well, you did bring it back from Las Vegas with crayons that said 'Treasure Island' on the package."

"That's right," Gloria chuckled. "Danny made us stop there to watch the pirate show."

"Donny."

"Who?" my mom asked, her raised eyebrows accentuating her confusion.

"Donny was the guy who took you to Vegas. I remember because Abuela kept referring to you as Marie that weekend."

"Who?" Her eyebrows shot up again.

I was in disbelief. "You know, Donny and Marie?" Gloria looked at me with a blank stare.

"She really didn't make you watch TV with her, did she?" I said and laughed into my hand.

Gloria shook her head. "Well, maybe I should start writing in a diary. You know, if I don't go blind."

"Mother," I groaned.

She laughed and held up her hand. "Sorry. I forget you're very sensitive. But you're going to have to get used to my kind of humor."

"And what exactly is your kind of humor?"

"The kind that makes you roll your eyes. That always makes me laugh, to be honest."

"All right, I'm going to bed," I said as I stood up.

She grabbed my hand and pulled me back down onto the couch. "Wait, I want to tell you something," she said.

"I don't know if I can handle any more surprises this year, Mom."

Gloria tightened her grip. "No more surprises. I promise. I just wanted to tell you that I think you answered Maya's question about David beautifully."

"Really?" I asked.

Gloria nodded and squeezed the hand she was holding. "You are a good mother, Claudia. That little girl is very lucky to have you."

I hadn't expected such a genuine compliment from her. I swallowed my emotions so I could talk. "She's lucky to have us both."

We nodded in agreement and just sat there for a few more minutes.

Then I turned to her and said, "How about we go buy me a new bed tomorrow?"

CHAPTER FORTY-SIX

THINGS I NEED TO REMEMBER #1: I'M STRONGER THAN I THINK

Dear Diary,

I know it's been a while. I guess I was waiting for some words of wisdom to share with future me or even some meaningful lessons learned. But I think all of that is still a work in progress. Just like me.

I'm starting this new journal to mark the beginning of my new life.

It has officially been one year since David left me, and I can't say I'm totally healed from all that happened. What I can say is that I definitely have more happy days than sad ones.

The divorce was finalized last month. I'm keeping the house and full custody of Maya. He's going to stay in San Francisco but will make a weekend trip back every other month to see our daughter.

He's also paying me child support. But I waived spousal support and any claim to his parents' vacation home in Oregon (his brother finally sold it to him) or any other of their properties in the event of his death. The spousal support—although I knew I deserved it—was the one thing he wasn't willing to budge on. In the end, it would've held up the divorce being finalized. It was more important for me to move on. I got my daughter, child support, and the house.

I'm still working with Mercedes at Tesoro. I'm proud to say she has been making a pretty good profit the past few months. And I'm even going with her to Oaxaca for her annual buying trip in September. With a year of updated experience as a business manager, I'm sure I could probably find another job with a higher salary. In fact, Mercedes keeps telling me to start looking. But I'm happy where I'm at for the time being. So many things in my life changed this past year. I kinda just want things to stay the same for a while.

Gloria is doing better. She ended up finding a specialist at City of Hope here in California and stayed with me for two more months while she recuperated from surgery. Doctors were able to remove the tumor without too many complications. But she is blind in that eye now, and she had a hard time at first. It helped, though, that Maya insisted on wearing an eye patch just like her grandma for several days. She's in Florida right now but plans to come back next month so she can stay with Maya when I go to Mexico with Mercedes. She'll also be here in December to spend Christmas with us. Even Carlos is going to come down one weekend so we can finally meet each other.

Nick moved into his new apartment in Pasadena a few weeks ago. The house sold quickly, as all property does in this town. He comes over every Sunday for dinner. He's basically family now. My mom still says she hopes we end up together. I don't know about that. We both have a lot of things to work on personally before I think we'd be ready to jump into another romantic relationship. But like my abuela always used to say, "Nunca digas nunca."

As for Rachel, I don't know where she is or what she's doing. David told me she broke up with him just a few days after New Year's. At my request, Nick doesn't talk about her. Ever. And I've asked him not to share any information about me—if she ever asked, that is. I just know that their divorce was finalized before ours and that they agreed to sell the house and split the money. Neither of them asked for or received any spousal support. It was as if they just wanted the marriage to be over as quickly as possible.

I doubt I will ever want to see or talk to Rachel again. Some days I hate her and some days I feel sorry for her. Gloria says whatever happens to her now, it's what she deserves. "Because you won't ever find true happiness at the expense of someone else's tears." Who knew that losing her sight in one eye would make Gloria look at things so philosophically now?

As for me, I choose to believe that some people come into our lives for only a season. They serve a purpose, whether it's to teach us a lesson about ourselves or just help us through things at that time. Then they're gone. Rachel came into my life when I needed a friend the most. And there's a small part of me that will always be grateful for that.

I never knew my best friend would be someone who could betray me in the worst way possible. What I do know now, though, is that if I survived that, then I can survive anything.

AUTHOR'S NOTE

Thank you so much for reading my book. I hope you enjoyed meeting these women and taking this journey of forgiveness and hope. This story was about the breakup of a marriage and the breakup of a friendship. Both can be equally hard, but there's something really heart wrenching about being betrayed by someone you thought was your best friend—your person.

As with all my books, I want to entertain but I also try to educate if I can. I especially love inserting pieces of history that feature the Mexican and Mexican American experience. And if I can do it in Los Angeles, then even better.

Although I grew up in the Inland Empire region of Southern California and still live there, I consider the city of Los Angeles to be my second hometown. It's where I would visit my grandma Chavez and my godmother Socorro (we called her "Nini") on Sundays. They lived in a small apartment in Lincoln Heights—just minutes from the hustle and bustle of downtown Los Angeles—before moving to a house in Highland Park. I also lived in the city just after college, and I loved being able to explore all the different neighborhoods as an adult.

This book also features a tiny piece of my own family's history—La Placita Church, a.k.a. Our Lady Queen of Angels, a.k.a. Iglesia Nuestra Señora Reina de Los Ángeles. Grandma Chavez began attending Mass there after she immigrated to the city from Mexico because it was one of the few churches she knew of that held services in Spanish. Because she didn't drive, she'd travel by bus there, sometimes with my aunt and sometimes all by herself. A very loyal parishioner, she eventually began working for the church, cleaning or helping out wherever she could. A photo of her praying inside La Placita was even featured in a *Los Angeles Times* article about the beginning of Lent season.

SATURDAY, FEBRUARY 16, 1991

Ash Wednesday Rites

Then in 1995, La Placita was where our family held her funeral Mass.

Two years later, we returned to baptize my oldest daughter—who would have been her first great-grandchild. And then my son three years after that. The priests still remembered my grandma Chavez fondly.

That's why it meant so much to me that my husband and I were able to baptize my nephew there last year. I want to believe that Grandma Chavez was there in spirit too.

We lost Nini in 2024, but I still have family who live in Los Angeles, so we always have a reason to go visit. And even when we don't, we still like to just make the drive down the 10 freeway when we're craving taquitos from Cielito Lindo or churros from El Mercadito.

And that's why the City of Angels will always hold a special place in my heart.

Thank you again for reading.

ACKNOWLEDGMENTS

Writing is hard.

There are days when you love your book, and there are other days when you can't stand one word of it.

And then there are other days when you wonder if you should be doing this at all, because impostor syndrome is an author's kryptonite.

Those are the days when you need your support system. They're the people who give you advice and tell you to keep going. They're the ones who remind you that the sacrifices and sleepless nights will all be worth it in the end.

I want to thank my amazing author friends, agent Sarah Younger, and editors Maria Gomez and Mackenzie Walton and the rest of the Montlake team for being a part of that support system.

Also, I couldn't do what I do without the love and encouragement of my family.

Finally, thank you to my readers. It's because of you that I am able to continue to write books about Mexican American characters who just want to be loved and fulfill their dreams.

I'm so grateful for you all.

ABOUT THE AUTHOR

Photo © 2021 Sabrina Kay Vasquez

Annette Chavez Macias writes stories about love, family, and following your dreams. She is proud of her Mexican American heritage, culture, and traditions, all of which can be found within the pages of her books. For readers wanting even more love stories and guaranteed happily ever afters, Macias also writes romance novels under the pen name Sabrina Sol. A Southern California native, Macias lives just outside Los Angeles with her husband, three children, and their dogs.